Their paths had crossed again.

And, ever since, Jake had felt increasingly drawn to Maggie, this woman who had long ago claimed his heart.

At first he had looked upon their reunion as a chance to ease the guilt that had plagued him for so long. He'd even told Maggie that he hoped they could be friends.

But now, as he stood beside her, Jake knew that his interest in this woman wasn't motivated by guilt...and that his feelings went far beyond friendship.

He still loved her. Had always loved her. And only her.

God help him, it was as simple—and as complicated—as that.

Books by Irene Hannon

Love Inspired

Home for the Holidays #6
A Groom of Her Own #16
A Family to Call Her Own #25
It Had to Be You #58

*Vows

IRENE HANNON

has been a writer for as long as she can remember. This prolific author of romance novels for both the inspirational and traditional markets began her career at age ten, when she won a story contest conducted by a national children's magazine. Today, in addition to penning her heartwarming stories of love and faith, Irene keeps quite busy with her "day job" as senior manager of corporate communications for a Fortune 500 company. In her spare time, she enjoys performing in community musical theater productions.

Irene finds writing for the Love Inspired line especially rewarding because, "Inspirational romances allow me to focus on the three things that last—faith, hope and love. It is a special pleasure for me to write about people who find the greatest of these without compromising the principles of their faith."

The author and her husband, Tom Gottlieb—"my own romantic hero"—reside in St. Louis, Missouri.

It Had to Be You
Irene Hannon

Love Inspired®

Published by Steeple Hill Books™

STEEPLE HILL BOOKS

Steeple
Hill™

ISBN 0-373-87058-2

IT HAD TO BE YOU

Copyright © 1999 by Irene Hannon

This edition published by arrangement with Steeple Hill Books.

Printed in U.S.A.

Remember not the events of the past, the things of long ago consider not.

—*Isaiah* 43:18

With deepest gratitude to the One who
makes all things possible.

Prologue

❧

"I'm sorry, Maggie, but...I just can't go through with it."

Maggie Fitzgerald stared in shock at the man standing across from her, his words echoing hollowly in her ears. He looked like Jake West, the man she'd loved since she was sixteen years old. But he didn't sound like that Jake. Not even close.

Maggie felt a cold chill crawl up her spine despite the Midwest heat and humidity, and she wrapped her arms around her body for warmth. He was only an arm's length away, close enough to touch, and yet she suddenly felt more alone than ever before in her life. Because always, through all the losses in her life—her mother, her father, and just three weeks before, the tragic deaths of her sister and brother-in-law in a small-plane crash—she'd still had Jake. He'd been her friend for as long as she could remember, and though their relationship had transitioned—quite unexpectedly—to romance, their friendship remained strong and sure.

But now he was leaving—less than five weeks before she was scheduled to walk down the aisle as his bride. It was inconceivable. Incomprehensible. But true. The stoic expression on his face told her so more eloquently than his words.

The knot in Maggie's stomach tightened as she sank down onto the couch, her legs suddenly too shaky to support her willowy five-foot-six, hundred-and-ten-pound frame. Nothing in her twenty-four years had prepared her for this...this *betrayal*. Maybe that was a harsh term. But what else could you call it when the man you loved bailed out just because things got a little rough?

Even in her dazed state, however, Maggie had to admit that "a little rough" wasn't exactly an accurate description of the situation. The sudden responsibility of raising six-year-old twins—one of whom needed on-going medical care—wasn't a minor complication. Not when they'd planned to spend the first ten years of their marriage child-free, exploring some exotic new corner of the world each year on vacation, living the adventures they'd always dreamed of. It was a situation that demanded huge compromises, and Maggie knew it marked the death of a dream for both of them. But she had wanted to believe that Jake would realize there simply was no other option. As their only living relative, Maggie *had* to take her sister's girls. But clearly Jake hadn't been able to accept it. And where did that leave her?

Apparently alone.

As Jake sat beside her and reached for her hand, she glanced at him with dazed eyes, blind to the anguish in his. The strongly molded planes of his dear, familiar face were only a misty blur. When he spoke, the appealing, husky cadence of his voice—edged with that smoky quality that was distinctly his—sounded suddenly foreign to her ears, and his words seemed to come from a great distance.

"Maggie, I'm sorry," he whispered, knowing the words were inadequate, his gut twisting painfully at the wretched, abandoned look in her eyes.

So was she. Ever since her sixteenth birthday, when their relationship changed forever—from childhood friends to sweethearts—she'd never even looked at another man. She'd built her whole future around Jake. A future that was now crumbling around her.

"This...situation...doesn't change how I feel about you," he continued when she didn't respond. "But...well, I guess I never expected a ready-made family. It would be bad—" He cut himself off and deliberately changed the term. "Hard...enough if they were normal kids. But they've just lost both parents, and Abby has years of medical treatment ahead of her. And what about our plans for seeing the world? For not being tied down by responsibilities, at least in the beginning? And I'm not ready to take on the responsibilities of parenthood. I just feel so...trapped," he finished helplessly. With a sigh, he reached for her cold hands, his gaze locked on hers. "Do you understand at all?"

Slowly Maggie shook her head, trying desperately to restrain her tears. "No," she replied brokenly. "No, Jake, I don't. I thought...well, I know we haven't actually said the vows yet, but I thought, in our hearts, we'd already made a commitment. For life. For better or for worse. What if this had happened six weeks *after* the wedding instead of six weeks before? Would you have walked out then, too?"

Jake cringed, and he felt his neck grow hot. He de-

served that. It was more or less the same question his
father had coldly asked. Though his mother had been
less vocal in her disapproval, he had seen the look of
disappointment in her eyes, as well. But if the vows
had actually been spoken, he would have stuck it out.

"You know better, Maggie."

She looked at him, suddenly skeptical. "Do I? I'm
not so sure anymore, Jake." She shook her head and
gave a short, mirthless laugh. "But I guess it was a
lucky thing for you it happened now. You won't be
put to that test. You're free to walk away."

God forgive him, but he'd thought that very thing.
That he *was* lucky this had happened *before* the wedding. He felt like a heel for even thinking it, but he
couldn't deny that he'd been relieved.

Maggie watched his face, realized that though her
words had been spoken harshly, they did, in fact, mirror his thoughts. Her stomach clenched even tighter.
Until this very minute she'd half expected him to rethink his decision and do what she considered the honorable thing. But as her gaze searched his eyes, she
knew he wasn't going to bend, and a powerful wave
of fear suddenly crashed over her.

When she spoke again, her voice was tinged with
desperation. "Jake, I—I don't want to lose you. I don't
know why the Lord gave us this burden, why He's
testing our commitment like this. I wish I did. I wish
there was an easy answer to this problem. But I can't
see any other option. Can you?"

He stared at her helplessly. There was only one other
option as far as he could see: put the two bereft six-
year-olds into the hands of a foster family. But leaving
them in the care of strangers would be wrong, and he
knew it. That was why he hadn't asked her to choose

between that or him. After much soul-searching he had decided that the best solution was for him to break the engagement. He didn't feel particularly noble about it, and his father's few choice words about duty and honor were still ringing in his ears, but in the end he had to make his own decision. And as much as he loved Maggie, he feared that if he went into this marriage feeling trapped, it would lead to resentment and, ultimately, heartbreak.

But now, sitting here with her ice-cold hands in his, her vulnerable eyes pleading with him to reconsider, he wondered if this was any better.

"Maggie, are you sure Charles didn't have any relatives who might take the girls?" he asked, already knowing the answer. They'd been over this before.

She shook her head. "He was an only child, born late in life. His parents died years ago. There isn't anyone else, Jake."

With a sigh of frustration, Jake rose and strode restlessly across the room, stopping at the window to stare unseeingly into the night.

Maggie watched him, frantically searching for words that might change his mind. She couldn't lose Jake! Since her sixteenth birthday, all she'd wanted out of life was to be Mrs. Jake West. Maybe modern women were supposed to want a career and independence. But those things paled in comparison to being Jake's wife. What better "career" could she find than spending her life loving Jake, first traveling with him all over the world and then creating a home for him and their children? Her throat tightened painfully, and she choked back a sob.

"Jake...maybe we should just postpone things. Maybe if we give it a little time..."

Her voice trailed off as he turned to face her. There was a tightness to his jaw, a sudden resolve in his face, that made her realize there was something he hadn't told her yet, something that she knew intuitively was going to seal their fates.

"That's not really an option, Maggie. I..." He paused, and she could see the struggle on his face as he searched for the words to tell her the thing that was going to make her world fall completely apart.

"Jake." The panic in her voice was obvious, even to her own ears. She didn't want to hear what he was going to say. "Please, can't we think about this a little more?"

She heard him sigh, saw the sudden sag in his shoulders, watched with trepidation as he walked slowly back to the couch and sat beside her again. More than anything in the world she wanted him to pull her into his arms and tell her that everything was going to be all right, as he had on so many other occasions through the years. But she could see that wasn't his intent. He kept himself purposely at a distance and made no attempt to touch her.

Jake lifted a hand and wearily rubbed his forehead, then drew in a deep, unsteady breath. When he spoke, his voice was gentle but firm. "Maggie, I joined the navy. I leave in five days."

Maggie stared at him blankly, her eyes suddenly confused. "Leave?" she parroted. "You're leaving? You joined the navy?"

"Yes. I signed all the papers this morning. I've known for a week I was going to do it, but I just couldn't seem to find the words to tell you."

"But...but why?"

"It's my chance to see the world, Maggie. It won't

be the same as if we were going together, I know, but with my advanced degree I should get plum assignments. That's what they told me at the recruiting office, anyway. I go directly to officer training school. It's a great opportunity.''

''But…but you have a job already.''

''I know. But it's just a job, Maggie. In two years the most exciting thing I've done with my engineering skills is design hydraulic systems for elevators. I don't want to do that the rest of my life.''

''But…but why the navy?'' she asked, still trying to make sense of this unexpected twist.

Because I knew if I didn't do something irrevocable like that, I wouldn't be able to go through with the breakup, not when you look at me like this, he thought in silent anguish. But he couldn't say that.

He studied her now, this woman he loved, as he debated how to answer. From the first time he kissed her, Maggie had been the only woman he ever wanted. They'd played together as toddlers, hung around as teenagers and fallen in love that one magical day on Maggie's sixteenth birthday when he'd suddenly begun to realize that she was growing up. For the first time, he had really looked at her—the way a man looks at a woman who attracts him. Maggie wasn't exactly a great beauty, with her wavy, flyaway red hair and turned up nose. But those attributes were more than offset by her gorgeous, deep green eyes and porcelain complexion. Suddenly she wasn't just a ''pal'' anymore, but a woman who brought out unexpected feelings and responses in him.

And as time went by, he'd begun to notice other things, too. Like how close to the surface her feelings lay, how transparent they were, clearly reflected in her expressive eyes. And he'd noticed something else in her eyes, too—a maturing passion, flashes of desire, that set his blood racing. But she had a discipline he could only admire. For, in an era of questionable morals, she made no apology for her traditional Christian values, believing that the ultimate intimacy should be reserved for marriage, expressed only in the context of a lifetime commitment. He'd always respected her for that.

Yet despite Maggie's strong faith, she had a certain air of fragility, an aura of helplessness, that always brought out his protective instinct. And it was this latter quality that he knew would do him in tonight unless he had an airtight out, an ironclad escape—like joining the navy.

And *escape* was an accurate word, he admitted. He was running away because he was running scared. It was as simple as that. But he couldn't very well tell her all that.

"The navy seemed to offer some great career and travel opportunities," he replied, the reason sounding lame—and incomplete—even to his own ears.

Maggie stared at him, wide-eyed and silent. She'd hoped he'd at least help her get settled with the twins. She'd even begun to think that maybe he would change his mind if he saw that caring for them wasn't so bad after all. But he wasn't going to give himself that chance. He was bailing out.

An aching sadness overwhelmed her as she recalled all the tender words they'd said to one another, all the plans they'd made with such eager anticipation. She thought of the hours they'd spent poring over maps, dreaming of places that would take them far from their Midwest roots, planning their future travels around the world—beginning with their honeymoon in Paris. A honeymoon now destined never to take place, she realized. Cold fingers clutched at her heart and tightened mercilessly, squeezing out the last breath of hope. He'd made his decision. It was done. There was nothing more to say.

She gazed at Jake, and suddenly she felt as if she was looking at a stranger, as if the man she'd fallen in love with had somehow ceased to exist. That man had been caring and kind, someone who could be relied upon to stand beside her, no matter the circumstances. The stranger sitting beside her seemed to possess none of those qualities. He'd said he loved her. And maybe he thought he did. But his actions didn't even come close to fitting her definition of love.

Maggie took a deep breath, struggling to make sense of everything that was happening. Her life had changed so dramatically in the last three weeks that there was an air of unreality about it. She'd lost her only sister. She'd been given responsibility for two young, newly orphaned children, one of whom needed ongoing medical care. And now the final blow. She was losing the man she loved. Only her faith kept total despair at bay. But even *with* her faith, she was finding it hard not to give in to self-pity. Why was the Lord testing her this way? she cried silently. She just couldn't see any purpose to it.

Unless…unless it was the Lord's way of letting Jake show his true character now, before they formalized their commitment, she thought, searching desperately for an explanation that made *some* sense. She supposed it was better to find out now how he reacted in adversity. But frankly, at this moment, it didn't give her much consolation.

"Maggie?"

Jake's concerned voice drew her back to the present. The familiar warmth and tenderness were back in his eyes, and for just a moment she was tempted to tell him she'd do whatever he wanted, just so long as they could be together.

But with sudden resolve, she straightened her shoulders and lifted her chin. She'd already practically begged him to rethink his decision, and he'd rejected her plea. Well, she had *some* pride. If Jake didn't love her enough to stick by her through this, then she didn't want him, either. She could survive on her own. Okay, so maybe she'd relied too much on Jake to take care of things, make all the decisions. That didn't mean she couldn't learn to do those things herself. Especially since it was clear she *had* to. She needed to take her life in her own hands. Beginning right now.

Abruptly Maggie rose, and Jake stared up at her, startled by her sudden movement.

She took a deep breath, willing herself to get through the next few minutes without breaking down. Her heart might be tattered, but there would be time for tears later, when she was alone. Plenty of time, in fact. Like the rest of her life.

"Jake, I don't see any reason to prolong this, do you? You've said what you came to say. It's obvious you've set a new course for your life. I have to accept that. And I wish you well."

Jake rose more slowly, his face troubled. There was a quality in Maggie's voice he'd never heard before—a quiet dignity, tinged with resignation. This wasn't at all the reaction he'd anticipated. He'd expected tears and pleading right up to the final goodbye.

"Look, Maggie, I don't want to just walk out and

leave you to totally fend for yourself. I'd like to at least help you out financially, make sure you're settled.''

As far as Maggie was concerned, offering money was the worst thing Jake could have done. Maybe it would appease his conscience, but she wanted nothing from this man who, until half an hour ago, had been the center of her world, whose love she had mistakenly believed to be unshakable and true.

"I don't want your money, Jake. I have a job. A good job. Graphic design is a growing field. I might even branch out into illustration. And Becky and Charles had insurance, so the girls will be well provided for. We'll be fine."

Jake looked at Maggie, noting the uncharacteristic tilt of her chin. She'd always been so compliant, so accepting of his help, that he was a bit taken aback by her refusal. And he was even more surprised when she removed her engagement ring and held it out to him.

"I think this is yours."

"Keep the ring, Maggie," he protested, surprised at the unevenness of his own voice.

"Why? It's a symbol of something that no longer exists. I'd rather you take it back." She reached over and dropped it into his hand. Then she walked to the door, opened it and turned to face him. "I don't think we have anything else to say to each other, do we?"

Jake looked at Maggie. Her beautiful eyes were steady, and for once he couldn't read her feelings in their depths. But he knew she was hurting. Knew that she must feel exactly as he felt—devastated and bereft. But she was hiding it well. Slowly he followed her to the door.

"I'll take care of canceling all the...arrangements." He could at least spare her that.

"Thank you," she said stiffly.

"I'm sorry, Maggie." He knew words were inadequate. But they were all he could offer.

"So am I." Her voice caught on the last word, and for a moment he thought she was going to lose it. He almost wished she would. He didn't know how to deal with this aloof, controlled Maggie. He wanted to take her in his arms one last time, wanted to cry with her at the unfairness of life, wanted to mourn the passing of their relationship. It was clear, however, that she had a different sort of parting in mind.

"Well…I guess there's nothing left to say."

"No."

"Maggie, I hope…" His voice trailed off. What did he hope? That someday she would find it in her heart to forgive him? Unlikely. That she would eventually be able to remember with pleasure their good times? Again, unlikely. That a man worthy of her love would one day claim her heart?

That thought jolted him. No, that wasn't at all what he wanted. His Maggie in the arms of another man? The idea repelled him. And yet, how could he wish her less? She deserved to find happiness with a man who would love her enough to stand by her through the tough times as well as the happy ones. Someone who would do a much better job at that than he had.

"What do you hope?" she asked curiously, a wistful note creeping into her voice.

He considered his answer, and settled for one that didn't even come close to expressing the myriad of conflicting emotions in his heart. "I wish you happiness, Maggie."

The smile she gave him was touched with bitterness,

telling him more eloquently than words that she considered that a vain hope. "Thanks, Jake. Goodbye."

And then she very gently, very deliberately, shut the door behind him.

Maggie walked numbly back to the couch and sat down. She felt chilled to the bone and suddenly she began to tremble. For the first time in her life she was truly alone. She'd told Jake that she would be all right. But those words had been spoken with more bravado and pride than confidence. She didn't have a clue how she was going to cope. Not without Jake.

Jake, with his gentle touch and laughing eyes, his confidence and optimism, his sense of adventure. He had filled her world with joy and brightness. The events that had transpired in this room during the last hour couldn't erase the memory of all they'd shared, of the love she had felt for him. Without Jake, the future stretched ahead like a dark, aching void, filled with overwhelming responsibilities, yet empty of the warmth and companionship and love that made all trials bearable. How could she go on alone?

And then she thought of the twins. They needed her. Desperately. They, too, had been deprived of the people they loved most. She had to be strong for them, if not for herself. Together they would move forward. For the three of them, love had died—for the twins, physically; for her, emotionally. But the death was equally final in both cases.

Which meant that, for the first time her life, her future lay solely in her own hands. She had no one to consult, no one to make decisions for her, no one to reassure her that she could handle the task before her. It was up to her alone.

Well, maybe not quite alone, she reminded herself

suddenly. There *was* Someone she could rely on, Someone who would stand by her through whatever lay ahead. And so she took a moment, before the demands of her new life came crashing down on her, to close her eyes and ask for His guidance.

Please, Lord, show me what to do. Help me be strong. Help me to know that I'm never truly alone. That You're always with me. And help me to accept, even without understanding, the hardships You've given me, and to believe in my heart that You would never give me a cross too heavy to bear.

The short prayer brought Maggie a momentary sense of peace and renewed confidence. She could almost feel the Lord's loving presence beside her. And for that she was immensely grateful. For she knew, beyond the shadow of a doubt, that she would need Him desperately in the months and years to come.

Chapter One

Twelve Years Later

*G*ive it up.

The word's echoed in Jake's mind as the swirling Maine mist wrapped itself around his small rental car, effectively obscuring everything beyond a thirty-foot radius. He frowned and eased his foot off the accelerator. Should he continue the short distance to Castine or play it safe and pull in somewhere for the night?

A sign appeared to his right, and he squinted, trying to make out the words. Blue Hill. He glanced at the map on the seat beside him. Castine was less than twenty miles away, he calculated. But he suspected that these narrow, winding—and unfamiliar—roads weren't too forgiving, and dusk was descending rapidly. Not a good combination, he decided. Besides, he was tired. He'd driven up from Boston, then spent what remained of the day exploring the back roads and small towns of the Blue Hill peninsula. If he wanted to feel rested and fresh for his interview at the Maine Maritime Academy tomorrow, it was time to call it a day.

As if to validate his decision, a sign bearing the words Whispering Sails B&B providentially loomed out of the mist. Talk about perfect timing! he mused. He pulled into the gravel driveway and carefully followed the gradual incline until he reached a tiny parking area, where one empty space remained. Hopefully, the space was a good sign.

Jake eased his six-foot frame out of the compact car and reached into the back seat for his suit bag, slinging it effortlessly over his shoulder. As he made his way up the stone path, he peered at the house, barely discernible through the heavy mist. The large Queen Anne-style structure of weathered gray clapboard was somewhat intimidating in size, its dull color offset by the welcome, golden light spilling from the windows and the overflowing flower boxes hugging the porch rail. Definitely a haven for a weary traveler, he decided.

Jake climbed the porch steps, read the welcome sign on the door and entered, as it instructed. A bell jangled somewhere in the back of the house, and he paused in the foyer, glancing around as he waited for someone to appear. The house was tastefully decorated, he noted appreciatively, with none of the "fussiness" often associated with this style of architecture. In fact, the clean, contemporary lines of the furnishings set off the ornate woodwork beautifully, and he found the subtle blending of old and new eminently pleasing. A soft, warm color palette gave the house a homey feel—no small accomplishment for high-ceilinged rooms of such grand proportion. Clearly the house had been decorated by someone with an eye for design and color.

His gaze lingered on the ample fireplace topped by

a marble mantle, which took up much of one wall, and he was sorry the month was July instead of January. He wouldn't mind settling into the large overstuffed chair beside it with a good book on a cold night. There was something...restful...about the room that strongly appealed to him.

As Jake completed his survey, a door swung open at the back of the foyer and a young woman who looked to be about twenty hurried through.

"I thought I heard the bell," she greeted him breathlessly, her smile apologetic. "I was on the back porch changing a light bulb. Sorry to keep you waiting."

He returned the smile. "Not at all. I was hoping you might have a room for the night. I was trying to make it to Castine, but the weather isn't cooperating."

She made a wry face and nodded. "Not exactly Maine at its best," she concurred sympathically as she slipped behind a wooden counter that was half-hidden by the curving stairway. "You're in luck for a room, though. We're always booked solid in the summer, but we just received a cancellation." The young woman smiled and handed him a pen. "If you'll just fill out this card, I'll help you with your bags."

"No need. I just have a suit bag. But thanks."

He provided the requested information quickly, then waited while the young woman selected a key and joined him on the other side of the desk.

"I'll show you to your room. It has a private bath and a great view of the bay—well, it's a great view on a clear day," she amended with a rueful grin over her shoulder as she led the way up the steps. "Maybe by tomorrow morning it will be clear," she added hopefully. "Anyway, breakfast is between eight and nine in the dining room, which is next to the drawing room.

Checkout is eleven. My name's Allison, and I'll be on duty till ten if you need anything. Just ring the bell on the desk.'' She paused before a second-floor door at the front of the house and inserted the key, then pushed the door open and stepped aside to let him enter.

Jake strolled past her and gave the room a quick but thorough scrutiny. It seemed that the hand of a skilled decorator had been at work here, as well. The room was done in restful shades of blue. A large bay window at the front of the house would afford a panoramic view of the sea in clear weather, he suspected, and a cushioned window seat beckoned invitingly. A four-poster bed, antique writing desk, intricately carved wardrobe and comfortable-looking easy chair with ottoman completed the furnishing. His gaze paused on the fireplace, noting the candle sconces on the mantle, and again he wished it was cool enough for a fire.

"I hope this is all right," Allison said anxiously.

He turned to her with a smile. "Perfect. The room is very inviting."

Allison grinned. "My aunt has a way with color and such. Everybody says so. And she makes all the guests feel real welcome. That's why we have so many regulars. You know, you're really lucky to get this room. It's the most requested one. Especially with honeymooners."

Jake grinned. "I can see why. It's quite…romantic."

Allison blushed and fumbled with the doorknob. "Well, if you need anything, just let me know. Have a pleasant evening, Mr. West."

As the door clicked shut, Jake drew a deep breath and stretched tiredly, flexing the tight muscles in his neck. He'd been on the road since early morning, but the time had been well spent. Before he decided to make this area his permanent home, he intended to check it out thoroughly.

He strolled over to the window and stared out thoughtfully into the gray mist. Home, he repeated silently. Surprisingly enough, the word had a nice sound. After twelve years of roaming the globe, his worldly possessions following him around in a few small boxes, the thought of having a home, a place to call his own, had a sudden, unexpected appeal. But he shouldn't be too surprised, he supposed. For the last couple of years he'd been plagued with a vague feeling of restlessness, of emptiness, a sense of "Is this all there is?" Even before his brother's phone call, the notion of "settling down" had crept into his thoughts, though he'd pushed it firmly aside. It wasn't something he'd seriously considered—or even *wanted* to consider—for a very long time. In fact, not since he was engaged to Maggie.

Jake frowned. Funny. He hadn't really thought much about Maggie these last few years. Purposely. During the early years after their breakup, she'd haunted his thoughts day and night, the guilt growing inside him with each passing month. It was only in the last three or four years that he had met with some success in his attempts to keep thoughts of her at bay. So why was he thinking of her now? he wondered, his frown deepening.

His gaze strayed to the chocolate-chip cookies, wrapped in clear paper and tied with a ribbon, resting between the pillows on the bed. He'd noticed them earlier, had been impressed by the thoughtful touch. Maybe they had triggered thoughts of the woman he'd once loved, he reflected. She used to bake him chocolate-chip cookies—his favorite—he recalled with a bittersweet smile.

But Maggie was only a memory now, he reminded himself with a sigh. He had no idea what had become of her. She'd moved less than a year after their parting, breaking all ties with the town which held such unhappy memories for her. Even his parents, to whom she had always been close, had no idea where she went. It was better that way, she'd told them. They understood. And he did, too. But though he'd initiated the breakup, he had nevertheless been filled with an odd sense of desolation to realize he no longer knew Maggie's whereabouts. He didn't understand why he felt that way. Didn't even try to. What good would it do? All he could do was hope she was happy.

Jake walked over to the bed and picked up the cookies, weighing them absently in his hand. Here he was, in the honeymoon suite, with only memories of a woman he'd once loved to warm his heart. For a moment, self-pity hovered threateningly. Which was ridiculous, he rebuked himself impatiently. His solitary state was purely his own doing. He'd known his share of women through the years, even met a few who made him fleetingly entertain the idea of marriage. But that's as far as it ever went. Because, bottom line, he'd never met anyone who touched his heart the way Maggie had.

He sat down in the chair and wearily let his head fall against the cushioned back. He'd never really admitted that before. But it was true. Maybe that was the legacy of a first love, he mused, that no one else ever measured up. Most people got over that, of course, moved on to meet someone new and fall in love again. He hadn't. As a result, he'd never regretted his decision to remain unmarried. Until now. Suddenly, as he contemplated a future that consisted of a more "normal" land-bound existence instead of the nomadic life he'd been living, the thought of a wife and family was appealing. For the first time in years, he felt ready to seriously consider marriage—and fatherhood.

Of course, there was one little problem, he thought with a humorless smile. He hadn't met the right woman.

Then again, maybe he had, he acknowledged with a sudden, bittersweet pang of regret, his smile fading. But it was too late for regrets. To be specific, twelve years too late.

"I mean, this guy is gorgeous!"

Abby looked at her sister and grinned as she scrambled some eggs. "Are you sure you're not exaggerating?" she asked skeptically.

"Absolutely not." Allison peeked into the oven to check the blueberry muffins, then turned back to her twin. "Tall, handsome, dark hair, deep brown eyes. And you know what? I think he's single."

"Yeah?" Abby paused, her tone interested. "How old is he?"

Allison shrugged. "Old. Thirty-something, probably. But for an older guy, he's awesome."

"Let me serve him, okay?" Abby cajoled.

"Hey, I saw him first!" Allison protested.

"Yes, but you had your chance to talk to him last night. It's my turn. That's only fair, isn't it, Aunt Maggie?"

Maggie smiled and shook her head. "You two are getting awfully worked up about someone who will be checking out in an hour or two."

Allison sighed dramatically. "True. But we can dream, can't we? Maybe he's a rich tycoon. Or maybe he's lost his beloved wife and is retracing the route they traveled on their honeymoon. Or maybe he's a Hollywood producer scouting the area for a new movie. Or..."

"Or maybe you better watch those muffins before they get too brown," Maggie reminded her with a nod toward the oven.

Allison sighed. "Oh, Aunt Maggie, you have no imagination when it comes to men."

"I have plenty of imagination. Fortunately, I also have a good dose of common sense."

"But common sense is so...so boring," Allison complained.

"He just came in," Abby reported breathlessly, peering through a crack in the kitchen door. She grabbed the pot of coffee before Allison could get to it, and with a triumphant "My turn," sailed through the door.

Maggie smiled and shook her head. One thing for sure. There was never a dull moment with the twins. At eighteen, the world for them was just one big adventure waiting to happen. And she encouraged their "seize the moment" philosophy—within reason, of course. Because she knew that life would impose its own limitations soon enough.

When Abby reentered the kitchen a few minutes later, she shut the door and leaned against it, her face flushed.

"Well?" Allison prompted.

"Wow!"

"See? Didn't I tell you? What's he wearing?" Allison asked eagerly.

"A dark gray suit with a white shirt and a maroon paisley tie."

"A suit? Nobody ever wears a suit here. He must be a business tycoon or something."

"Sorry to interrupt with such a mundane question, but what does he want for breakfast?" Maggie inquired wryly.

"Scrambled eggs, wheat toast and orange juice," Abby recited dreamily.

Maggie was beginning to regret that she'd missed this mysterious stranger's arrival. But the church council meeting had run late, and their unexpected guest had apparently retired for the night by the time she arrived home. It *was* unusual for a younger, apparently single, man to stay with them. Most of their guests were couples. Maybe she ought to check this guy out herself, she thought, as she placed two of the freshly baked blueberry muffins in a basket. Just for grins, of course. It would be interesting to see how she rated this "older guy" the twins were raving about.

Maggie picked up the basket of muffins and a glass of orange juice and headed for the door. "Okay, you two, now the mature woman of the world will give you her expert opinion."

The twins giggled.

"Oh, Aunt Maggie. You've never been anywhere but Missouri, Boston and Maine," Abby reminded her.

Maggie felt a sudden, unexpected pang, but she kept her smile firmly in place. "True. But that doesn't mean I haven't had my romantic adventures."

"When?" Allison demanded pertly.

When, indeed? There'd only been one romantic adventure in her life. And that had ended badly. But she'd never told the girls much about it. Only when they reached the age when boys suddenly became fascinating and they'd begun plying her with questions about her own romantic past had she even mentioned it. And then only in the vaguest terms. Yes, it had been serious, she'd told them. In fact, they'd been engaged. But it just hadn't worked out. And that was all they ever got out of her, despite their persistent questions. She never wanted them to know that it was because of their arrival in her life that her one romance had failed. They'd had a hard enough time adjusting to the loss of their parents; she never wanted to lay the guilt of her shattered romance on them, as well. And she wasn't about to start now. "I think I'll remain a woman of mystery," she declared over her shoulder as she pushed through the door to the sound of their giggles.

Maggie paused on the other side, taking a moment to compose herself. For some reason their innocent teasing had touched a nerve. She'd always claimed she had no time for romance, that she was perfectly happy living her life solo. She'd pretty much convinced them of her sincerity through the years. She'd almost convinced herself, as well. In many ways, her life *was* easier this way. Only occasionally did she yearn for the life that might have been. But she'd learned not to waste time on impractical "what-iffing." Her life was the way it was, and for the most part she was happy and content and fulfilled. The Lord had blessed her in many ways, and she was grateful for those blessings. In fact, she had more in the "blessings" department than most people.

Her spirits renewed, she glanced around the small dining room. All the tables were filled, but it was easy to spot their "mystery" guest. He sat alone, angled away from her, his face almost completely obscured by the daily paper he was reading. Yet she could tell that for once her assessment matched that of the girls'.

They'd been right on target in their description of his physical attributes. He was impeccably dressed, his dark hair neatly trimmed above the collar of his crisp white shirt. His long legs stretched out beneath the table, and his hands seemed strong and capable.

As Maggie started across the room, the man lowered the paper and reached for his coffee, giving her a good view of his strong, distinguished—and very familiar—profile.

It was *Jake!*

Even as her mind struggled to reconcile his presence with the astronomical odds of him appearing in her dining room, her heart accepted it. She knew that profile—the firm chin, the classic nose, the well-shaped lips. It was him.

Maggie felt suddenly as if someone had delivered a well-placed blow to her chest, knocking every bit of wind out of her lungs. Her step faltered and the color drained from her face. She had to escape, had to get back to the kitchen and regain some control, before he spotted her.

But it was too late. As he lifted the coffee cup to his lips he glanced toward her, and their gazes connected—Maggie's wide with shock, Jake's changing in rapid succession from mild interest to curious to stunned.

Jake stared at the red-haired woman standing less than ten feet away from him and his hand froze, the coffee cup halfway to his lips. His heart stopped, then raced on. *Maggie!*

Maggie didn't even realize her hands were shaking until the basket of muffins suddenly slipped out of her grasp. She tore her gaze from his and bent down, just as he rose to join her. Some of the juice sloshed out of the glass, leaving a sticky residue on her fingers as it formed a puddle on the floor. She looked at it helplessly, but a moment later Jake was beside her, wiping it up even as he retrieved a wayward muffin. Then he reached over and took her hand.

Her startled gaze collided with his, their eyes only inches apart.

"Let me," he said softly, the husky cadence in his voice exactly the same as she remembered it. With difficulty she swallowed past the sudden lump in her throat as he carefully wiped the sticky juice off her fingers with the clean side of the napkin. She stared down numbly, watching his strong, bronzed hand gently hold hers. She used to love the way he touched her, she recalled, her breath lodging in her throat. His hands—possessive, sure, tender—could work magic. A sudden, unexpected spark shot through her, and in confusion she jerked free of his grasp and rose unsteadily to her feet.

He stood up, as well, and then gazed down at her, his eyes warm, a shadow of incredulity lingering in their depths.

"Maggie." The way he said her name, gently and with wonder, made her heart lurch into triple time. "It's been a long time."

"Yes. It has." A tremor ran through her voice, but she didn't care. She was just grateful she could speak at all.

"Is this your place?"

"Yes. Listen, I'm sorry about the muffins and juice. I'll go get you some more. Excuse me." And then she turned and fled.

Jake watched her go, aware for the first time that the two of them were drawing curious looks from the other guests. With one last glance toward the kitchen, he slowly turned and walked back to his table. His first inclination had been to follow Maggie, but he understood that she needed some time to adjust to this strange turn of events. He knew he did.

Jake reached for his coffee, noting that his hand was trembling. He wasn't surprised. A bizarre coincidence like this was more than a little unsettling. Only yesterday he'd been thinking of Maggie, and his dreams last night had been filled with her. Then he'd awakened to a reality that didn't include her, reminding himself that she was part of his past. Until now.

For twelve years, Jake had felt as if the two of them had unfinished business. Now, after all these years, it seemed he was being given a second chance to make amends. And he intended to take it. He didn't expect her to welcome him back with open arms. But he hoped they could at least find some sense of resolution and inner peace.

Peace wasn't exactly the word Maggie was thinking as she burst through the kitchen door, breathless and pale. Her emotions were anything *but* peaceful. Her heart was banging against the wall of her chest as furiously as if she'd just finished a hundred-yard dash. She felt strangely light-headed. And more than a little annoyed. What was wrong with her? Why should a man whom she hadn't seen in twelve years, who had walked out when she'd needed him most, still have such a powerful effect on her? It didn't make any sense. And Maggie didn't like things that didn't make sense.

"Aunt Maggie?" Allison's concerned voice penetrated her thoughts, and she glanced up.

"What's wrong?" Abby asked, her face alarmed at her aunt's pallor.

Maggie forced herself to take a deep breath. "I'm fine. I just…well…that man you two have been talking about, I—I used to know him."

"You *know* him?" Allison repeated incredulously. "How? When?"

"A long time ago. I haven't seen him in years. It was just a…shock, that's all. I'll be okay in a minute."

Abby sent Allison a worried frown. Maggie never got rattled. "So who is he?" Abby persisted.

Maggie walked over to the center island and put two new muffins in the basket, then filled a glass with orange juice, aware that her hand was shaking. She knew the twins would notice. She also knew they weren't going to let her get away without explaining this uncharacteristic behavior. With a sigh, she turned to find them staring at her, their expressions intent—and concerned.

"He's a man I used to date…a long time ago."

Suddenly the light dawned on Allison's face. Though Maggie teased them about her past beaux, as far as they knew she'd only been really serious about one man in her entire life. Certainly none since they could remember. And it would take someone who had once been important to her to make their aunt…well, come unglued.

"Aunt Maggie, this is *him*, isn't it?" Allison's voice was slightly awed.

"Him who?" Abby demanded.

Allison turned to her twin, suddenly excited. "*Him*. You know, the guy Aunt Maggie was engaged to once."

Now it was Abby's turn to look incredulous. "Aunt Maggie, is that true?"

Maggie had always been glad that the twins had

grown into insightful, perceptive young women. Until now. She might as well admit the truth, she thought with a sigh. They'd get it out of her sooner or later.

"Yes, it is."

"Wow!" Allison breathed.

"Yeah, wow!" Abby echoed. "It's so romantic!"

Maggie could think of other words to describe it. *Disruptive,* for one. *Upsetting,* for another. *Scary,* for a third, although why that word popped into her mind she had no idea. She turned to the twins and gave them a stern look.

"Now look, you two, the man is leaving shortly. It's just sheer coincidence that he turned up on our doorstep last night. I'll admit I was surprised. Shocked, even. But don't make a big deal out of this."

"But Aunt Maggie, don't you think it's...well, like a movie or something, that he appeared out of the mist at your B&B after all these years? You know, where long-lost lovers are reunited and rekindle an old romance?" Abby asked dreamily.

"First of all, we are *not* long-lost lovers. We didn't get lost. We broke up. On purpose. And second, neither one of us has any interest in rekindling an old romance. I'm perfectly content with my life just as it is. And even though he's not wearing a ring, Jake could very well have a wife and five kids somewhere."

"I'll bet he doesn't," Allison predicted smugly.

"Now why on earth would you say that?" Maggie demanded impatiently, turning to find the other twin peeking through the crack in the door.

"Because he keeps looking this way, like he's waiting for you."

"He probably just wants his orange juice," Maggie

pointed out, trying desperately to keep her voice from reflecting the turbulence of her emotions.

As she picked up the glass and added it to the tray with the basket of muffins she could feel the twins' gazes on her back, knew they were silently communicating with each other about this exciting development in their aunt's lackluster love life. But in truth, she didn't want to go back out there. Talking to Jake would only stir up old, painful memories best left at rest. Yet, refusing to see him would be childish. Their relationship was history, after all. Whatever they once felt for each other had long since evaporated. They would simply carry on a calm, mature conversation, and then she'd bid him farewell. She could handle that, she thought as she lifted the tray and walked toward the door.

Couldn't she?

Chapter Two

Jake was on his feet the moment Maggie stepped through the door, but when she was detained by guests at another table, he slowly sat back down. In a way he was grateful for their intervention, because as they engaged her with questions about local sights, he had a chance to look at her unobserved.

She's changed, he reflected, as his discerning gaze swept over her. She was still slender, her trim figure shown to good advantage in a pair of well-fitting khaki slacks and a green, long-sleeved cotton blouse that was neatly tucked in and secured with a hemp belt. But the girlish figure he remembered had changed subtly—and attractively—as she'd matured.

His appreciative eyes moved to her hair. The vibrant red color had mellowed slightly, but was no less striking, he noted with pleasure. He'd always been partial to red hair, and Maggie's was especially beautiful, shot through with gold highlights. Apparently she'd never quite tamed its waves. Despite her efforts to pull it sedately back, loose tendrils had escaped around her face, giving the no-nonsense style a winsome, feminine appeal. She still had her freckles, too, he observed with a smile, but they appeared to have faded slightly. He assumed she was grateful for *that* change, recalling how she'd always complained about them.

But there was something else...different...about her, he realized. The Maggie he remembered had been dependent, always waiting for him to take the initiative. The woman he now observed seemed anything *but* dependent. She was gracious, poised and self-confident. A woman who not only took charge of *things* but was quite capable of taking care of *herself*. It was a surprising—but intriguing—transformation.

There was one thing, though, that hadn't changed at all, he discovered a moment later when their gazes connected and his pulse flew into overdrive. He found her every bit as attractive as he had twelve years before. His spirits took a swift and surprisingly strong upswing—only to nose-dive a moment later. Just because *he* felt the old chemistry didn't mean *she* did. And even *if* she did, he doubted that she'd want to renew their friendship, let alone anything more. Why should she, after what he'd done to her twelve years ago? Yet, he couldn't quite stifle the hope that suddenly surged through him.

Maggie moved toward him then, and he stood as she joined him, noting the slight flush on her cheeks. One more thing that hadn't changed, he tallied with pleasure. She still blushed. It was a quality he'd always found endearing.

"I wasn't sure you'd come back out," he confessed quietly.

She served the juice and muffins, avoiding his gaze. "Why wouldn't I?"

There was a moment of silence before he responded. "I wouldn't have blamed you if you hadn't," he told her, instead of replying to the question.

She risked a glance at him then, praying that her fragile composure would hold. "That was a long time ago, Jake." Much to her surprise—and relief—her voice was steady, and she congratulated herself for sounding so calm and controlled when her insides were churning.

Jake eyed her speculatively, debating whether to pursue the subject. "Maybe so," he responded carefully. "But some things are hard to forget."

A shadow crossed her eyes, come and gone so quickly he almost missed it. Anyone else would have. But once he had been keenly attuned to the nuances of her emotions. Apparently he still was. No matter what she said next, he knew that the hurt was still there, possibly buried so deeply in her heart even *she* didn't realize it still existed. But it clearly did, and his gut twisted painfully as he came face-to-face with the lingering effects of his actions twelve years before.

Instead of responding directly to his comment, she shrugged, and when she spoke, her tone was straightforward. "Life goes on, though. We all learn to cope."

He wanted to ask if life had been good to her, if she'd found the happiness she deserved, if she'd had much trouble raising the twins…if her heart belonged to another man. She wore no ring. He'd noticed that right away. But you didn't ask someone personal questions after twelve years. Not when you'd long ago forfeited the right. He had to settle for a less probing query. "So you've managed all right, then, Maggie?"

Maggie looked into his eyes—warm and compelling and intense—and remembered with a bittersweet pang how easily she used to get lost in his dark gaze. How, with a simple look, he could make her heart soar. His eyes were still expressive, still powerful, she realized. But she wasn't susceptible to their magnetism anymore, she told herself resolutely. A lot of things had changed. She'd changed. And this man, once the center of her world, was really nothing more than a stranger to her now.

She tucked the tray under her arm and forced herself to smile. "Well, as you can see, I have a business. The girls are well. We've done fine. I hope your career has been as satisfying as mine."

"The navy has given me a good life," he acknowledged. "I have no regrets about that choice, anyway."

But he had regrets about other choices? Better not to ask, though, she decided quickly.

"Well, I have things to attend to, Jake," she said brightly. "I hope your stay with us has been pleasant—"

The words died in her throat as he reached out and touched her arm.

"I know this situation is somewhat…awkward…but I can't help thinking our paths crossed again for some reason." He paused, searching for a convincing way to phrase his request. Finally he drew a deep breath, his eyes reflecting the intensity of his feelings. "I don't want to walk away without at least talking to you," he told her honestly, his gaze steady and direct. "Will you give me half an hour or so? For old times' sake, if nothing else?"

Maggie tried to ignore the entreaty in his eyes as she considered his request. But it was hard to think rationally when the warmth of his hand was seeping through the sleeve of her blouse. She really didn't want to talk to him. What good would it possibly accomplish after all these years? It seemed far...safer...to leave the past where it belonged—in the past.

But she had to admit that, like him, she was thrown by the odd coincidence that had brought them together. A coincidence so odd that it seemed somehow more than coincidence. She recalled how she'd prayed for just such a "coincidence" more often than she cared to admit in the early years, when she was struggling to earn a living and cope with the challenges of single parenthood. There were so many times when a simple touch, a warm, caring hand holding hers, would have lightened her burden immeasurably. But the Lord hadn't answered those prayers. Not in the way she'd hoped for, at least. Instead, He had helped her find hidden reserves of strength, spirit and determination that had seen her through the rough times. In the end, she'd made it on her own, and in so doing, discovered that she was a capable and competent woman who didn't need to rely on a man to survive. The experience had bolstered her self-esteem, and she had learned to make choices and plans decisively and with confidence.

So why had the Lord sent Jake now, long after she'd stopped asking? Why disrupt her world now, when she had not only resigned herself to a solitary life, but made her peace with it? Maggie didn't have a clue. But there must be a reason for this unexpected meeting, and maybe she should at least try to find out what it was.

"Please, Maggie," Jake persisted. "It would mean a lot to me."

She drew a deep breath and nodded. "All right, Jake. The girls can finish up the breakfast."

His answering smile was warm and grateful—and

relieved. "Thank you." He glanced at his watch. "I need to make a quick call. Then we can talk."

"There's a phone in the drawing room. Next to the fireplace."

He nodded. "I'll be right back."

Maggie watched him leave, then sank down into the closest chair. Her seat afforded her a discreet view of the drawing room. He was turned slightly away from her as he used the phone, and she took advantage of the opportunity to observe him.

He's changed, she noted thoughtfully. He'd filled out, the lanky frame she remembered maturing into a trim, well-toned body. The style of his dark brown hair was familiar, though shorter than it used to be. And a faint brush of silver at both temples gave him a distinguished air. The few lines on his face, which hadn't been there when they parted, spoke more of character than of age. Maggie had to admit that he was even more handsome now than he had been twelve years before.

But there was something else different about him, something beyond the physical that she couldn't quite put her finger on, she realized with a frown. He radiated a quiet confidence, a decisiveness, a sense of determination and purpose. It was reflected in his body language, in the very way he moved, she thought, as he hung up the phone and made a few quick notes on the pad beside it. The Jake she had known was eager, restless and searching. This Jake was polished, self-assured and at peace with his place in the world.

And yet…there was a certain indefinable sadness in his eyes, a world-weariness, that tugged at her heart. It was almost as if he'd searched the world for something but had come up empty, and ultimately had resigned himself to that fact.

Maggie had no idea where that insight came from, or even if it was accurate. Nor did she have a clue what it meant. Still, she knew instinctively there was a void of some sort in Jake's life that troubled his soul.

But the state of Jake's soul was *not* her concern, she reminded herself sternly as he walked toward her. Her energies would be better focused on conducting a civil, rational conversation.

Jake smiled as he sat down across from her. "Well, that buys me an hour."

"You have an appointment?"

"Mmm-hmm. But I wish I didn't."

His comment, as well as the familiar tone in his voice, startled Maggie. She didn't know how to respond, so she remained silent, uncomfortably aware that he was studying her.

"The years have been good to you, Maggie," he said finally. "You look great."

This wasn't at all the polite, impersonal conversation she'd expected, and the warm, husky note in his voice rattled her. "Th-thanks. So do you," she replied, berating herself for letting him fluster her.

"So tell me about this place." He made an all-encompassing gesture. "Have you been doing this long?"

That was more like it, she thought with relief. Questions like that she could handle. "Eight years. I moved to Boston about a year after..." She started to say, "after you left," but changed her mind. The less she talked about *them*, the better. "...after I got the twins," she continued. "I worked in a graphic design firm there for three years. By then Abby was finished with all her

operations and therapy, so there was less need to stay
in a big city. And I thought it would be better for the
girls to grow up in a small town. We'd visited Maine
on vacation once and loved it, so we came up and
looked around one summer. This place happened to be
on the market at a good price. It had been vacant for
a while, and even though it was structurally sound, it
needed lots of cosmetic help and some updating. Before I knew it, I was the proud owner of a B&B. I did
freelance design work for a while to tide us over until
we established a clientele, and I still sell some of my
watercolors to a greeting card company."

She paused and took a deep breath. "The early years
here were a little rough, and it took a lot more hard
work than I expected to get established, but I've never
regretted the move," she finished.

Jake eyed her speculatively, making no attempt to
conceal his admiration. "I'm impressed, Maggie. It
took a lot of courage to make such a radical life-style
change. Not many people would have risked it."

She shrugged dismissively, but was oddly pleased
by the compliment. "I did a lot of research before I
made the move. This is a popular area, and the B&Bs
do well. I drew up a pretty solid business plan, so it
wasn't too difficult to get a loan for the necessary im-
provements. And I found ways to keep the capital expenditures reasonably low."

Jake stared at the woman across from him, struggling
to reconcile the Maggie he knew with this savvy busi-
nesswoman. His Maggie would not have had a clue
about business plans or capital expenditures. Apparently she'd changed even more than he suspected. But
it wasn't an unpleasant change, he realized, a faint
smile touching his lips.

Maggie noted the smile and eyed him cautiously. "What's wrong?"

"Nothing. It's just that the Maggie I remember had very little interest in business. I'm surprised, that's all."

"The Maggie you knew didn't *need* to be interested in business, Jake. This one does."

There was no hint of recrimination in her matter-of-fact tone, but the old, familiar guilt tugged at Jake's conscience. If he'd honored his commitment to her, Maggie wouldn't have had to struggle alone to build a life for herself and the twins. It couldn't have been easy, though she'd downplayed the difficulty. Which only made him admire her more.

"You seem to have done a good job," he said quietly. "This place is obviously a success. And the twins seem like fine young women. Abby looks as if she's recovered fully from the accident."

Maggie nodded. "She has. She needed two more operations after…after I took them in, and therapy after that for three years. But she's fine now." She glanced toward the kitchen, her eyes softening. "They've been a tremendous help to me through the years. I couldn't have made this place a success without them. And they've brought a great deal of joy to my life."

Now was the perfect opening to ask the question that was most on his mind. He reached for his coffee and took a sip, trying to phrase it the right way. "Has it just been the three of you all these years, then?"

Maggie turned and looked at him directly. "If you're asking me whether I'm married, or have ever been married, the answer is no."

"Why not?" The indiscreet question came out before he could stop it, and he felt hot color steal up the back of his neck. He shook his head and held up his hands. "Listen, forget I asked that, okay? It was way out of line."

She toyed with the edge of a napkin, then gave a little shrug. "It's all right. The simple fact is, you weren't the only one who didn't want to take on a ready-made family, Jake. Especially one with medical problems."

He flinched. She'd scored a direct hit with that comment, whether she intended to or not. "I guess I deserved that," he admitted.

She frowned. "I didn't mean it that way. It's just that I eventually realized my situation was an awful lot for anyone to take on, especially in the early years. And as time went by, I simply lost interest in romance. I have a nice life. Why should I change it? But tell me about you," she urged, adroitly shifting the focus before he could pursue the subject. "What are you doing here?"

He took her lead readily, grateful she hadn't taken offense at his rash question. "Actually, I'm interviewing this afternoon at the Maine Maritime Academy."

Her eyes widened in surprise. "For a job?"

"Yes. To make a long story short, I'm leaving the navy and Dad is coming to live with me."

"What about your mom?"

"She died five years ago, Maggie."

"Oh." Her face looked suddenly stricken, and he reached across and laid his hand over hers. Maggie had always gotten along famously with his parents. They'd held a special place in her heart, especially after her own parents died.

"It was a shock to all of us," Jake continued gently. "She had a stroke about five years ago. She lived for about six months after that, and Dad took care of her at home. That's where she wanted to be. Mom was a great believer in families taking care of their own. In fact, before she died, she made Rob and me promise that if Dad ever got to the point where he couldn't live alone, one of us would take him in rather than relegate him to a retirement or nursing home.''

"And he isn't able to live alone now?"

Jake shook his head regretfully. "No. He had a heart attack about eight months ago and went down to stay with Rob and his family in Atlanta while he recovered. Except that he never did recover very well. He's gotten pretty frail and a little forgetful, and Rob and I finally realized that he couldn't ever go home. Rob was perfectly happy to have Dad live with them—the kids love having their grandpa around—but three weeks ago he lost his job in a corporate downsizing, and Jenny— Rob's wife—had to go back to work. What with three kids and lots of uncertainties, life has been pretty stressful for them. And they really can't give Dad the attention he needs. So the younger son—namely me— was called in to pinch-hit. That's why I'm here.''

"You mean you're giving up your navy career to take care of your dad?"

Jake dismissed the implied sacrifice with a shrug. "I never intended to spend my life in the service. And even though it was a good life in many ways, I have to admit that I'm getting a little tired of being a nomad. The idea of settling down in one place is beginning to appeal to me. Rob may be having some career problems at the moment, but I'm starting to envy his life— the wife, the kids, the picket fence.''

"So you've been...alone all these years?" she said tentatively.

"I never married, either, Maggie," he told her quietly.

A strange feeling of lightness swept over her, but she ignored it and focused on a less volatile topic. "So how does your dad feel about this move?"

Jake's face grew troubled. "Not happy, I'm afraid. You know how independent Dad always was. He hasn't taken kindly to having to rely on his kids to take care of him. Rob says it wasn't too bad at first, when Dad thought he'd eventually be able to go home. But since we decided that's not an option, he's been pretty despondent. He knows we're right, but that hasn't made it any easier for him to accept. And it's even worse now that he realizes he'll be stuck with me instead of Rob, at least for a while."

Maggie eyed Jake assessingly. His last comment had been made lightly, but she suspected his tone masked deeper feelings. She knew his parents hadn't been happy when he'd walked out on her. They'd apologized on his behalf more times than she could count. But surely, after all these years, his father didn't still hold a grudge against his son on her behalf. There had to be more to their troubled relationship than that.

"I take it you and your dad don't get along that well," she probed carefully.

Jake gave a short, mirthless laugh. "You might say that. As I'm sure you know, Dad was very disappointed in me after I...after we broke up. And he didn't hold back his feelings on the subject, either. So I made fewer trips home, which only seemed to fuel the fire. I did go home more often after Mom's stroke, but not enough to suit Dad. He figured I'd abandoned them, too, I guess."

Maggie looked at him in surprise. Abandoned them,

too? That was an incriminating word choice. Did it mean that he regretted his decision twelve years ago to break up with her? Had guilt followed him all these years as he roamed around the world? She'd never really considered that. She figured once he'd made his decision he's simply gone on with his life, that eventually memories of her and their time together had faded. But his words implied otherwise.

"Anyway, like it or not, we're stuck with each other," Jake continued. "And I'm determined to make the best of it. In fact, to be perfectly honest, I hope we can mend the rift between us. Dad and I used to be close, and…well, I've missed that all these years."

Once again, Maggie was taken aback by Jake's admission. He'd never been the kind of man who talked much about feelings. Maybe the willingness to do so had come with maturity, she speculated. Once you felt comfortable with your life and had proven your abilities, it was easier to admit other limitations without feeling threatened. Jake struck her as being a very secure man in most aspects of his life. Confident and in control. Yet he'd been unable to reestablish a good relationship with his father. And he wasn't too proud to admit it.

"Well, the opportunity will certainly be there now," Maggie pointed out encouragingly. "I'm sure your dad will come around."

Jake shook his head skeptically. "I'm not so sure. But I have to try at least. Rob has his hands full, and we can't go back on our promise to Mom. Besides, Rob's done more than his share with Dad since Mom died. It's only right I take my turn."

Maggie stared at Jake. The man was full of surprises. Through the years she'd gradually convinced herself that he was a self-centered, spoiled, irresponsible man who had probably grown even more so with age. But the decisions he'd made regarding his father, his acceptance of his duty, his willingness to honor the promise to his mother at the expense of his career, weren't the actions of a selfish man. They spoke of integrity and principal and dependability. Maggie had to admit that his behavior was admirable. But it was a grudging admission, and certainly not one she cared to verbalize.

"Excuse me, but there's a call for you, Mr. West," Abby interrupted, pausing beside the table, her gaze blatantly curious as it moved from Jake to Maggie. "A man named Dennis Richards."

Jake frowned. "He must not have been able to switch the time for the first interview after all. Will you wait, Maggie? I'll be right back."

"Yes."

"You can take the call on the phone in the foyer, at the desk," Abby told him.

She watched Jake leave, then turned to Maggie, her eyes shining. "Were you really engaged to him once?" she asked incredulously.

Maggie briefly glanced in the direction Jake had disappeared and nodded. "It's a long story, honey. And it happened a long time ago."

"But he's back now," Abby pointed out eagerly. "Who knows? Maybe—"

"Maybe we should try not to let our imaginations run away with us," Maggie advised, cutting off her niece's fanciful speculations.

"But what's he doing here?" Abby persisted.

"He's on his way to Castine. He's considering a job at the Maritime Academy."

"You mean he might be living less than twenty miles away?" Abby was clearly elated.

"Maybe," Maggie admitted reluctantly.

"Wow!" Abby repeated. "Wait till I tell Allison!"

Before Maggie could respond, Abby turned on her heel and disappeared into the kitchen. Maggie shook her head helplessly, then propped her chin on her hand, a pensive frown on her face as she considered the situation.

Jake had reappeared in her life after twelve years. "Shock" was hardly adequate to describe her reaction. But somehow she'd made it through the last half hour or so. Perhaps the Lord had taken pity on her and sent an extra dose of courage her way. Still, it had taken every ounce of her willpower and fortitude to act as if Jake's presence hadn't been a jolting experience that left her reeling emotionally.

She had succeeded, though, and congratulated herself for that. But a thirty-minute encounter was one thing. How on earth would she cope if the man lived just down the road? If she knew every time she went out that she might run into him—at the grocery store, on the street, in the park? The thought unnerved her completely.

What unnerved her even more was the realization that the man still had the *power* to unnerve her. She resented that. After all, he was nothing to her anymore. Her life was full and rich as it was. She had two loving "daughters," an artistic talent that gave her great joy, a satisfying career and a solid faith that continued to sustain her. What more could she ask for?

But Maggie knew the answer to that question, she admitted with a sigh. Though she'd long ago reconciled herself to the fact that the single life seemed to be

God's plan for her, deep in her heart she still yearned for someone to share it with. Having once loved deeply, she knew what joy love could bring. She didn't think about it often, though. Idle wishing was fruitless. But seeing Jake again had reawakened those yearnings, made her recall the heady feeling of being in love.

Her lips curved up into a wistful smile as she thought back. It had been a wonderful time, those days of awakening emotions and eager plans for a future together, when the world stretched before them, infinite in its possibilities. How differently her life would have turned out if those plans had come to fruition. But the Lord had had a different future in store for her. And she shouldn't complain. Her life had been blessed in many ways.

"It looks like I'll have to leave sooner than I wanted to." Jake's regretful voice interrupted her reverie.

"I understand."

"Listen, Maggie, I'd like to continue our conversation. We barely got started. Can I call you tomorrow?"

She frowned and slowly shook her head. "I'm not sure that's a good idea."

"I guess you've been kinder to me already than I have any right to expect," he acknowledged soberly. "You probably still hate me, and I can't say I blame you."

"I never hated you, Jake. I was just…hurt. But I got over that a long time ago."

He looked at her, wanting to believe that was true, but finding it difficult to accept. In her place, he doubted he'd be that forgiving. "Really?"

She nodded. "Really."

"Then why won't you talk to me?"

Because I'm scared, she cried silently. *I feel like a*

tightrope walker who's about to lose her balance. And I don't want to fall, Jake. Not again. Not ever again.

But of course she couldn't say that. "It's awfully busy this time of year. I just don't have the time to socialize."

"How about a phone call, then? Surely you can spare a few minutes for that."

They both knew she could. And Maggie didn't want to give Jake the impression that she still held a grudge. That would make her seem small and unforgiving. Not to mention un-Christian. With a sigh, she capitulated.

"All right, Jake. Give me a call when you have a few minutes."

She was rewarded with a smile so warm it seemed like sunshine on a lazy summer day. "Thank you, Maggie. I appreciate it. I've already taken care of my bill and loaded my car, so I'll say goodbye for now." He stood up and held out his hand. She had no choice but to take it, trying to still the rapid beating of her heart as her fingers were engulfed in his firm, warm grip.

"I know this encounter has upset you, Maggie," he murmured, the familiar husky timbre of his voice playing havoc with her metabolism as his discerning gaze locked on hers. "And I'm sorry for that. I never want to upset you again. But I'm not sorry our paths crossed. I think it happened for a reason."

Maggie didn't respond. She couldn't.

Jake held her gaze a moment longer, then released it—as well as her hand. "I'll call you soon," he promised. With that he turned and strode away.

Maggie sank back into her chair, his words echoing in her mind. He'd said he thought their paths had crossed for a reason. She couldn't dispute that. It was too odd a coincidence to accept at face value. He'd also said he was glad it had happened. On that point she disagreed. Maggie wasn't glad at all. Because now that Jake had walked back into her life, she somehow knew it would never be the same again.

Chapter Three

"Earth to Maggie, earth to Maggie. Are you with me over there?"

Maggie abruptly returned to reality, blushing as she sent Philip, her lunch partner, an apologetic look. "Sorry about that," she said sheepishly.

"No problem. So what if you don't find my company fascinating? Why should I be insulted?"

Maggie grinned at his good-natured teasing. "You're a good sport, you know that?"

"So I've been told. So what gives?"

She shifted uncomfortably. "What do you mean?"

"Maggie, I've known you for what...seven, eight years? In all that time I've never once seen you distracted. So I figure something's happened—something pretty dramatic. Therefore, I repeat...what gives?"

Maggie looked down and played with her fork. She should have known she couldn't hide her inner turmoil from Philip. He was way too perceptive. And maybe it wasn't such a bad idea to tell him about Jake. Philip had been a trusted friend and firm supporter for years.

Without his encouragement, she might never have taken up serious painting again. Even now he had several of her pieces displayed in his gallery. He'd been a good sounding board through the years, too. A widower with two grown daughters, he'd offered her valuable advice about the girls on numerous occasions. Maybe it wouldn't hurt to run this situation by him, get his take on it.

"Okay, you win," she capitulated. "Something pretty…dramatic…did happen today."

He tilted his head and eyed her quizzically. "Well, I can't say you look unhappy exactly. It must not be anything too terrible."

"I'm not so sure about that," she murmured, shaking her head. She stirred her ice tea and took a deep breath. "You remember I mentioned once that years ago I was engaged?"

"Mmm-hmm."

"Well…Jake—that was his name—he…he stayed at the inn last night."

Philip frowned. "You mean he came to see you?"

"No, nothing like that," she said quickly. "He got caught in the fog and just happened to stop at our place. Allison checked him in. I didn't even know he was there until this morning at breakfast, when the girls kept talking about this…this nice-looking man who'd checked in. It turned out to be Jake."

Philip stared at her. "That must have been a terrible shock."

Maggie gave a short, mirthless laugh. "That's putting it mildly. I've been off balance ever since it happened. Which is odd, since my relationship with him was over long ago. I can't figure out why his reappearance has disturbed me so much."

Philip studied her for a moment. "It does seem strange," he concurred. "After all, whatever you two shared is obviously history."

"Right."

"And it isn't as if he even means anything to you anymore."

"Right." This time there was a hint of uncertainty in her voice.

"What was he doing here, anyway?"

"He's interviewing for a job at the Maritime Academy."

"You mean he might actually move up here?"

"Yes. And that makes me even more nervous. Which is ridiculous, because we're really no more than strangers to each other now."

"It's probably just the shock of seeing him," Philip reassured her. "Where has he lived all these years?"

"All over, I guess. He's been in the navy. I think he still would be if it wasn't for his father." Maggie briefly explained the situation to Philip.

"Hmm" was his only cryptic comment when she finished.

Maggie tilted her head and looked at him quizzically. "What's that supposed to mean?"

He shrugged. "I guess I'm a little surprised. And impressed. Not many people would give up their career, start over, change their whole life to keep a promise basically made under duress. He sounds like a very honorable man."

Maggie frowned. "Yes, he does," she admitted. "And it's so at odds with the image I've had of him all these years."

"Well, people do change."

"I suppose so," she admitted reluctantly. "I just wish I didn't feel so off balance."

"Things will work out, Maggie," he told her encouragingly. "They always do. You've successfully weathered a lot of storms though the years, and you'll ride this one out, too. I know. And I'm always here if you need a sympathetic ear. Don't forget that." He touched her hand lightly and smiled, then switched gears. "In the meantime...when do I get a preview of the new painting?"

"Will next week be okay?"

"Perfect. I'll reserve a spot right near the front for it. You know, you have a large enough body of work now to consider your own show."

Maggie grimaced. "I just don't feel...well...good enough...to have an official show."

"Why don't you let me be the judge of that? Besides, you'll never know till you try. It's not like you to back off from a challenge."

"I know. But my painting is so...personal. If I got bad reviews it would be devastating. I'm not sure I'm ready to face that."

"First of all, they wouldn't be bad. And second of all, you can face anything, Maggie Fitzgerald. Because you are one of the strongest women I know."

Maggie wanted to believe him. As recently as yesterday she might have. But a lot had happened since then. And at this particular moment, she didn't feel very strong at all—thanks to one very unforgettable man named Jake West.

"Jake called twice. Will call again tomorrow."

Maggie's heart leapt to her throat as she read the note on the kitchen counter. She should have figured he'd call while she was out. She hoped the girls had explained where she was. She didn't want him to think she was trying to avoid him. It was just that she led a very busy life. Her days—and evenings—were filled. Like tonight. The zoning board meeting had run far later then she expected, because of some heated discussion. And she still had a few breakfast preparations to make, even if it was—she glanced at her watch and groaned—ten-thirty. There always seemed to be too much to do and not enough time.

As Maggie methodically set about assembling the egg and cheese casseroles that were tomorrow's breakfast entrée, she reflected on the hectic pace of her life. For most people, simply running an inn and raising twins would be a full-time job. But she had made other commitments, as well. Like serving on the church council. And on the zoning board. Not to mention the watercolors she did for the greeting card company and, in recent years, pursuit of more serious art in her limited "spare" time. Why did she take so much on? she wondered with a frown. Could it be that she wanted to keep herself so busy that she had little time to dwell on the one thing that was lacking in her life?

With an impatient shake of her head, Maggie beat the eggs even harder. She didn't usually waste time trying to analyze her life choices. If some of them were coping mechanisms, so be it. They worked, and that was all that mattered. Or they'd worked up until today, she amended. Jake's reappearance had changed everything and, much to her surprise, rattled her badly.

But what surprised her even more was the fact that when she looked at him, it wasn't the hurt she remembered, but the intense, heady joy of being in love. In some ways, it would almost be easier to remember the pain. Because that had no appeal. But love—that was a different story. That had a whole lot of appeal. It was just that the opportunity had never come along again. And it wasn't here *now,* she reminded herself brusquely as she slid the casseroles into the refrigerator. Jake had had his chance. She wasn't about to give him another.

Abby looked up from her seat in a wicker chair on the porch and grinned as she saw Jake stride up the path.

"Did you come to see Aunt Maggie?" she asked eagerly, laying her book aside.

"Please don't tell me I missed her again?" He'd been trying unsuccessfully for the past two days to reach her, and the frustration was evident in his voice. If every minute of his stay in Castine hadn't been packed, he would have simply driven over and planted himself in her drawing room until she had time to talk to him. But he knew one thing for sure. He wasn't leaving Blue Hill until he saw her again, even if that meant tracking her down wherever she might be now.

"Don't worry, you didn't. She's in the studio, Mr. West."

He felt the tension in his shoulders ease, and he smiled. "Call me Jake. And where's the studio?"

"It's the little room off the kitchen."

"Would it be all right if I go back?"

"Sure. Aunt Maggie won't mind," Abby said breezily, ignoring the worried look that Allison sent her way as she stepped outside. "It's just down the hall and through the door at the end."

"Thanks." Jake turned to find Allison in the doorway.

"Hello, Mr. West," Allison greeted him.

Jake grinned at her. "No one's called me 'Mr.' in years. Just Lieutenant. And both of those sound too formal now. So how about we just make it Jake?"

Allison smiled. "Okay."

"Good. I'll see you ladies later."

Allison watched him disappear, then turned to her sister with a worried frown. "Why did you send him back there?" she demanded urgently. "You know Aunt Maggie said never interrupt her when she's painting, unless it's an emergency."

Abby gave her sister a condescending look. "Allison, Aunt Maggie's love life *is* an emergency."

Allison clamped her lips shut. How could she argue with Abby—especially when her sister was right?

Maggie tilted her head and frowned. She wanted the seascape to convey restlessness, inner turbulence, the sense of impending fury. But she wasn't quite there yet. Considering her firsthand knowledge of the ocean, and given that her own emotional state paralleled the scene she was trying to paint today, it ought to be easy to transfer those feelings to canvas. But the mood was eluding her, and that was frustrating.

A firm tap sounded on the door, and Maggie glanced toward it in annoyance. Why were the twins bothering her? They were old enough now to handle most of the so-called crises that occurred at the inn. But maybe there truly was an emergency of some kind, she thought. In sudden alarm she reached for a rag to wipe her brush, psyching herself up to deal with whatever crisis awaited her. "Come in."

The "crisis" that appeared when the door swung open was *not* one she was prepared for, however. What on earth was Jake doing here, in her private retreat?

She stared at him in surprise as her heart kicked into double time. Try as she might, she couldn't control the faint flush that crept onto her cheeks, or stop the sudden tremble that rippled over her hands.

Jake smiled engagingly. "Abby said I could come back. I hope you don't mind. But I'm on my way back to Boston, and this was my last chance to see you before I left. We didn't seem to have much success connecting by phone."

"Y-yes, I know." Why did her voice sound so shaky? "Sorry about that. I was at a zoning board meeting the first night you called, and running errands the other times." That was better. Steadier and more in control.

"So the girls told me." He propped one shoulder against the door frame and folded his arms across his chest. "You continue to amaze me, Maggie. I don't remember that you ever had any interest in politics or government, local or otherwise, and now you're on the zoning board?"

She carefully set the brush down and reached for a different rag to wipe her hands on, using that as an excuse to escape his warm, disquieting gaze. "Well, I'm part of the business community of this town. It's my home. I feel a certain sense of responsibility to do my part to make sure Blue Hill retains the qualities that attracted me in the first place."

"Once again, I'm impressed."

"Don't be. A lot of people do a whole lot more than me."

He didn't agree, but rather than debate the point, he strolled into the studio, his gaze assessing. It was a small room, illuminated by the light from a large picture window on one side. Unlike his image of the stereotypical messy artist's studio, however, this one was neat and orderly. A couple of canvases in various stages of completion stood on easels, and several other finished works were stacked against one wall.

But what captured his attention most were the posters. Vienna. Florence. Rome. Paris. London. Athens. As his gaze moved from one to another, he realized that these were the places he and Maggie had planned to visit together. And he realized something else, as well. He'd seen most of them, while Maggie had been confined to rural Maine, coping with responsibilities that even now her slender shoulders seemed too fragile to bear. His dream of travel had become reality; hers had remained a dream.

He looked down at her slim form silhouetted against the window, the sun forming a halo around her hair, and his throat tightened. He wished with all his heart that he could take her to all the exotic places pictured on her walls. She would love them, he knew, would be as awed as he had been on his first visit. But maybe…maybe she'd managed to see one or two, he thought hopefully.

He nodded toward the walls. "Nice posters," he remarked casually. "Are any of them souvenirs?"

She gave him a wry smile and shook her head, dashing his hopes. "Hardly. B&B owners may cater to travelers, but they do very little traveling themselves. Especially with two girls to raise. I've stayed pretty close to home all these years. I expect you've made it to some, or all, of these spots, though."

He nodded, trying to stem the surge of guilt that swept over him. "Yes."

"Are they as wonderful as we…as people say?" she

asked, the slightly wistful note in her voice producing an almost physical ache in his heart.

"Mmm-hmm." He cleared his throat, but still the huskiness in his voice remained. "I'm sorry you never got to see them, Maggie."

"Oh, but I will," she said brightly, suddenly aware that he felt sorry for her. She didn't want his sympathy. "I'm going to Europe right after Christmas. Actually, the trip's been in the works for years. I decided what with the twins going away to college this fall, it was time I started a new phase of my life, as well. I'm going to close the B&B for four months and visit all the museums and take some art classes and just soak up the ambiance. It should be wonderful!"

The sudden spark of enthusiasm in her eyes lit up her face, giving it a glow that warmed his heart. "That sounds great. I know you'll enjoy it, especially with your art background." He nodded toward the canvases stacked around the room. "I guess I never realized just how talented you are. I remember you sketching and doing some watercolors, but not painting. I don't know that much about art, but these look very impressive to me."

Despite herself, Maggie was pleased by his compliment. "Thanks. I'm not that good, though. I really don't have any formal training. But Philip—he owns a local gallery—has encouraged me. He even displays some of my work. And he's been trying for the last year to convince me to have a show at a gallery in Bangor that's owned by a friend of his. But I'm just not sure I'm ready for that."

"You look ready to me," Jake told her sincerely. There was a quality to her work, an emotion, a power, that radiated compellingly from the canvases. Even with his untrained eye he could sense it.

"Philip says so, too. But I haven't committed to it yet."

"Is this Philip someone whose judgment you trust?"

She nodded confidently. "Absolutely. About everything except my painting, that is. We've been friends for a long time, and I'm afraid he may not be completely impartial."

An alarm bell rang in Jake's mind. Maggie had used the term *friend*, but when she spoke of this Philip, the warmth and familiarity in her voice implied something more. And that possibility disturbed him. Which was wrong. He certainly had no claim on her heart. He should be glad that she'd found a male companion. Considering all the love she had to offer, Maggie wasn't the kind of woman who should spend her life alone. But even as he acknowledged that his reaction was selfish and wrong, he couldn't change the way he felt. The thought of Maggie in love with another man bothered him. It always had.

"Well, I think he's right," Jake said, biting back the question that he longed to ask her about Philip.

"We'll see," Maggie replied noncommittally. "So...you're heading back to Boston. How did the interview go?"

"I'll tell you all about it in exchange for a cup of coffee," he bartered with a smile.

"Oh! Sure. I thought maybe you only had a few minutes."

"I've got an early flight out of Boston tomorrow morning, so I'd like to get back at a reasonable hour. But I can stay for a little while," he told her as he followed her into the large, airy kitchen.

"Flight?" she asked over her shoulder as she filled two cups.

"Rob and I are meeting at the old house. Before we put it on the market we have to sort through everything and decide what we want to keep. The rest will be sold at an estate sale."

Maggie turned to him with a troubled frown. "This must be awfully hard on your dad."

"I'm sure it is," he agreed with a frown. "He's accepted the necessity of it, though, and other than a few specific items he's asked us to save, he's pretty much left the disposition of everything in Rob's and my hands."

"That won't be an easy job, Jake," Maggie empathized.

Jake hadn't really thought that far ahead. But he'd been gone from his childhood home for a long time. The emotional ties had loosened long ago. He expected he'd cope just fine. He couldn't very well say that, though. It would sound too coldhearted somehow.

"Well, Rob and I will be doing it together. That should help," he replied.

She placed his coffee on the table and sat down, motioning for him to join her. "So how did the interview go?"

"I guess it went well. They offered me the job."

Her breath caught in her throat as her heart stopped, then lurched on. "So you'll be moving to Castine?" she said carefully.

He nodded. "In about three weeks."

Three weeks! That hardly even gave her time to adjust to the idea! "That fast?"

"Well, Rob's in a bind. The sooner I take Dad off his hands, the better. And I think I'll like the job a lot.

I've been an instructor for a few classes in the navy, and I enjoy teaching. And this job will let me stay close to the sea, which is a real plus.''

His voice had grown thoughtful, and Maggie looked at him curiously while he took a sip of coffee, again struck by the sense of maturity and quiet confidence that he radiated. The high energy she remembered—exhilarating but sometimes undirected—seemed to have been tamed and channeled toward specific goals.

"So, since I had a lot of leave accumulated, I'm taking a month off while they process my discharge—to get things squared away for my new life. I found a nice two-bedroom cottage that's available right now and signed the papers yesterday,'' he finished.

"It seems like you have everything pretty much under control.''

"Logistically, yes. Dealing with my father…that's another story.''

"Well, he's had an awful lot to adjust to, Jake. Maybe he just needs some time.''

"Time I can give him. I'm just not sure that's all it will take.'' He glanced at his watch regretfully and drained his cup. "I've got to go. It's a long drive back to Boston. But I'll be back, Maggie. And I was hoping…well, I thought maybe we could have dinner then to finish catching up and celebrate my new job.''

She looked into warm brown eyes that, with a single glance, had once been able to fill her heart with light and hope and promise. But that was then. This was now. And she wasn't the starry-eyed bride-to-be that she'd been twelve years ago.

And yet…sitting here with him now, she felt an awfully lot like the young girl she used to be. Which was not a good sign at all. Her best plan would be to avoid him until she straightened out the emotional tangle she'd felt ever since his reappearance.

"So what about it, Maggie? How does a dinner celebration sound?"

She looked down and ran a finger carefully around the rim of her cup. "I'm not sure that's a good idea, Jake."

He didn't respond immediately, and she refused to meet his gaze, afraid that if she did, her resolve would waver. Finally she heard him sigh, and only when he made a move to stand up did she look at him.

"Would you think about it at least?" he asked quietly. "Don't give me an answer now. I'll call you when I get back. And I'm sorry about interrupting your work. I'll let myself out."

Maggie didn't protest. And as she watched him disappear through the door, she took a sip of her cold coffee. She had no intention of changing her mind. For one very simple reason. She wasn't at all sure there was anything to celebrate.

Chapter Four

With a weary sigh, Jake flexed the muscles in his shoulders, then reached for yet another dusty box. Thank heavens Rob hadn't been called back to Atlanta for that job interview until all of the big items at the house had been dealt with. Only a couple of closets remained for Jake to clean out alone. But it was slower—and more difficult—going than he'd expected.

It seemed that Maggie had been right. Even though he'd cut most of his ties with this small house and the town where he grew up, for some reason he found it surprisingly difficult to be in his childhood home for the last time. He'd come to realize that though his ties to this place were few, they were stronger than he'd suspected. The process of cutting his roots with such finality was unexpectedly unsettling.

As he and Rob pored over the old scrapbooks, sometimes laughing, sometimes lapsing into quiet, melancholy remembrance, the good days came back to Jake with an intensity that startled him. The days when they'd all lived here together under this roof, happy and content. The days when he and his dad were not only father and son, but friends.

He'd lingered longest over the faded photos. The photos of himself, flanked by his parents at high school graduation, their eyes shining with pride. Photos older still, of his dad teaching him to ride a bike and to pitch a baseball. For years, Jake hadn't allowed himself to remember those happier times. The memories only made him sad. Though he'd denied it to himself for more than a decade, the truth was he'd always cared what his father thought about him. But he'd failed him twelve years ago, and many times since in the intervening years.

Jake sighed. He almost wished he didn't care. It would make things easier. But he did. He still loved his father, despite the older man's opinionated views and stubborn disposition. Not that he'd done much to demonstrate that in the last decade, he admitted. After his father's sound rejection of his initial overtures, he hadn't wasted time or energy on further attempts.

His mother was a different story. She had been disappointed in his choices, as well, but she'd never let that interfere with her love for him. The rift between her youngest son and husband had always caused her distress, and in her quiet way she'd tried—unsuccessfully—to bring them together on several occasions. One of her greatest disappointments was that she hadn't lived to see a reconciliation.

Maybe his father would have softened over time if Jake had admitted he'd made a mistake. And maybe Jake would have admitted his mistake if his father's attitude had softened a little. But instead it became a standoff. It was a shame, really, Jake thought with a pang of regret. Because as he'd grown older he'd come to realize the enormity of his betrayal in walking out on the woman he had professed to love.

Jake had considered admitting that to his father a few times through the years, but the older man had never offered him an opening. And Jake didn't want it thrown back in his face.

Sometimes he wondered if his father harbored regrets, too. If he did, he'd never let on. Jake suspected that pride was at the root of their problem. But knowing the source didn't necessarily suggest a solution. And dwelling on the past wasn't helping him finish today's job, he reminded himself.

Jake glanced at the box he had just withdrawn from the closet and was surprised to find his name written on it in his mother's neat, careful hand. As he sifted through the contents, he realized that she had saved every letter he'd written, as well as every clipping he'd sent. He blinked rapidly to clear the sudden film of moisture from his eyes. His mother's death had been hard on him. He missed her deeply, as well as the direct link she had provided to home. Although he'd continued to write, his father never responded. It was only through Rob that Jake kept tabs on him. He wasn't sure if his father even opened his letters.

Suddenly Jake's gaze fell on the clipping announcing his promotion to lieutenant two years before. His mother couldn't have put that in the box. Nor the article about the special commendation he'd received last year, he realized, shuffling through the papers. Which only left one possibility. His father had not only *opened* his letters, but *saved* them. Which must mean he still cared.

With a suddenly lighter heart, Jake worked his way steadily through the remaining boxes, eating a hastily

assembled sandwich as he made one more circuit of
the house to ensure that none of the furnishings had
gone untagged. Most items were to be sold. A few were
to be shipped to his cottage in Maine. Everything
seemed to be in order, he thought with satisfaction, as
he stepped into the garage and glanced around. There
really wasn't much of value out here, certainly nothing
he planned to take to Maine. Unless...

His gaze lingered on the boxes containing his father's woodworking tools. He knew from Rob that they
had lain unused since his mother's death. But why not
hang on to them, just in case? Without stopping to
reconsider, Jake quickly changed the instructions on
the boxes, then headed back inside.

By the end of the emotionally draining day, Jake had
reached the last "box"—a small fireproof safe stored
in the far corner of the closet in his parents' bedroom,
under the eaves. He read the label, written in his
mother's hand, with a puzzled frown. "Important Documents." As far as he knew, he and Rob had already
located and dealt with all the "important documents."

But the mystery was cleared up a moment later when
he opened the lid. He should have guessed the kinds
of things this box would contain, knowing his mother's
definition of "important," he thought with a tender
smile. Carefully, one at time, he withdrew the items.
Her own mother's handwritten recipe for apple pie. A
poem she'd clipped from the newspaper about taking
time to enjoy a quiet summer night. Jake's kindergarten
"diploma." An embossed copy of the Twenty-third
psalm, given to her on her wedding day by her father.
These sentimental items were his mother's real trea-
sures, Jake knew. These "important documents"—not
expensive rings or necklaces—had been her jewels.

Every item touched his heart—but none more so than the last one. As he withdrew the single sheet of slightly yellowed paper, memories came flooding back of a hot summer day more than a quarter of a century before. The document contained few words, but as his eyes scanned the sheet he remembered with bittersweet intensity the strong emotions and deep sincerity that had produced them.

It had been a long time since that document had seen the light of day. But as he carefully replaced the paper and gently closed the lid, he hoped that its time would come again soon.

"Is Maggie here?"

The unfamiliar woman behind the desk at Whispering Sails shook her head. "No, I'm sorry. Is there something I can help you with?"

Jake sighed wearily. It had been a hectic and emotionally taxing three weeks since he'd left Maine, and he'd had a very long drive up from Boston. He should have just gone directly to his cottage in Castine and contacted Maggie tomorrow. This was obviously a wasted detour.

"No. I was just hoping to see her for a minute. I should have called first."

The woman looked at him uncertainly. "Are you a friend of hers?"

"Yes." Jake wasn't sure Maggie would agree, but from his perspective the statement was true.

"Well...then I guess it's okay to tell you what happened. Allison was in a car accident, and Maggie's at the hospital."

Jake's face blanched. "How badly is she hurt?"

"I don't know. Maggie got the call about two hours ago, and I haven't heard from her yet."

"Where's the hospital?"

The woman gave him directions, and with a clipped "Thank you," he strode out the door and to his car. Less than a minute later he pulled out of the driveway in a spray of gravel, his foot heavy on the gas pedal, oblivious to the speed signs posted along the route.

By the time he reached the hospital, his body was rigid with tension. He scanned the emergency room quickly, but there was no sign of Maggie.

"Sir…may I help you?"

He glanced at the woman behind the desk. "I'm looking for Maggie Fitzgerald. Her niece, Allison Foster, was brought in some time ago. A car accident."

"Oh, yes. Ms. Fitzgerald is just around the corner." She inclined her head to the right.

"How is Allison?"

"The doctor is still with her, sir. We'll let you know as soon as we have any word."

He acknowledged her reply with a curt nod, then covered the length of the hall in several long strides, pausing when he reached the door to the cold, sterile waiting room. It was empty except for the lone figure huddled in one corner.

Jake's gut clenched as he looked at Maggie's slim form, every muscle in her body tense, her face devoid of color. He tried to swallow, but it was difficult to get past the sudden lump in his throat. How many of these kinds of crises had she endured alone, without even the reassuring clasp of a warm hand for comfort?

Jake had never thought of Maggie as a particularly strong woman. But his assessment of her had changed radically in the last few weeks. She was clearly capable of handling emergencies alone. If she wasn't, she couldn't have survived the last twelve years. But that didn't mean she had to, not anymore. Not if he had anything to say about it, he decided, jamming his hands into his pockets, fists clenched, as a fierce surge of protectiveness swept over him.

The sudden movement caught Maggie's eye and she jerked convulsively, half rising to her feet as she turned to him. The frantic look in her eyes changed to confusion as his identity registered. Was that Jake? she asked herself uncomprehendingly. And if so, why was he here? She hadn't prayed for him to miraculously appear to comfort her, to hold her, to help her survive, as she had so many times in the past during times of trauma. And yet…here he was. Or was it just a dream? she wondered, closing her eyes as she wearily sank back into her chair and reached up to rub her forehead.

The warm hand that clasped her icy one a moment later wasn't a dream, though, and her eyelids flew open.

"Jake?" Her voice was uncertain, questioning, as if she couldn't believe he was really there.

"Yeah, it's me," he confirmed softly as he reached over and pried a paper cup of cold coffee out of her other hand, then took that hand in his warming clasp, as well.

"But…what are you doing here?"

"I stopped by Whispering Sails, and the woman on duty told me you were here. What happened, Maggie?"

She drew a deep, shuddering breath and spoke in short, choppy sentences. "Some guy ran a stop sign. Rammed Allison's car on the passenger side. He walked away. But her…her head hit the window. It knocked her out. She was still unconscious when they brought her in. They haven't told me anything yet. But I'm afraid.... She's so young, and... Oh, Jake!'' A sob rose in her throat and she bowed her head as a wave of nausea swept over her. *Dear God, please let Allison be all right,* she prayed fiercely. *Please! She has her whole life still to live!*

Jake watched helplessly as Maggie's slender shoulders bowed under the burden of desperate worry. Without even considering what her reaction might be, he put his arm around her and pulled her close.

For a moment, Maggie was sorely tempted to accept the comfort of his arms. A part of her longed to simply let go, to burrow into the haven he offered, to let his solid strength add stability to a world that at the moment seemed terribly shaky. Part of her wanted that badly.

But another part sounded a warning. *Don't get used to this, Maggie. Don't even think about leaning on this man. You did that once, remember, and where did it leave you? Alone, to pick up the pieces. You've handled crises before. You don't need him to make it any easier. Because even if he helps you through this one, he won't be there the next time. And it will be that much harder to face if you accept his support even one time.*

Jake felt her go absolutely still, and he waited, holding his breath. He hoped she would simply let him hold her, that she would accept his actions at face value—as the compassion of a friend. But when her body grew rigid and she pulled away, he knew he'd lost this round. Reluctantly he let her go.

''Ms. Fitzgerald?''

Maggie's head shot up and she was on her feet instantly. ''Yes.''

The white-coated figure walked into the room and held out his hand. "I'm Dr. Jackson." He turned to Jake quizzically as he took Maggie's hand.

"Th-this is Jake West," Maggie told him. "He's a...a friend of the family."

The two men shook hands, and then the doctor turned his attention back to Maggie. "Let's sit down for a minute, okay?"

Jake watched her carefully. He could tell from the rapid rise and fall of her chest that she was scared to death, and despite her rejection moments before, he decided to risk taking her hand. Maybe she'd allow that minimal intimacy. He wanted—needed—her to feel a connection between them, a tactile reassurance that she was not alone. And this time she didn't protest his touch, he noted with relief. In fact, she almost seemed unaware of it, though she gripped his hand fiercely.

"Your niece has a slight concussion, Ms. Fitzgerald, and a bruised shoulder. Nothing more, it appears. She was very lucky that the other driver hit the passenger side of the car. We'd like to keep her overnight for observation, but she should be fine."

Jake could sense Maggie's relief as her body went limp. "Thank God," she whispered fervently.

"You can see her now if you'd like."

"Yes." She nodded and rose quickly. "If you'll just show me the way, Doctor..."

"Of course."

"I'll wait here for you," Jake told her.

She stopped and turned back to him with a frown. "You don't have to."

"I want to."

Maggie was too exhausted to argue. Besides, she had

a strong suspicion it wouldn't do any good anyway. "I'm not sure how long I'll be."

"I'm in no hurry." Before she could argue further, Jake settled into one of the chairs and picked up a magazine.

Short of telling him to get lost, Maggie was left with no choice but to follow the doctor.

She reappeared in thirty minutes, and Jake looked at her in surprise, rising quickly when she entered. "Is everything all right?" he asked.

"Yes. Allison's all settled now. She wanted me to go home and get some rest." She didn't tell him that when Allison found out Jake was there, she'd just about pushed her aunt out the door.

"I think she's right. You look done in, Maggie."

"Yeah, well, it's been a long day." She brushed a hand wearily across her eyes, and Jake noted that her fingers were still trembling. She was clearly in no condition to drive, he realized.

"Listen, Maggie, why don't you let me take you home?"

Her startled gaze flew to his. "But...my car is here."

"Do you need it for anything else today?"

"No."

"Then leave it here. I'll bring you back tomorrow to pick up Allison."

"That's too much trouble, Jake. I couldn't let you do that."

Couldn't or wouldn't? he wondered, deciding to try a different tact. "Come on, Maggie," he cajoled. "I know you're a strong woman and very capable of running your own life, but it's okay sometimes to let other people help. Besides, my mother always taught me to do at least one good deed a day. If you cooperate, I can count this for today."

Maggie was torn. In all honesty, she felt too shaky to drive. And she *was* exhausted. But she definitely did *not* want to feel indebted to Jake, didn't want to owe him *anything*.

"Look, Maggie, this is an offer with no strings, okay?" he assured her, as if reading her mind. He'd been pretty good at that once, she recalled. It was rather disconcerting to think he still was. "And if you feel that you have to do something to repay me, here's a suggestion. You can go with me to pick up Dad at the airport next week. A familiar face might help smooth over what's sure to be a rocky beginning."

Maggie considered his request. It seemed like a reasonable trade.

"Okay," she agreed. "That seems fair."

A relieved smile chased the tension from his face. "Great. Let's head home."

When he took her arm and guided her toward the door, she didn't pull away as she had earlier. His protective touch felt comforting. Not that she'd let it happen again, of course. Tomorrow, after a good night's sleep, she'd feel stronger. And then she'd keep her distance.

"Well, this is it."

Maggie turned to look up at Jake as they waited near the exit ramp of the plane, noting his tense expression. She wanted to reassure him that everything would be all right, but she wasn't sure that was true. From what Jake had told her, he and his father wouldn't have an easy time of it. Still, she wished there was some way to ease his mind, offer him some hope. With sudden inspiration she reached up and touched his arm.

"Jake, do you remember the verse from Proverbs? 'Entrust your works to the Lord, and your plans will succeed.' It's been a great comfort to me through the years. I know you face an uphill battle with your dad, and I'm not sure anyone can make it any easier for you. But there is a greater power you can turn to, you know. Prayer might help."

Jake glanced down at her with a wry smile and covered her hand with his. "Well, it sure couldn't hurt."

Just then the passengers began to emerge, and Maggie felt Jake stiffen, almost as if he was bracing for a blow.

A few moments later Howard West appeared. At least she thought it was Jake's father. But the frail figure trudging wearily toward the waiting area bore little resemblance to the robust man Maggie remembered. There was nothing in his dejected posture or delicate appearance to suggest the man she had once known. Maggie's grip on Jake's arm tightened, and she felt a lump rise to her throat.

Jake looked down at her. He should have prepared Maggie for his father's deteriorated appearance, he realized.

"He's changed a lot since Mom died," Jake murmured gently. "And even more since the heart attack."

She nodded silently and he saw the glint of unshed tears in her eyes. "I guess I should have expected something like this," she admitted, a catch in her voice. "But somehow I never thought that...well, I don't know, he just seems so...so lost..."

Jake glanced back toward his father and nodded. When he spoke, his own voice was slightly uneven. "I know. He should have made a better recovery. But after Mom died, he lost interest in a lot of things, and once he had the heart attack he just sort of gave up on life. He keeps getting more frail. It's hard to accept sometimes. He was always so strong.''

Howard looked up then. His gaze fell first on Jake, and his eyes were so cool, Maggie could almost feel the chill. His mouth tightened into a stubborn line and he lifted his chin slightly, defiantly as the two men looked at each other across a distance that was more than physical. They remained like that for several seconds, until finally, sensing a need to break the tension, Maggie took a step forward and smiled.

Howard transferred his gaze to her, and the transformation in his face was astonishing. The glacial stare melted and the line of his lips softened as a genuine smile of pleasure brightened his face.

''Hi, Pop,'' she greeted him, using her pet term of endearment for him.

''Maggie.'' He held out his arms. ''Nobody's called me that in years. Aren't you going to give this old man a hug?''

She stepped into his embrace, and his thin, bony arms closed around her. There was almost nothing to him, she realized in alarm as she affectionately returned the hug. When they finally drew apart there was a telltale sheen to his eyes.

''Maggie girl,'' he repeated, still holding her hands. ''You look wonderful. A sight for sore eyes, I can tell you. I heard you were here, but I didn't expect you to come and meet me. I'm glad you did, though. It does a body good to see such a friendly face in a strange place.''

Maggie knew Jake was right behind her, knew he'd

heard his father's comment. She was sure it had cut deeply. And she was equally sure that was Howard's intent. Clearly the gulf between the two of them had widened dramatically through the years, she thought in dismay.

"Hello, Dad."

Howard reluctantly transferred his gaze from Maggie to Jake. "Hello," he said flatly.

"Did you have a good trip?"

"It was bumpy. And long."

"Then let's get your luggage and head home so you can rest."

"I don't need to rest."

Before Jake could respond, Maggie tucked her arm in Howard's and began walking toward the luggage carousels. "You're a better traveler than me, then," she declared with a smile. "I'm always tired after a long plane trip. And Atlanta to Maine certainly qualifies."

"Well, I might be a little tired," he admitted.

"Maybe a short nap would be nice when you get home."

"Maybe it would."

Although Howard conversed readily enough with Maggie, and his eyes even took on their old sparkle a couple of times, she quickly became aware that he was doing his best to ignore his son. Several times she tried to draw Jake into the conversation, but Howard would have none of it. Finally she gave up.

When Jake pulled into the parking lot of Whispering Sails, Howard leaned forward interestedly. "Is this your place, Maggie?"

"Yes. And the bank's," she teased.

"Well, it's mighty pretty. And a nice view, too."

"Thanks, Pop. It's been our home for a long time now. We love it here."

"I can see why. What's that over there?" He pointed to a small structure of weathered clapboard about a hundred yards from the house.

"That's our cottage. It's a little roomier and more private than the house. Some of our guests come back and stay there every year. I'll give you a tour soon, if you'd like."

He nodded eagerly. "That would be great."

She reached back then, and clasped his hand warmly. "You take care now, okay, Pop?"

He held on to her hand as if it was a lifeline, the strength of his grip surprising her. "Is that tour a promise, Maggie?"

The plea in his eyes made her throat tighten, and her heart was filled with compassion and affection for this man she'd once loved like a father. Cutting her ties with Jake's parents had been very painful, but at the time it had seemed the best way to preserve her sanity and start a new life. She'd never stopped missing them, though. And she was more than willing to do what she could to ease the difficult transition for this man who had lost not only his wife, but his health, his home and now his independence.

"Of course. Give me a call once you're settled and we'll have lunch."

"I'd like that." When he at last reluctantly released her hand, she reached for the door handle.

"I'll walk Maggie to the door, Dad."

"That's not necessary, Jake," she said quickly.

"I insist."

"At least some of your good manners stuck with you," Howard muttered.

A muscle in Jake's jaw clenched, but he didn't respond. Maggie quickly stepped out of the car and met him at the path to the house, deciding not to protest when he took her arm. She wasn't going to give him the cold shoulder, too.

"It's pretty bad, isn't it?" she conceded quietly.

"And not apt to get much better any time soon, I'm afraid."

He paused when they reached the porch and raked his fingers wearily through his hair. "Thanks for going today, Maggie. I think it was good for Dad to see a friendly face, as he so bluntly put it."

There was a touch of bitterness—and despair—in Jake's voice, and though Maggie had her own unresolved issues with this man, she couldn't help but feel compassion for his plight. Impulsively she reached over and laid a hand on his arm. "I'll keep you both in my prayers, Jake," she promised with quiet sincerity.

"Thanks. We could use them. Goodbye, Maggie."

As he walked back to rejoin his father, Jake thought about Maggie's last comment. He wasn't much of a praying man, not anymore. In fact, it had been so long since he'd talked to the Lord that he doubted if his voice would even be recognized. But maybe the Lord would listen to Maggie.

Jake hoped so. On his own, he wasn't sure he could ever make peace with the stony-faced man waiting in his car. It would take the intervention of a greater power to bring about such a reconciliation. In fact, it would take a miracle. And unfortunately, Jake thought with a sigh, he hadn't witnessed many of those.

Chapter Five

Jake slowly opened his eyes, glanced at the bedside clock with a groan, then pulled the sheet back over his shoulder and turned on his side. Even after all his years in the navy, living by rigid timetables that often included unmercifully early reveille, he'd never adjusted to getting up at the crack of dawn. Okay, so maybe eight o'clock didn't exactly qualify as the crack of dawn. But it was still too early to get up on a Sunday morning.

He had just drifted back to sleep when an ominous clatter in the kitchen rudely awakened him. Obviously his father was up, he thought wryly. As he'd discovered in the last couple of days, Howard was an early riser. But he usually tried to go about his business quietly until Jake appeared. Clearly, however, his father was in no mood to humor him this morning.

With a resigned sigh Jake swung his feet to the floor. He supposed he should look on the bright side. At least they hadn't come to blows yet. On the other hand they'd barely spoken since Howard's arrival. Jake had tried to engage his father in conversation, but the older man's responses were typically monosyllables or grunts.

Jake frowned as Howard noisily dropped something onto the counter. For whatever reason, his father appeared to be in a worse mood than usual today.

Jake pulled on his jeans and combed his fingers through his hair. Might as well find out what was in the old man's craw. Whatever it was, Jake had a sinking feeling that it had something to do with him.

He padded barefoot toward the kitchen, pausing on the threshold to survey the scene. Howard had apparently already eaten breakfast, judging by the toast crumbs on the table and the almost-empty cup on the counter. A crusty oatmeal pot added to the unappetizing mess. Jake jammed his hands into his pockets and took a deep breath.

"I would have made breakfast for you, Dad."

"I might starve waiting for you to get up," the older man replied brusquely.

Jake felt a muscle tighten in his jaw, but he tried to maintain a pleasant, civil tone. "I spent a lot of years in the navy getting up early, Dad. I like to sleep in when I can. I'll be on my new job in less than a month, back to a regular schedule. I'm enjoying this while I can."

"At the expense of God, I see."

Jake frowned. "What's that supposed to mean?"

Howard spared him a disparaging glance, disapproval evident in his eyes. "It doesn't look to me like you plan on going to church today. I guess you've turned your back on God, too."

So that explained why his father was wearing a tie, Jake thought distractedly as he considered Howard's caustic remark. The fact was, the older man was right—and Jake felt guilty about it. Since he'd left home, he'd slowly drifted away from his faith. Oh, he still believed all the basics. He just hadn't seen much reason to demonstrate those beliefs by going to church. And gradually, as time went by, his faith had become less and less a part of his life. But clearly it was still very much a part of his father's.

"Give me a few minutes to get dressed," he said shortly, turning on his heel and retreating to his bedroom.

"What time are the services?" his father called.

Jake ignored the question—because he didn't have a clue. But Maggie would. He knew beyond the shadow of a doubt that her faith still played a pivotal role in her life. There was probably a church somewhere near Castine, but if he had to go, he figured he might as well use it as an excuse to see her. He reached for the phone, praying she hadn't left yet.

By the time Jake reappeared in the kitchen fifteen minutes later, in a navy blue blazer and striped tie over khaki slacks, his father had cleaned up the kitchen and was sitting at the table reading the paper. He looked up and adjusted his glasses when Jake stepped into the room, and for the briefest second Jake could have sworn he saw a flash of approval. But it was gone so fast, he couldn't be sure.

"So what time are services?"

"Ten o'clock."

"When do you want to leave?"

"Nine-thirty should be fine. I'm going to grab some breakfast first."

His father silently perused the paper as Jake toasted a bagel and poured some coffee. Except for the rustle of paper as he turned the pages, the house was quiet. Jake didn't even try to converse with him this morning. The last few days had been draining, and he was tired. The tension in the air between them was so thick, he could cut it with the proverbial knife. Jake found himself on edge all the time, constantly bracing for his father's next dig.

The drive to the church also passed in strained silence. But the sight of Maggie waiting outside for them, just as she'd promised, brought a wave of relief. Funny. As far as he was concerned, Maggie had more reason than his father did to treat him badly. Yet despite her wariness and her obvious attempts to keep him at arm's length emotionally, she was at least civil. That was more than he could say for his father.

"Hello, Pop. Hi, Jake."

Jake smiled at Maggie as they approached. She looked especially lovely today, in a teal green silk dress that clung to her lithe curves, her hair sending out sparks in the sun when she moved. In the soft morning light, she hardly looked older than she had twelve years before.

"Hi." He smiled at her, and their gazes connected for a brief, electric moment before hers skittered away.

"Maggie, you're a sight for sore eyes." Howard's tone was warm, and for the first time since the day they'd picked him up at the airport, the older man smiled. It was amazing how that simple expression transformed his face, Jake reflected. Gone was the cold, prickly, judgmental man who shared his house. In his place was a congenial stranger, easygoing and good-natured. He seemed like the kind of person who could get along with anybody. Anybody but his youngest son, that is, Jake thought grimly.

"How have you been, Pop?"

He shrugged. "Kind of hard to adjust to a new place. I'm looking forward to that lunch and tour you promised me, though."

"How about tomorrow?"

"That would be great!" His eyes were actually shining and eager, Jake noted.

"Jake, would you like to come, too?" Maggie asked politely, turning to him.

The idea of spending time with Maggie under any circumstances was appealing to Jake. But he knew his presence would ruin the treat for the older man. Slowly he shook his head. "I'm afraid I can't. I need to go over to school and get some things squared away." Without even looking, he could sense his father's relief.

"Another time, then," Maggie replied.

Did she mean it? he wondered. She'd done little to encourage his attention since that first morning at the B&B when he'd reappeared in her life. She was polite, pleasant, completely civil. But he sensed very clearly that she'd also posted a No Trespassing sign on her heart. She would be nice to him because she was a lady and because she'd been brought up in a faith that taught forgiveness. But he suspected that she had set clear limits on their relationship.

Maggie took Howard's arm and led him into the church, leaving Jake to follow in their wake. In Maggie's presence Howard stood up straighter, walked more purposefully, Jake realized. It was obvious that Maggie was good for his father. And maybe...maybe that was why their paths had crossed, he speculated. Not because the two of them were destined to renew a failed romance, but because Maggie would be able to help Howard.

It was a sobering thought, and not one Jake especially liked. It wasn't that he begrudged his father the joy Maggie seemed to give him. But somehow he'd hoped that...well, he didn't know exactly what he'd hoped would come out of their chance meeting. He only knew it had something to do with him and Maggie—*not* Maggie and Howard.

As Jake took a seat beside Maggie, he tried to recall the last time he'd been to a Sunday service. Eight or ten years ago, maybe? Probably during one of his few visits home on leave. It felt strange to be back. Strange, and yet... He couldn't quite put his finger on it. It was just that here, in this peaceful place, with the familiar words of Scripture ringing in his ears and Maggie and his father beside him, he felt oddly as if he'd come home. Which made no sense, given that his father hated him, Maggie—though polite—was distant, and he hadn't darkened a church door in years. The Lord probably didn't even recognize him. Nevertheless, he couldn't shake the sense of homecoming. For whatever reason, being in this place with these people felt good. And right.

When the service ended, Maggie accompanied them outside, then turned to say goodbye. But Jake didn't want her to leave, not yet. She was the only bright spot in his day, and he was in no hurry to return to the silent, tension-filled house with his father.

"Where are the girls today?" he asked, trying to buy himself a few more minutes in her presence.

"Minding the store. We take turns going to services on Sunday. What time would you like me to pick you up tomorrow, Pop? We don't take guests on Sunday night, so my Monday mornings are free.''

"I'll drop Dad off, Maggie. It will save you a trip," Jake said.

She considered his offer for a moment, then gave a shrug of concession. "All right. How about ten o'clock, Pop?"

"The sooner the better as far as I'm concerned."

"I'll see you tomorrow, then." She reached over impulsively and gave Howard a hug, and for a moment Jake actually envied the older man. Though she was only a whisper away from him, she was as distant as some exotic locale where he'd been stationed. The breeze sent a whiff of her perfume his way, and he inhaled the subtle, floral scent. Nothing dramatic or sophisticated, just refreshing and filled with the promise of spring. It seemed somehow to capture her essence.

"Goodbye, Jake," she said pleasantly as she stepped out of his father's embrace. The sizzling connection was there again as their gazes met, sending a surge of electricity up his spine. His eyes darkened, and her own dilated ever so slightly under the intensity of his gaze, her lips parting almost imperceptibly. How was it possible that she could move him so after all these years with no more than a look?

"See you tomorrow, Maggie," Howard said brightly.

With a nod, she turned and walked rapidly away. Too rapidly, Jake thought. It was as if she was running away from him. He knew she didn't want to feel anything for him. He understood that. He also understood that she had no choice. *They* had no choice. The emotional ties that had once bound them might be tattered. But the chemistry was most definitely still there.

"She always was a real special girl," Howard declared warmly as he watched her disappear around the corner. "It sure is nice to see that some things never change."

Jake glanced at his father, prepared to take offense. But for once the older man's potentially barbed remark didn't seem to be directed at Jake. His eyes were thoughtful, sad even, as he stared after Maggie. Maybe his father was thinking of all the things that had changed in his life these last few years, Jake mused. Death, illness, loss of independence—they'd all taken their toll.

Both his father and Maggie had clearly changed through the years. And so had he. For the better, he thought. The challenge was to convince these two very special people of that.

"This sure is a wonderful place, Maggie," Howard complimented her as they finished their tour of Whispering Sails. "And you did all this yourself?"

"All the decorating. And a lot of the minor renovations. It's amazing what you can learn from a library book. Plumbing, wallpapering, electrical repairs, carpentry—it's all there."

Howard shook his head. "I would never have believed it. I don't recall you ever showing an interest in that kind of thing in the old days."

"Well, what's that old saying—'Necessity is the mother of invention'? You can learn an awful lot when you have to. And it's a whole lot more economical than paying someone to do it. So how about a quick look around town before we have lunch?"

By the time Maggie pulled up in front of Jake's cottage to drop Howard off, it was nearly three o'clock.

She could tell that the lonely older man was reluctant to see their outing come to an end, and her throat tightened in empathy. If only he and Jake could reach some understanding. This rift had to be hard on both of them.

"Maggie, would you come in and have a cup of coffee?" Howard asked, the plea in his eyes tugging at her heart. "Jake's not back yet. His car's still gone."

Maggie hesitated, but only for a moment. As long as she didn't have to worry about running into Jake, she could spare a little more time for Howard. And maybe she could find some words that would help these two strong-willed men breach the gap between them. "All right. For a few minutes," she agreed.

Half an hour later, sitting at the kitchen table with Howard, Maggie carefully broached the subject. "So how have you and Jake been getting along?"

Howard's response was a wry face and a shrug. Which pretty much confirmed her suspicion. She took a sip of her coffee, then wrapped her hands around the mug, choosing her words carefully. "You know, Pop, it would be easier if you and he could find a way to make some sort of peace."

He glanced down at his coffee. "Not likely."

"I feel guilty about the two of you, you know. Like the rift between you is my fault."

"That's not true, Maggie. At least not now. Jake's decision to walk out on you did *start* everything. What kind of man would do a thing like that? I thought I raised him better." He shook his head sadly and sighed. "But things just went downhill from there. I guess I made my feelings pretty clear—I never have been one to mince words—and he just quit coming around. Oh, once in a while on leave he'd show up for a few days. More for his mother than anything else.

He did love her, I'll give him that. But he should have come around more often. She was always sad he didn't. It was almost like he cut us off because we reminded him of something he was ashamed of. Even when Clara was sick, we didn't see much of him. Not till the end. Barely made it home before she died, in fact. That wasn't right.''

"Where was he at the time, Pop?" Maggie asked gently.

"Japan."

"That's pretty far away," she reflected. "I don't suppose the navy would have looked kindly on too many trips home."

Howard studied her curiously. "Seems strange, you defending him, Maggie. After what he did to you."

She shrugged and took a sip of her coffee. "It was a long time ago, Pop. We were different people then. I was devastated for a long time. But in the end I put it in the hands of the Lord, asked for His help. And eventually I was able to leave the past behind and move on. I won't lie to you, Pop. The scars are still there. It was a very tough road alone. But the girls, and my faith, helped a lot."

"I can see you've made a nice life for yourself, Maggie. But…well, I hope you won't think I'm being too nosy…I just wondered how you feel about living this close to Jake again after all these years."

Maggie took a moment to consider that question as she poured herself another cup of coffee. It was the same question she'd been asking herself for weeks. And it was a question that became even harder to answer after Sunday services, when one sizzling look from Jake had not only sent her blood pressure skyrocketing, but made her feel as shaky as a newborn colt.

So far she hadn't come up with an adequate answer. Her feelings were all jumbled together…shock, anger, trepidation. She was nervous and jumpy and confused. Mostly confused. Because she'd long ago relegated her relationship with Jake to history. She'd even gotten to the point where weeks went by when she didn't think of him. She had finally convinced herself that he no longer meant anything to her. So she had been stunned and unsettled to discover that the powerful attraction between them hadn't died after all. It had simply lain dormant—and undiminished. She felt it spark to life every time he was near her. She sensed that he did, too. And she didn't like it. Not in the least. But she didn't know what to do about it.

Maggie glanced up and realized that Howard was still waiting for an answer. "I really don't know, Pop," she replied honestly as she stood and gathered up their cups. "I'm still trying to sort it out." She deposited the cups in the sink and turned on the faucet. "I suppose I'm still in…" She paused and peered down. "Say, Pop, did you know your sink isn't draining too well?"

He rose and joined her. "Yeah. We called the owner but he hasn't done anything about it yet."

"This could back up anytime. Let me take a quick look in the garage. There might be a few tools."

Howard showed her the way, but after poking around between the boxes Jake had shipped from his father's house, she gave up. "I don't see anything. But I have some in the… Pop, what's this?" she asked curiously, leaning close to examine a label on a box. "Do you still do woodworking?"

Howard peered at the box. "Haven't in years. Not since Clara died. Hmmph. Can't imagine why Jake brought all that stuff. Guess I ought to look around and see what else he dragged up here." He glanced at the small accumulation of boxes, and his shoulders sagged dejectedly. "Not much to show for a lifetime, is it? A couple dozen boxes of junk."

Maggie reached over and gently touched his arm. "Pop, you know the important things aren't in boxes. They're here." She laid her hand on her heart.

He nodded. "You're right about that. But I haven't done too well on that score, either, I guess."

"It's never too late."

He considered that in silence for a moment, then turned to her and planted his hands on his hips. "But first things first. What about my clogged-up sink?"

She smiled. "I have some tools in the car. Let me run out and get them."

A few minutes later Maggie was wedged under the sink, Howard standing over her. "Can you hand me the wrench?" she asked, her voice muffled.

He rummaged around in her toolbox and passed it to her. "Maggie, are you sure you know how to do this?"

She grinned. "Trust me. Now, do you think you could round up some rags or old towels? There's probably water in here that will run out when I loosen the pipes."

"I'm pretty sure there are some rags out in the garage. I'll check."

Maggie shifted into a more comfortable position as she waited. It was too dark under the sink to get a clear view of the pipes. When Howard returned she'd ask him to hold the flashlight while she worked. In the meantime, she might as well see how tight the corroded connections were, she decided, reaching up to clamp the wrench onto the pipe.

When Jake pulled up in front of the cottage, he was pleasantly surprised to discover Maggie's car still parked in front. He had expected her to be long gone by the time he returned. He had no idea how his father had convinced her to come inside, but he owed the older man one for that coup. Just seeing her would brighten up his otherwise mundane day.

Jake strolled into the house, pausing in the living room to listen for voices. But the house was totally silent. Maybe they were sitting out back.

Jake strode quickly through the living room, heading toward the back door. But he came to an abrupt halt when he reached the kitchen doorway and his gaze fell on a pair of long, clearly feminine legs, in nicely fitting tan slacks, extending out from under his sink. Maggie, of course. But what in heaven's name was...

"Pop? Listen, could you hold the flashlight for me? It's pretty dark under here. And hand me the rags. I think the wrench did the trick. It's starting to give."

Silently Jake walked over to the sink, sorted through the items in the unfamiliar toolbox on the floor and withdrew a flashlight. He clicked it on, then squatted beside the prone figure, impressed by her deft handling of the wrench. She was full of surprises, that was for sure. As he recalled, she didn't know pliers from a screwdriver in the old days. With a smile he pointed the light toward the tumbled mass of red hair. "Sorry. I don't have any rags," he said in an amused tone.

Maggie's startled gaze flew to his, and she tried to sit up, whacking her forehead on the pipe in the process. "Ouch!" She clapped her hand to her head and let the wrench drop to the floor.

Jake was instantly contrite. "Maggie, are you all right?" Without waiting for a reply, his hands circled her slender waist and he gently tugged her into the open until she sat on the floor beside him, her head bowed.

"I can't believe I did that," she muttered, rubbing her forehead. "After all the sinks I've been under, to pull a stupid stunt like that..."

"I shouldn't have startled you. Let me check the damage." He pried her hand off her forehead and frowned at the rapidly rising lump. "This needs ice right away." He rose and reached for her hand, drawing her swiftly to her feet in one smooth motion, then guided her to a chair. "Sit tight. What were you doing under there, anyway?" he asked over his shoulder as he headed toward the freezer.

"Pop said it was clogged. I figured I could probably fix it. I was checking it out when you walked in."

"I found some rags, Maggie. They were right where..." Howard stopped abruptly at the garage door. "What happened?" he asked in alarm.

"I hit my head," Maggie explained quickly. "Jake is fixing me an ice pack."

"I knew I shouldn't let you tackle that plumbing. That's not woman's work," Howard fretted.

"Oh, Pop, don't be silly. I do this all the time at home. Women are liberated these days, you know." Jake handed her the homemade ice pack—ice cubes in a plastic bag wrapped in a dish towel—and she clamped it against her head, wincing as the cold made contact with her tender skin. "Thanks. I think."

Howard snorted in disgust. "Liberated! You mean

free to do all the dirty work? Doesn't sound very liberating to me.''

Maggie chuckled. "I've never heard it put quite that way, but you have a point," she conceded.

"We seem to be in short supply when it comes to tools around here, Maggie, but if you'll let me borrow a couple of these, I'll fix the drain," Jake said.

"Are you sure? I really am pretty good at this. I don't mind finishing up."

"Let Jake do it," Howard told her. "He should have done it in the first place anyway."

Maggie looked at Jake, saw his lips compress into a thin line at the criticism, and decided that this was a good time to make her exit. "Well, in that case, I'll head home. We have a full house tonight, and I need to be on hand to greet the guests."

"I'll bring the tools back in a day or so," Jake promised as he walked her to the door.

"No hurry. Hopefully I won't need them before then anyway." She turned and smiled at Howard, who had followed them. "Goodbye, Howard."

"Goodbye, Maggie. Thank you for the tour. And lunch. It was real nice."

"You're very welcome. I enjoyed it a lot."

Maggie turned to go, only to find Jake's hand at her elbow. She looked up at him questioningly.

"I'll see you to your car."

Maggie shrugged. "Suit yourself."

They walked in silence, and even though Maggie's head was starting to throb, she was acutely conscious of Jake's nearness, of the warmth of his hand on her bare skin and the faint, woodsy scent, uniquely his and achingly familiar. She had all but forgotten that scent. But standing so close to him now, she was reminded with startling intensity of all the times this man had held her in his arms, had caressed her face, had claimed her lips. But how could she still find him attractive after what he'd done to her? She'd been burned once. Shouldn't she be immune to his appeal?

Jake glanced down at Maggie's bowed head as they approached the car. She seemed lost in thought. *Where are you, Maggie?* he asked silently. *Are you remembering, as I am?* Gently, as unobtrusively as possible, he rubbed his thumb over the soft skin on her arm, recalling a time when she'd welcomed his touch. His happiest memories, his times of greatest contentment, were linked with this woman, he realized.

His gaze lingered on her glorious hair, as beautiful as ever. It was the kind of hair a man could get lost in—full and thick and inviting his hands in to play. But those old, sweet days were gone, he reminded himself. And yet…he felt the same as he had twelve years before. The astounding attraction—physical, emotional and intellectual—was still there. Did she feel it as intensely as he did? he wondered. And was it real? Or was it just fed by memories of what had once been, reawakened temporarily by the strange coincidence of their reunion?

"I'll hang on to the ice bag, if that's all right," Maggie interrupted his thoughts when they reached the car, trying with limited success to keep her voice steady.

With an effort he forced his lips up into a grin as he opened her door. "Such as it is. And thanks for taking time for Dad today. I know he appreciated it."

"It was no effort. He's a good man, Jake. He's just dealing with an awful lot right now."

"I know it's tough for him. I wish I could make it easier. But I can't reach him, Maggie. He shuts me out.'' He sighed and raked the fingers of one hand through his hair as he glanced back toward the cottage. ''I had hoped that if we actually lived under the same roof he might come around. But I'm beginning to lose hope.''

''Give it some time,'' she urged, impulsively laying her hand on his arm. ''You and he have been apart for so long that you need to get to know each other again before you can feel comfortable together.''

Jake smiled gently as he glanced down at her hand resting on his arm, then covered it with his. ''You know, when I talk to you, I don't feel quite so hopeless. Why is that, Maggie?''

Her gaze locked with his, and for just a moment, the tender look in his eyes, the warmth of his voice, made her feel sixteen again. Made her want to *be* sixteen again. Which was bad. What was past could never return. She needed to remember that. She was not going to get caught up in the romantic fantasies that Abby and Allison were weaving. They were eighteen. She was almost thirty-seven—far to old to believe in fairy tales and happy endings.

With an abruptness that momentarily startled Jake, Maggie removed her hand and stepped away.

''I don't know. But maybe I should bottle it,'' she said with forced brightness as she slid into the car. ''Call it Dr. Maggie's elixir. See you later, Jake.'' She started the engine, put the car in gear and drove away without a backward look.

Jake watched her go, a troubled look on his face, then slowly walked back to the house. His father met him at the door.

''She going to be all right? That was a nasty bump.''

''She'll be fine, Dad.'' Physically, at least. Emotionally, he wasn't so sure. About either of them.

Chapter Six

Great. Just great.

Maggie stared down in disgust at the decidedly flat tire. Naturally this couldn't have happened in town. That would be too easy. It had to happen in the middle of nowhere—namely, an isolated spot on the remote Cape Rosier loop.

A drop of water splashed onto her cheek, and she closed her eyes with a sigh of resignation. Now it was raining. That figured. And it only made sense that the air would take a turn toward the chilly side. Where was the warm sun and lovely light she'd had earlier while she was painting?

Gone, obviously, she thought with a disgusted glance at the rapidly darkening sky. As were her hopes of anyone appearing along this stretch of deserted road, she concluded. Other than walking two or three miles to a house, her only option was to change the tire herself. Suddenly she sneezed, groping in her pocket for a tissue as she sniffled. On top of everything else, she seemed to be coming down with a bug of some kind.

So what else could go wrong today? she wondered in dismay.

Maggie climbed back into the car, allowing herself a moment to regroup before tackling the job ahead of her. She put her forearms on the wheel and wearily rested her cheek against them, angling her head away from the bruised spot on her temple that was a souvenir of her plumbing adventure the week before. She hadn't seen Jake since then, although Howard had called once in the middle of the week. He said he was just checking to see how she was, but she suspected that he was simply lonely. It was so sad, the two of them sharing a house yet both so alone. Jake was trying—she knew that. But his attempts at reconciliation were rebuffed at every turn. In a way she felt sorry for him.

It was odd, this feeling of sympathy she had for Jake. And it was certainly a surprising—and ironic—twist, considering their history. But what surprised her even more was the spark between them. How could her response to him suddenly reactivate after lying in disuse for so long? One smoky look from those deep brown eyes was all it had taken to make her feel sixteen again. It has been so long since she'd felt the tremulous, breathless sensation of physical attraction that she'd even forgotten how to handle it. And she didn't want to relearn that lesson. What she *wanted* to do was turn those feelings off. That, however, didn't seem to be an option, she admitted with a sigh. But she *could* choose not to act on them. And she so chose.

For the moment, though, she would do better to focus her attention on a more pressing problem. The flat tire wasn't going to fix itself, after all. So, with a resigned sigh, she got out of the car and opened the trunk.

Maggie eyed the spare tire and jack uncertainly.

She'd changed a tire before, of course. Once. A long time ago. In a basic car-maintenance class she'd taken. Under the watchful eye of the instructor. The procedure was a bit hazy after all this time. But it would come back to her, she told herself encouragingly.

Maggie removed the spare tire without too much difficulty, then got down on her hands and knees to look under the car, trying to figure out where to put the jack. She was so intent on her task that she didn't even realize a car had stopped until she heard a door shut. Before she could fully extricate herself from under the car to check out the new arrival, an amused voice spoke beside her.

"How is it that I always seem to find you repairing things?"

Maggie scooted back and turned to stare up at Jake.

"What are you doing here?" she asked in surprise.

"I think the more important question is, what are *you* doing here?"

"At the moment, changing a tire," she replied dryly.

"I can see that. What I meant was, what are you doing on this road? It's pretty isolated."

She shrugged. "I come here to paint. There are some lovely coves out this way." Suddenly she sneezed again, then reached into the pocket of her jeans for another tissue.

Jake frowned. He'd noticed right off that her voice was a bit husky, and a closer look revealed that her eyes were red. "Are you sick, Maggie?"

She wiped her nose and shook her head. "Of course not. I never get sick."

He reached for her hand then, and before she could protest he drew her to her feet and placed a cool palm against her forehead. It was warm—too warm—and his frown deepened.

"You have a temperature."

"No, I don't. I'm fine." She pulled away, disconcerted by his touch. If her face hadn't been flushed before, it was now. She walked around him toward the trunk and started to reach for the jack, but his hand firmly restrained her.

"Yes, you do. And standing out here in the drizzle isn't going to help matters. Go wait in my car while I change your tire."

"You don't have to do that," she protested.

He sighed in frustration. "Maggie, just accept the help, okay? I would have stopped no matter who it was."

In all honesty, she really wasn't feeling that great. In fact, she was fading fast. With a sigh, she capitulated. "All right. Thank you."

Maggie couldn't believe that she actually dozed in Jake's car while he changed her tire, but he had to nudge her shoulder gently to wake her up when he finished. Her eyelids felt extraordinarily heavy as they flickered open.

"All done," he declared as he slid in beside her.

The drizzle had escalated into a steady rain during her brief nap, producing a soft, rhythmic cadence on the roof. Her gaze flickered to Jake's blue shirt, which had darkened in color with moisture and now clung damply to his broad chest, and stuck there as her pulse accelerated.

"How are you feeling?" he asked solicitously.

"Your shirt's wet," she murmured inanely, her gaze still on his chest.

He shrugged her concern aside. "It'll dry. I'm more worried about you. Are you okay to drive?"

With a supreme effort, she transferred her gaze to his face. "Sure. I—I guess I picked up a bug or something. I felt fine this morning. This just came over me in the last hour or two. I'll be okay by tomorrow."

"I don't know," he replied doubtfully. "You look pretty under the weather."

"As opposed to under the sink? Or under the car?" she teased.

That drew a brief smile in response, but then he grew more serious. "You don't have to put on an act in front of me, you know. I can tell you're feeling rotten. You always got a certain look when you were sick. Something in your eyes…" His gaze locked on hers, and for a moment her heart actually stopped beating. Here, in this cocoon of warmth, sheltered from the rain, she felt as if they were alone in the world. He was only a few inches away, close enough to touch, to lean on, to kiss…

Her breath caught in her throat as the impulse to do just that intensified. This was all wrong. She didn't want to feel this way, not about Jake. How could she even consider letting herself get involved with him again? Yes, he seemed different. More responsible, more mature. But it was too soon to know. Far too soon. But even though her mind accepted that logic, her heart stubbornly refused to listen.

Jake watched Maggie's face, his perceptive gaze missing nothing. She had always been easy to read. She wanted him to kiss her just as badly as he *wanted* to kiss her. But it was too soon. One of the things he'd learned in the navy was to control his impulses, think things through. An impulsive move in battle could cost you your life. And an impulsive move right now could cost him Maggie. Intuitively he knew that, and it wasn't a risk he was willing to take.

Reluctantly he released her gaze and turned to look at the road, which was now partially obscured by fog. He took a deep breath, willing his pulse to slow down, struggling to control his erratic respiration. He didn't want to scare Maggie away by revealing the depth of his attraction.

"I think we'd better head back or we might be marooned here," he said conversationally, striving for a light tone. "Not that I'd mind, you understand, but I think you need to change into some dry clothes and get some rest."

Maggie drew a shaky breath and reached for the door handle.

"You're right." She started to push the door open, then turned back to him with a frown. "By the way, you never did tell me how you happened to be out here today. It's not exactly a well-traveled route."

He sighed and wearily shook his head. "Dad and I had an argument. Again. I decided to go for a drive until I cooled down, and this road caught my eye. Lucky for you, I guess."

"I take it things haven't improved much in the last week between you two?"

"I think that would be a fair assumption."

"I'm sorry, Jake. I wish there was something I could do."

He shrugged. "We'll just have to work it out between the two of us. But I appreciate your concern."

"Well, tell Pop I said hi. And…thanks, Jake."

"You're welcome. Now go home and get some rest."

"I'll try, although I do have a business to run, Jake. But Eileen—you met her the night Allison was in the hospital, remember?—she comes by to fill in when we need someone, and she helps with the cleaning every day for a couple of hours. So I don't have to do much when I get home. Since I don't take guests on Sunday night, I'll actually be a lady of leisure until tomorrow afternoon."

"Good. Take advantage of it. The best way to fight a virus is to rest."

"Yes, Doctor," she teased.

"Hey, I learned a lot in the navy. One of my best buddies was a medic." He reached across to push her door open, and as his arm brushed against hers her heart lurched.

"I'll follow you until we get to the main road." Did his voice sound huskier than usual, or was it only her imagination? she wondered. "And Maggie...don't worry about my problems. I'll deal with the situation. I'm sure you have enough problems of your own to handle."

He was right, of course, she thought, as she dashed through the rain to her own car. She did have her own problems. And a glance into the rearview mirror revealed her biggest one.

With a sinking feeling, Maggie played back the answering machine again. As she listened a second time, her spirits nose-dived. Eileen had the flu, too, and wasn't going to be able to come over in the morning to help with the cleaning.

Maggie hit the erase button and wearily pushed her hair back from her face. This had most definitely *not* been a good day, she decided. A flat tire, a flu bug and four guest rooms plus the cottage to clean before two o'clock tomorrow. If the twins were here it would be manageable. But they had signed up months ago to volunteer for a week at a camp for disadvantaged children, and they wouldn't be home until tomorrow afternoon. Which meant the housecleaning chores fell squarely on her shoulders.

She trudged into the kitchen to make herself a cup of tea, detouring for two aspirin on the way. She was generally able to overlook minor aches and pains and work right through normal fatigue, but this was different. She honestly felt that if she didn't lay down, she might fall down. Maybe Jake was right. A little rest might help. Perhaps if she gave herself an hour or so she'd feel good enough to tackle a couple of the rooms tonight. Then she could finish up in the morning.

Maggie dragged her protesting body up to the third floor, which had been divided into two dormer bedrooms—one for her, one for the girls. She sank down onto her bed, too tired even to remove her shoes as she stretched out. The twins would give her a hard time about that, she thought with the ghost of a smile as her eyelids drifted closed. She'd always been such a stickler about keeping shoes off beds and furniture. But the thought didn't linger long. In less than fifteen seconds she drifted into oblivion.

As consciousness slowly returned, Maggie lifted her heavy eyelids and stared at the ceiling feeling disoriented. Then she turned her head to look at the clock on her bedside table. When it finally came into focus, she frowned. Eight o'clock? She'd slept for two hours? But no, the light wasn't right, she thought in confusion, glancing toward the dormer window. It was at the wrong angle.

With a sudden jolt, the truth hit home. It was *morning!* Propelled by panic, she quickly sat up and swung her legs to the floor. The room tilted crazily, and she dropped her head into her hands as she waited for everything to stop spinning.

The sudden ringing of the phone on her nightstand made her jump, and she groped for the receiver with one hand.

"Hel..." Her voice came out in a croak and she tried again. "Hello?"

"Maggie? Is that you?"

"Yes," she replied groggily. "Hi, Jake."

She could hear the frown in his voice. "You sound awful."

"Thanks a lot."

"How are you feeling? Or does your voice tell the story?"

Yes, she thought to herself, it does. The numbing lethargy still had a grip on her body, and her aches hadn't dissipated much, if at all. "I'll live," she assured him, striving for a flippant tone. "It's just a flu bug or something. And in this business there are no sick days. The guests just keep coming." She reached for a tissue and tried to discreetly blow her nose.

Jake realized that he'd never really thought about that. The few times he'd been under the weather in the navy he'd simply gone on sick call. But Maggie didn't have that luxury. In fact, as far as he could see, she didn't have many luxuries, period. And that bothered him. "I guess you're right," he admitted. "But the girls can help, too, can't they?"

There was no way to avoid such a direct question.

"They could if they were here. But they've been gone all week and won't be back until late this afternoon. So I'm the official greeter today."

"But your cleaning woman is coming today, isn't she?"

"Monday is one of her regular days to come," Maggie hedged.

"Well, try to take it easy, okay?" he replied.

"I'll try," she said, knowing that she could try all she wanted to—the house still had to be cleaned. It was a daunting task when she was well; "impossible" was a more appropriate descriptor today, considering how she felt. But she'd manage somehow. She always did.

"I'll check back with you later, Maggie."

"Okay. Thanks for calling, Jake."

Slowly she replaced the receiver. Then, summoning all her reserves of energy, she forced herself to stand up. At least she was already dressed, she thought wryly as she made her way unsteadily down the stairs to the utility closet. *You can do it*, she encouraged herself. *The girls will be back to help later today. Just make it through the next few hours, take it one room at a time, and you'll be fine.*

And with that she reached for the mop.

By the time Maggie started on the third room, however, she was on autopilot. She went through the motions mindlessly, every movement more of an effort than the last. In fact, she was so out of it that it took several rings before she realized someone was at her front door. Her gaze flew to the steps in panic. *Please, Lord, not a guest*, she prayed as she made her way stiffly down the stairs. *Not yet. Not this early.*

This time her prayers were answered. When she swung the door open, she found Jake, not a guest.

In one swift, assessing glance he came to the obvious conclusion. She was sick as a dog and, judging by the faint scent of disinfectant cleaner drifting his way and the mop in her hand, she was *not* resting. Without a word he took her arm and ushered her inside, forcing her to sit in the closest chair before he knelt beside her. He put his hand on her forehead, and this time it was not only hot but clammy. A muscle in his jaw clenched and he frowned.

"What are you doing with that mop?" he demanded.

"Cleaning."

"What happened to Eileen?"

"She has the bug, too."

"Why didn't you tell me that earlier?"

"What good would that have done?"

He ignored that comment for the moment. "Have you called the doctor?"

"It's just a bug, Jake. Something's been going around. I was just lucky till now. I guess it was my turn."

He didn't look convinced, but he didn't argue the point. Instead, he stood up and held out his hand. "Come on. You're going back to bed."

She shook her head. "Jake, you don't understand. I have ten guests arriving this afternoon beginning at two o'clock. I've only cleaned two of the four rooms and I still have the cottage to do. I'll barely make it as it is. I can't lay down now."

"Maggie, you're sick. You should never have gotten up today in the first place."

She sighed, blinking away the tears of weariness that sprang to her eyes. "Jake, try to understand. Eileen and the girls are my only backup. There isn't anyone else I can call.''

''Yes, there is.''

She gave him a puzzled look. ''Who?''

''Me. I learned to wield a pretty mean mop in the navy. They don't tolerate slobs, you know,'' he said, flashing her a brief grin.

She stared at him. Jake West cleaning a house? It was incomprehensible. As she recalled, he had always put housekeeping duties on a par with going to the dentist.

''Don't look so shocked,'' he admonished her gently, with that disconcerting habit he had of reading her mind. ''Times change. People change. You can trust me to do a good job. I promise your guests won't complain.''

''It's not that...'' She was still having a hard time comprehending his generous offer. And even if he was sincere, it was too much to ask. ''Jake, I can't let you do my work. It's not right. And don't give me that good deed business. This goes way above and beyond that.''

He crouched down beside her once again, his warm, brown eyes level with hers, and took her cold hand in his. ''Maggie, I *want* to do this, okay? You're sick. You'll only get sicker if you push yourself.'' He paused a moment, then took a deep breath. ''Look, I know that you're still trying to grapple with this whole situation between us. To be honest, so am I. But fate, or whatever you care to call it, brought us back together. I don't know why. But at the bare minimum I'd like to be your friend—whatever that takes, and despite the fact that I don't deserve it. And friends take care of each other. Let me take care of you today, Maggie. As a friend.''

She listened to Jake's heartfelt speech in silence, unable to doubt the sincerity in his eyes—or ignore the tenderness. He cared for her, that was clear. And, God help her, she was beginning to care for him again. She didn't want to. She told herself it was unwise. That it was risky, that she could get hurt again. But she couldn't help it. Because the Jake that had walked back into her life not only had all the good qualities she remembered, he had become even better. Under other circumstances, he was the kind of man she could easily fall in love with. There was nothing in his present behavior to make her cautious.

It was his past behavior that worried her. His track record wasn't good. And that made her *very* cautious. Her wariness wasn't something that could be overcome in a week, or a month, or maybe even a year. She'd been burned once before by this man and left with scars—plus a very real fear of fire.

Jake scrutinized her face, but for once he couldn't read her thoughts. He didn't want to push himself on her, but he'd already decided he wasn't going to walk away and let her face the housecleaning task alone. If necessary, he would insist—and deal with the consequences later. But he hoped she would just accept her limitations and be sensible.

"Maggie?" he prodded gently, exerting slight pressure on her hand when she didn't respond.

Jake's voice brought her back to the present. She was deeply touched by his offer, whatever his motivation. And like it or not, she needed help today. The Lord had obviously seen that need and provided for it. Maybe the help wasn't in the form she would have chosen, but who was she to question His motives?

"All right, Jake. Thank you. To be honest, I—I'm not sure I could have made it anyway."

Considering how she prided herself on her self-reliance, Jake knew she must be a whole lot sicker than she was letting on, to admit that she wasn't able to handle the task in front of her. Once more he stood and gently reached for her hands, drawing her to her feet. He put his arm around her shoulders, and as they walked slowly up the stairs she leaned on him heavily—another indication of her weakened physical state. No way would she lean on him—literally or figuratively—unless she was in bad shape.

He paused at the landing, giving her a chance to catch her breath.

"Where's your room?"

She nodded toward the back stairway at the end of the hall. "Third floor."

By the time they made it up the much narrower stairway to her bedroom, he could feel her quivering. They passed an open door that revealed a spacious, gaily decorated dormer room with two twin beds. Obviously the twins' domain, he thought with a smile, noting the posters of the girls' latest movie heartthrobs.

Maggie's room was much smaller, squeezed under the eaves near the front of the house. It was very simply furnished and decorated, as if she'd poured all of her attention into the rest of the house and simply not bothered with her own little piece of it. As he gently eased her down onto the narrow twin bed, his throat contracted with tenderness and admiration for this woman who had struggled against all odds to overcome traumas and challenges that would have overwhelmed most people. Jake didn't know where she had found the strength to face each day, especially in those early years. But as he knelt to remove her shoes, his eyes fell on the Bible on her nightstand, and he suspected that was probably its source. She'd always had a strong faith, and it clearly had sustained her spiritually through the difficult years.

But how had she managed emotionally? he wondered. Maggie had so much love to give. Had it all been directed to the girls? He suspected so. As he tucked the covers around her shoulders, he felt that the single bed in the small attic room spoke more eloquently than words of her solitary state. He started to speak, then realized that she had already fallen asleep. Gently he reached down to brush a wisp of hair off her forehead, his fingers dropping to linger on her cheek. As he gazed at her pale face, a fierce surge of protectiveness washed over him.

Ever since their paths had crossed, Jake had felt increasingly drawn to the woman who had once, long ago, claimed his heart. At first he'd looked upon their reunion as a chance to at last find a way to ease the guilt that had plagued him for so long. Only a few minutes ago, he'd told Maggie that he hoped they could be friends. But now, as he stood beside her, he knew that his interest wasn't motivated by guilt, and that his feelings went far beyond friendship.

He loved her. It was as simple—and as complicated—as that.

As he gazed tenderly down at her, he thought of the Maggie he'd once loved. All the essential qualities he'd cherished were still there. But she'd changed, too. And he found that he loved the new Maggie, with her self-reliance and confidence and decisive manner, even more than he had loved the dependent young woman who had once deferred to his every decision. He liked her grit and her spunk and her strength—and her soft heart, which hadn't changed one iota.

Jake walked slowly to the door, pausing at the threshold to glance back once more at Maggie's sleeping form. She was quite a woman, he thought. She deserved to find a man who would love her and stand by her no matter what, who believed in honoring commitments and wasn't afraid of responsibility, who could be counted on to stand with her through good times *and* bad.

Jake had failed her once on that score, but he vowed silently that he never would again. The question was, how could he convince her of that?

Jake didn't have the answer. But he knew one thing with absolute certainty. He would find a way. Because suddenly a future without Maggie was not something he was willing to consider.

Chapter Seven

"See, Allison, I told you it was him!"

Abby's triumphant voice heralded the arrival of the twins at the kitchen door, and Jake glanced up from the pot he was stirring. "Hello, ladies," he greeted them with an engaging grin.

They simultaneously dumped their knapsacks on the floor and joined him.

"What are you doing here?" Abby asked curiously. "And where's Aunt Maggie?"

"She's in bed with the flu. I'm making her some soup."

"You're cooking?" Allison was clearly impressed.

Jake grinned. "I don't think heating up a can of soup exactly qualifies as cooking."

"How sick is she?" Abby asked with a frown of concern.

"Pretty sick."

"Where's Eileen?"

"She's got the same bug."

"But...but what about the cleaning?" Allison asked

in alarm. "What will we tell the guests when they arrive?"

"The guests have already arrived and they're all settled in," Jake informed them calmly as he transferred the soup to a bowl and put it on a tray. "Your aunt started the cleaning, and I finished up."

"You mean...you mean *you* helped clean the rooms?" Abby asked incredulously.

Jake gave them a look of mock indignation. "Don't you think I'm capable of wielding a mop and broom?"

"It's not that," Allison said quickly. "It's just that...well, guys don't usually offer to pitch in on stuff like that."

"Well, let me tell you ladies a little secret," Jake said conspiratorially. "Men know how to clean. They just pretend they don't. So keep that in mind whenever you meet Mr. Right."

"I bet you had trouble convincing Aunt Maggie to let you help," Allison speculated.

"A little," he admitted with a grin.

Suddenly Abby frowned. "Gosh, she must be really sick if she gave in and went to bed."

"It's just the flu," Jake assured them as he added a cup of tea and some crackers to the tray. "But she's probably not going to have a whole lot of energy for a few days. Do you think you two can pick up the slack?"

"Sure. No problem. This is our summer job, anyway. We'll just put in a little overtime. Aunt Maggie's done it often enough for us."

They really were good kids, Jake reflected. Maggie had raised them well. "Great. Now, if you two can get the breakfast preparations under way, I'll take this up to your aunt."

The twins watched him disappear through the door, then Allison sank down on a convenient chair and sighed. "Wow! Talk about Sir Galahad!"

Abby joined her on an adjacent chair and propped her chin dreamily in her hand. "Yeah."

There was silence for a moment while they both mulled over this latest turn of events, and then Allison turned to her sister. "Do you think maybe something might come of this after all? I mean, I know Aunt Maggie keeps saying that their relationship is in the past and all that, but how many guys would clean toilets for a woman they don't care about?"

"I think it has very interesting possibilities," Abby replied with a thoughtful nod. "I think Aunt Maggie still cares, too. She just won't admit it—to us or herself. But maybe we can find a way to give her a nudge."

"And how do you propose we do that?"

Abby smiled smugly. "Well, as a matter of fact...I have a plan."

Jake eased Maggie's door open with one shoulder and cast a worried glance toward the bed. He'd checked on her a couple of times during the afternoon, and she'd been sleeping soundly. Now, however, she was sitting up, bent over, struggling to tie her shoes.

He pushed the door all the way open and strode inside. "What are you doing?" he demanded with a frown. He deposited the tray on the dresser and turned to face her, clamping his hands on his hips.

She looked up, startled. "Jake, it's after five! I'm surprised none of the guests have arrived yet," she said, her voice edged with panic.

"They have arrived. All of them."

Her eyes widened in alarm. "Oh, no! What did you tell them?"

"I told them hello. Then I welcomed them to Whispering Sails and asked if I could help with their luggage. I think that's the spiel, isn't it?"

Her frantic hands stilled on the laces and she stared him. "You mean…you checked everyone in?"

"Mmm-hmm. I looked them all up in the guest book on the desk in the foyer. It was a piece of cake." He picked up the tray and came to sit beside her. "Dinner," he explained, placing it on her lap.

She stared down at the soup, then back at him. "Jake, I…" Her voice choked, and she looked down in embarrassment. She was usually able to keep her emotions under control, but she couldn't stop the tears that sprang to her eyes. It had been a long time since anyone had stepped in as he had to ease her burden. The twins were great, of course. And they certainly would have helped if they'd been here. But they were family. Family members did those kinds of things for each other. But Jake wasn't family. He was… Well, she wasn't sure exactly what he was. He said he wanted to be her friend. But a moment later, when he took her chin in gentle fingers and turned her head toward his, the look in his eyes said a whole lot more than friendship.

"Did I pick the wrong kind of soup?" he asked with a tender smile.

She shook her head. "No. Th-this is fine."

"Then, what's wrong?"

She swallowed with difficulty. "It's just that I—I appreciate all you did today, Jake. It was too much to ask."

"You didn't ask."

"No, but...well, I feel like you were sort of forced into this."

"I wasn't forced into anything," he assured her firmly. "I wanted to help."

"I guess I owe you now," she replied with a sigh. "Big-time."

Jake cupped her flushed face with both hands, and his gaze locked on hers. It was difficult to concentrate on his words when his thumbs began to stroke her cheeks. But she tried.

"Maggie, you don't owe me a thing. If I spent the rest of my life trying to ease your burdens, I could still never make up for what I did to you."

Maggie's spirits took a sudden, unaccountable nose-dive. Was that the only motivation for Jake's good deed—to make amends? Was that the reason he'd offered her his friendship?

Jake saw the sudden dark cloud pass over her eyes and frowned. "What's wrong now?"

She shrugged and transferred her gaze to her soup, playing with the spoon. "Nothing. Just tired, I guess."

Jake studied her a moment, then nodded toward the tray. "Well, eat your soup and get back in bed. Everything's under control downstairs. The girls will take care of breakfast."

"I feel better since I slept, Jake. I can—"

"Maggie." He cut her off, his voice gentle but firm. "I want you to promise me you'll take it easy until at least tomorrow afternoon. You need the rest." When she didn't reply, he sighed. "Look, if you won't do it for yourself, do it for me, okay? Otherwise I'll be awake all night worrying about you."

She looked at him curiously, started to ask "Why?" but stopped herself in time. She could deal with those kinds of questions later, when she'd regained her strength. In the meantime, after all he'd done for her today she could at least give him some peace of mind in return.

"All right, Jake," she agreed.

"Good." He glanced at his watch, then grinned ruefully. "Well, I better get home and put together some dinner for Dad and me. Or maybe I can convince him to go out. He hasn't been in the mood yet, but it's worth a try tonight," he mused. "Now eat your soup."

She gave a mock salute. "Aye, aye, sir."

He grinned sheepishly. "Sorry. I got used to giving orders in the navy. It's a hard habit to break. How about, please eat your soup?"

"That's better," she conceded.

He sat there for another moment, his eyes soft on her face, and Maggie felt her breath catch in her throat. She knew that look. It was the look he used to get at his most tender moments, right before he kissed her, and her pulse went into overdrive.

Jake's gaze dropped to her full lips and a surge of longing swept over him. With a supreme effort he forced his gaze back to hers.

His eyes had deepened in color, Maggie noted, and she stared back into their unfathomable depths as he reached over to stroke her cheek with a featherlike touch. A pulse began to beat in the hollow of her throat as he slowly, very slowly, leaned toward her.

Maggie knew she should resist while she still could. But instead of listening to logic, her eyelids fluttered closed and she leaned ever so slightly toward him, inviting his kiss. She felt powerless to stop herself.

And then his lips, warm and tender, gently—and briefly—brushed her forehead. That was it. The kiss was over in an instant, so quickly that Maggie, who had expected so much more, was momentarily left off balance. Her eyelids flew open and she stared at him as he abruptly stood up.

"Good night, Maggie. I'll call you tomorrow."

And then he was gone.

She stared after him, still trying to figure out what had just happened. She thought he was going to kiss her. Really kiss her. And she'd offered no resistance. But instead of the passionate kiss she'd expected, he'd given her a brotherly peck on the forehead.

Why? Was it because he really did care about her only as a friend? Or was he just being noble, refusing to take advantage of her weakened physical condition?

Maggie didn't have a clue. But she knew one thing very clearly. Jake's brotherly kiss on her forehead just hadn't cut it. For better or worse, she wanted more.

Jake pulled up in front of his cottage and turned off the engine. It had taken the entire drive from Maggie's place to his for him to regain some semblance of control over his emotions. And he was still shaken by how close he had come just now to blowing it with her. Thank God he had found the discipline to back off, to stop at that brotherly kiss on the forehead, when what he really wanted to do was claim her tender lips with a kiss that expressed all the passion and love that was in his heart.

As each day passed, he knew with greater certainty that his feelings for this special woman had never died. During all the years of separation they had simply been stored in a quiet corner of his heart, growing in intensity as they waited for the opportunity to be given full expression. Now that the opportunity was at hand, they were clamoring for release.

But he had to be cautious. He felt sure that Maggie wasn't yet ready to accept such an admission on his part, that she was still very confused about her own feelings, grappling with questions and doubts, just as he had been initially. She needed time. He needed patience.

Jake drew a slow, deep breath. Only now was his pulse returning to normal, his respiration slowing. He'd known any number of women through the years who attracted him, but he'd never come this close to losing control. The only woman who had ever been able to do that to him was Maggie, beginning that summer when he was seventeen. She obviously hadn't lost her power over him.

Jake stepped out of the car and walked toward the house, trying to psyche himself up for the long evening ahead with his father. He didn't feel up to that ordeal— or to cooking. Wearily, he pushed the door open, took one step inside, then stopped in surprise. Appetizing aromas were wafting his way, and he frowned in puzzlement. Warily he made his way to the kitchen door, where a quick survey revealed the table neatly set for two and his father at the stove.

"Dad?"

Howard turned in surprise. "Oh. Didn't hear you come in. Dinner will be ready in fifteen minutes. You have time for a shower if you want one."

His father turned back to the stove and Jake stared at him, speechless. "Dad…are you making dinner?"

"Looks that way, doesn't it?" he replied gruffly.

"But…why?"

The older man shrugged. "You worked all day over

at Maggie's. That was a nice thing to do, with her sick and all. Figured you'd probably be hungry when you got home. I didn't have anything else to do anyway.''

Jake struggled to grasp this unexpected turn of events. His father actually sounded…well, if not friendly, cordial at least.

"Dad…I bought some sparkling cider when you first arrived," he said on impulse. "I thought we could have it with our first dinner here in the cottage. But…well, things didn't quite work out. If you'd like to have it tonight, it's in the cabinet next to the dishwasher."

His father's only response was a grunt, which Jake couldn't interpret. But when he reappeared ten minutes later after a quick shower, dinner was on the table. And so was the cider.

"Maggie, my dear. How are you feeling today?"

Maggie glanced toward the familiar voice of Millicent Trent and smiled at the older woman seated in a wicker settee on the front porch.

"Hello, Millicent! Welcome back to Whispering Sails. I'm much better today, thank you. And I'm sorry I wasn't on hand to greet you when you arrived."

"Don't give it a thought. The young man who showed me to my room last night was very nice. And he seemed quite concerned about you."

Maggie flushed. "It was just a flu bug, I think."

"Well, I must say you still look a bit peaked," Millicent observed, peering over her glasses.

"I'm a little tired, but I feel fine," Maggie assured the older woman. "I'm sure I'll be completely back to normal by tomorrow. The girls won't let me lift a finger today, so I'm getting lots of rest."

"Well, then, can you spare a few minutes to visit with an old lady?"

Maggie smiled. "I don't know about an old lady, but I certainly have time to visit with you."

Millicent chuckled. "You do have a way with words, my dear. Oh, Allison, would you mind bringing your aunt and me some tea?" she called when the younger girl stepped outside.

"Not at all, Ms. Trent. I'll be back in a jiffy."

"Now then, we can have a nice visit. Let's start with that young man. Who is he, my dear? I've never seen him around here before, and you know I've been a regular since the first year you opened."

Maggie took a moment to settle into an adjacent wicker chair, trying to decide how to answer the older woman's question. Millicent had become almost part of the family through the years, her annual two-week visits as predictable as the tides. She'd retired ten years before, apparently from a very prestigious position in publishing, and she had no family to speak of, as far as Maggie knew. But although she and Millicent had shared many a cup of tea and discussed everything from philosophy to the latest books and plays, they never talked about more personal matters. But for some reason, Maggie felt comfortable confiding in her about Jake.

"Jake is…an old friend," Maggie replied carefully. "He's recently moved to this area, and our paths just happened to cross."

Millicent eyed her shrewdly. "A friend, eh? His interest seemed somehow more than friendly to me."

Maggie blushed. Millicent might be old in body, but her mind was still as sharp and perceptive as someone half her age.

"To be honest, Millicent, I'm not sure what his interest is," Maggie admitted. "The fact is, we were…well, we were engaged once, many years ago."

"My dear, I had no idea!" Millicent exclaimed, laying her hand on the younger woman's arm. "I always suspected there was an unhappy romance in your past, but I never wanted to pry."

"It wasn't an unhappy romance," Maggie corrected her. She leaned back against the cushions and gazed thoughtfully into the distance as Allison deposited their tea, her lips curving into a sweet smile as she retreated to memory, oblivious to the view of the bay spread out before her. "It was a wonderful romance. Jake was my first love. In fact, he was my only love. But a few weeks before we were to be married, he… Something happened, and we… The wedding was called off. Jake joined the navy and I left the Midwest and moved to Boston, then eventually here. I hadn't seen him in twelve years when he literally appeared out of the fog at the inn a few weeks ago."

"My!" Millicent breathed softly, clearly mesmerized by the story. "What an odd coincidence."

Maggie nodded. "I still have a hard time believing it myself."

"And he lives here now?"

"Yes. In Castine. He'll be teaching at the Maritime Academy in the fall." Maggie briefly explained the events that had precipitated his move.

"My!" Millicent repeated. "That's quite a story, my dear. I take it your Jake has never married?"

"No."

"Hmm. And what do you intend to do about the situation?"

"Do?" Maggie repeated with a frown.

"Yes. Do. I would say the man is quite taken with you still, my dear. I can see it in his eyes when he talks about you."

Maggie flushed. "You sound like the twins," she declared.

"Well, the young and the old often have a clearer vision of life than you people caught in the middle," Millicent observed. "But I suppose the most important thing is how you feel about this young man."

Maggie sighed. "I really don't know, Millicent. I loved him once. With all my heart. But…well, I got hurt. He…he wasn't there when I needed him the most. I'm afraid to…well, take that risk again."

Millicent nodded sagely. "I can understand that, my dear. Perhaps the best thing to do is give yourself some time to become acquainted again. People can change, you know. And twenty years from now you don't want to look back with regrets."

Maggie studied her curiously. The bittersweet quality in the older woman's voice tugged at Maggie's heart. "Millicent…I don't want to pry, either, but…well, it sounds like maybe you had a similar experience."

The older woman took a sip of tea and nodded slowly. "Yes, Maggie, I did. Many years ago. Long before you were born, in fact. It's one of the reasons I come back here each year, in fact. You see, this is where I fell in love."

"You lived in this area?"

The older woman smiled. "Actually…I lived in this house."

Maggie stared at her. "Here?" At the woman's nod of confirmation, Maggie frowned. "But…but I researched the history, and I never saw the name Trent."

"That's because I took my mother's name when I moved to New York. I thought it had more of a literary ring to it."

"You mean you actually lived at Whispering Sails?" Maggie repeated incredulously.

"Yes. It wasn't Whispering Sails then, of course. It was just home. My father owned a very successful shipping company, and Robert—that was my beau's name—was a merchant seaman who sometimes worked on my father's ships."

She paused, a smile of sweet remembrance lifted the corners of her mouth.

"We met the summer I was twenty-two. He was a handsome man, with sun-streaked brown hair, tall and strong, with the bluest eyes you could ever imagine. Bluer than the sea on a cloudless day. We fell in love, madly, passionately, with the intensity reserved for the very young. But my father would have none of it. His daughter deserved better than a seaman, he informed me. And what of the career I'd planned? He'd sent me to college, much against his better judgment, and now that I had the degree I'd so desperately wanted, he expected me to do something with it.

"Robert and I had a wonderful summer together, and when it was drawing to a close he asked me to marry him. I thought about it a long time, Maggie. I loved him as I had loved no one before or anyone since. But he was poor, and content with his lot, and I was wealthy and ambitious. I wanted to make something of my life outside of Blue Hill, and I had just been offered a prestigious position with a publishing company in New York. Plus, much as I hate to admit it, my father had finally convinced me that I was too good for a mere seaman. So in the end, I turned him down."

She gazed out over the water, and her voice grew quiet. "I regretted my decision within a year. New York wasn't nearly as glamorous as I'd expected, and living among so many different kinds of people made me realize how arrogant my attitude had been. I wasn't any better than anyone else. Not as good as most, in fact. And I missed Robert desperately. To love with such intensity…what a gift that is. And what a sin to waste it."

Her voice faded, and Maggie leaned toward her. "But why didn't you tell him you'd changed your mind?" she pressed.

Millicent turned to her with a smile of regret. "At first I was too ashamed—and too proud, I suppose—to admit my mistake. But eventually, after two years, I realized what a fool I'd been. And so I wrote to him, and asked him to meet me on his next trip to New York. I didn't tell him why, because I wanted to apologize in person, to beg him to give me one more chance."

"And did he come?"

She shook her head. "No. You see, by then he was engaged to another woman. He was an honorable man, my Robert, and I knew he wouldn't break his engagement. Nor would I ask him to. So I simply wished him well."

"And you never saw him again?"

"No," she replied sadly. "But we corresponded after that, each Christmas, until he died five years ago."

"So you…you never married, Millicent?"

She shook her head. "No. Not that I didn't consider it. But no one ever again touched my heart the way Robert did. And I wasn't willing to settle for less."

Maggie knew exactly what she meant. It was the same legacy Jake had left with her.

"I'm so sorry, Millicent," she murmured, deeply touched by the sad story.

The older woman nodded. "So am I. Especially after I received this." She withdrew a slender chain from beneath her blouse and fingered two jagged pieces of silver which, when fitted together, formed one heart. "Robert gave me half of this in the middle of our special summer," she related softly. "He said that part of his heart now belonged to me and asked me to keep this always, and that he would do the same with his. I've worn my half faithfully, all my life.

She paused and gently fingered the two pieces of silver. "When he died I received a package with the other half from his daughter, along with a letter saying that her father had always carried it in his wallet and had left instructions for it to be sent to me when he died."

Maggie's eyes filled with tears as Millicent brought her story to a close. Her heart ached for the older woman and the sailor named Robert, whose abiding love had never been fulfilled.

Millicent leaned toward her then, her gaze earnest and intent. "My dear, love is a precious and beautiful gift, but it's easily lost. Pride, ambition, fear—so many things can get in the way. I don't know what made you and Jake break up years ago. I don't know how deeply he hurt you. But a lot can happen in twelve years. People change. Circumstances change. But true love endures. And if that's what you have, don't let it slip away. Because not very many people get a second chance at love."

Chapter Eight

A second chance at love.

Those words had been playing over and over in Maggie's mind ever since Millicent Trent planted the thought. And especially so today. Birthdays always made her wonder what the next twelve months would hold. But even in her wildest imagination she'd never considered on her last birthday that before the next one Jake would be back in her life.

Maggie took a quick glance in the rearview mirror and shook her head. She didn't feel thirty-seven. Not physically, anyway. Emotionally...well, that was a different story. She'd lived through a lot, especially in the last dozen years. But she honestly didn't think she looked her age.

Obviously, though, the twins did, she mused with a rueful smile. Why else would they have given her a day of "rejuvenation" at the new one-day spa that had opened in Bangor? Frankly, she'd been taken aback by the gift—not to mention appalled at the cost. Maggie wasn't accustomed to such self-indulgence, had opened her mouth to point out that the money could have been better spent on more practical items for the upcoming school year. But the girls had been so excited about their gift, had received so much pleasure from the giving, that she couldn't dampen their spirits. So she'd bitten her tongue and accepted it with a smile.

Then they'd topped off the first indulgence with a second—they were going to cook her a special birthday dinner tonight. Since neither of the girls was particularly interested in cooking, the chore usually fell to Maggie. And she was pretty good at it, if she did say so herself. Jake had always liked her cooking, she recalled with a smile.

Jake. He'd been more and more in her thoughts these last few days. Did he remember that today was her birthday? she wondered wistfully. Probably not. In general, men weren't very good about those kinds of things. But he'd changed a lot in the last dozen years. She thought of Millicent's words. Was Maggie being offered a second chance at love? And if so, was it a chance she was willing to take?

She didn't have the answer to those questions. And she didn't even want to think about them for the next few hours. The twins had told her to relax and enjoy the spa experience, and she couldn't very well do that if she thought about Jake. So with a discipline that surprised her, she forced all disruptive thoughts from her mind and focused on the moment. She wanted to get her money's worth—make that the twins' money, she corrected herself—out of this extravagant gift.

And as it turned out, she did. She was coddled and massaged and manicured, then treated to a facial, makeup session and haircut and style. It was pure indulgence, pampering like she had never before experienced, but much to her surprise she enjoyed it. Thoroughly. She emerged feeling invigorated, renewed, pretty and—strangely enough—younger than when she went in. It was wonderful!

By the time she climbed into her car for the drive back to the inn, Maggie was completely relaxed and looking forward to the special dinner the twins were preparing. She loved them dearly for the effort, no matter the result.

They were obviously watching for her, because when she stepped inside they were waiting, their faces shining, eyes expectant.

"Wow!" they breathed in unison, their voices reflecting their awe at the glamorous transformation in their aunt.

Maggie grinned. "Not bad for a thirty-seven-year-old innkeeper, huh?" she teased.

"Aunt Maggie, you look great!" Abby enthused. "That makeup really brings out your coloring. And I love your hair!"

"Yeah," Alison agreed. "It's a great cut. It looks really...sophisticated."

Maggie smiled. The haircut *was* good, she had to admit as she glanced at her reflection in the oven door. Nothing dramatically different than before, but expertly shaped and tamed to bring out her gentle, natural waves. She rarely left it down around the inn, but now, as it softly brushed her shoulders and flatteringly framed her face, she had to admit that wearing it loose and full made her feel younger. And very chic.

"Thanks. And thank you both for today. I hate to admit this, since it was such a wild extravagance, but I loved every minute of it!"

The girls beamed.

"We hoped you would. Now go up and dress for dinner. We laid out your clothes. And take your time," Abby instructed. "We aren't going to eat for an hour."

"Well, I won't argue," Maggie replied, trying to ignore the chaotic mess. "I may not be going to a ball, but I must admit I feel a little like Cinderella at the moment. So I'll enjoy it while it lasts."

As Maggie closed the kitchen door she heard the girls begin to whisper, and she smiled indulgently. They were terrific young women, she thought, allowing herself a moment of pride. Despite her novice-level child-rearing skills, despite her many mistakes, despite the absence of a father figure in their home, the girls had turned out just fine. It hadn't been easy to raise them alone, she reflected, but she'd done okay.

Then again, she'd never been totally alone, she reminded herself, as she stepped into her room and her gaze fell on the Bible beside her bed. She'd turned to the Lord many times through the years, asking for His guidance and support. And He'd always answered her. Not necessarily in the way she expected, but always with a wisdom that it sometimes took her years to appreciate.

She picked up the volume and opened it to the well-worn pages in Matthew that had given her comfort and calmed her troubled soul on so many occasions. "Ask, and it shall be given you; seek, and you shall find; knock, and it shall be opened to you. For everyone who asks, receives; and he who seeks, finds; and to him who knocks, it shall be opened." She flipped forward a few pages. "Come to me, all you who labor and are burdened, and I will give you rest. Take my yoke upon you, and learn from me, for I am meek and humble of heart, and you will find rest for your souls. For my yoke is easy, and my burden light.''

Maggie couldn't remember the number of times through the years when she had read those pages before going to bed, asking the Lord to help her make the right decisions, to ease her burden. And always she had felt His loving presence beside her. She paused now to thank Him in the silence of her heart for His steadfast presence throughout her life, but especially during these last twelve, often tumultuous years.

When Maggie gently closed the book, she felt even more renewed. She replaced it on the nightstand, then turned her attention to the clothes the girls had laid out. Her eyebrows rose in surprise when she realized that they had chosen her fanciest dress—a black chiffon, with rhinestone-studded spaghetti straps and a straight-cut bodice softened with a cowl-like draping of fabric. The full skirt swirled softly beneath a wide belt that was also studded with rhinestones. It was a lovely outfit—but good heavens, what were the girls thinking? she wondered in amusement. This was a cocktail dress, better suited to an elegant black-tie affair than an at-home dinner, no matter how ''fancy'' they were trying to make it. In fact, she'd only worn the dress once before, to an opening at an art gallery Philip had invited her to a couple of years before. She smiled and shook her head. Obviously the girls were trying to make this as nice an evening as possible. She couldn't find it in her heart to disappoint them.

She reached for the dress, and discovered a small, gift-wrapped package from the girls. It was a bottle of her favorite perfume, one she rarely bought because of the high cost. The twins had really outdone themselves this year, she thought with a soft smile.

When she was dressed, Maggie paused to glance in the mirror behind her door. She felt a little silly, all dressed up and nowhere to go. But she had to admit that her rejuvenating day at the spa, her new makeup and expertly styled hair—along with the dress, which emphasized her trim figure—made her feel terrific.

Suddenly she wondered what Jake would think if he saw her now. Would he be awed by her "glamour"? Would that flame of desire she so clearly remembered from years ago spark to life in his eyes? Would he be tempted to pull her into his arms and kiss her fiercely, with the simmering, barely restrained passion she recalled so well?

Although Maggie impatiently dismissed those questions, the answers were nevertheless waiting for her a few moments later when she walked into the dining room and came face-to-face with the man himself. They were obvious from the look in his eyes—yes, yes and highly likely.

Jake rose slowly from the table set for two in the center of the dining room, his gaze smoldering, hers confused. What on earth...?

A movement to her left caught her eye, and she turned to find the twins watching the proceedings with undisguised glee.

"Surprise!" they chorused.

I'm going to ground them until they're thirty, Maggie thought fiercely, hot color suffusing her face as she realized what they'd done. Now everything made sense. The spa. The clothes. The perfume. The two conspirators had decided to fill their aunt's social vacuum by planning a romantic evening for her—down to the fresh flowers and candles on the table and the bottle of sparkling cider chilling in the silver cooler, she noted with a dismayed glance. What must Jake think? she wondered, her mortified gaze meeting his. But he didn't look upset. Not in the least. In fact, he seemed amused. He was wearing that lopsided smile he used to give her when they were sharing a private joke. Thank goodness he was being a good sport about the whole thing! she thought gratefully. But she was so embarrassed, she wished the floor would just open up and swallow her.

"There's cheese and crackers on the table to start," Abby announced. "Take your time. We'll bring in the salad in a little while."

And then the twins disappeared.

Maggie stared helplessly at the tall, distinguished man in the dark gray suit who stood across from her.

"Jake…I'm so sorry," she choked out apologetically, her blush deepening. "I had no idea…. This isn't at all what…." Her voice trailed off and she shook her head. "Wait till I get my hands on them," she added vehemently.

He chuckled, a deep, pleasing rumble that somehow helped soothe her tattered nerves. "Oh, don't be too hard on them. Their hearts were in the right place."

"Maybe. But I've explained to them over and over that we're…well, that our relationship was in the past…they knew better than to pull a stunt like…I just can't believe they did this," she finished in exasperation, realizing how inarticulate her disjointed jumble of words sounded. But she was so upset, she couldn't think straight, let alone form a coherent sentence.

Jake, on the other hand, seemed the epitome of calm as he strolled toward her. But his casual stance was at odds with the flames flickering around the edges of his eyes, and her breath caught in her throat. "Let's humor them,'' he said quietly. ''They've gone to a lot of trouble, Maggie. And it is your birthday. What will one dinner together hurt?''

Maggie was afraid it might hurt a great deal. But she couldn't very well say that. And Jake was right. The girls meant well, even if their intentions were misguided.

''I suppose you're right,'' she capitulated with a sigh.

He smiled, then tucked one of her hands through his arm as they strolled back to the table. He pulled out her chair with a flourish and wink before sitting down next to her. The girls had set the two places at right angles instead of across from each other, Maggie noted. Another transparent attempt to make this an intimate dinner.

Jake poured their drinks, then raised his glass in a toast. ''To Maggie—the most beautiful thirty-seven-year-old I've ever known—and the most memorable woman I've ever met,'' he murmured huskily.

Maggie watched as he took a sip, his gaze never leaving hers, and suddenly she found it difficult to breathe.

''You really are beautiful, you know,'' he said softly. ''Especially tonight. I like your hair down, Maggie. It's too lovely to pull back all the time.''

She swallowed with difficulty. ''Th-thanks.'' Despite her best efforts, she couldn't stop her voice from betraying her turbulent emotions. She glanced down and played with the edge of her fork. It had been a long time since anyone had treated her as a desirable woman. It had been an even longer time since she *felt* like one. But with Jake…it was different. He made her feel special…and alluring…and not at all like Maggie the aunt, or Maggie the innkeeper. With him she felt like Maggie the woman.

Suddenly his hand covered hers, stilling her restless fingers.

"Maggie?"

She took a deep breath and looked up.

"Do I make you nervous?"

Of course he made her nervous. But she couldn't say that without saying *why*, so she forced herself to smile. "I'm just embarrassed by this whole thing, Jake. It's very…awkward. You must feel very uncomfortable."

"Frankly I don't."

She looked at him in sudden suspicion. "Did you know about this?"

"No. The girls just invited me to a birthday dinner. I had no idea it was only going to be the two of us. But to be honest, I'm not sorry. I've been wanting to…"

Suddenly soft music began to play, and Jake paused as Maggie uttered a soft groan. "Oh, no! Now we have music, too."

He listened for a moment, then another chuckle rumbled out of his chest. "Mmm-hmm. Can you place this singer?"

Maggie focused on the music, and then she, too, had to smile. The vocalist was one who had been popular in her parents' courting days.

"Just how old do they think we are?" Jake asked in a low tone, his eyes glinting with mirth.

"Ancient," she replied dryly, struggling to contain her own smile.

"Oh, well." He stood up and held out his hand. "I have a feeling the twins conveniently cleared the floor so we could…do the minuet maybe? That's a little beyond my capabilities, but I have mastered a pretty mean fox-trot. So...may I have this dance?''

"Jake, you'll only add fuel to the fire," she admonished him. "The girls' imaginations are active enough without any encouragement."

"Oh, come on, Maggie. One dance. It's a nice song—even if it *is* old."

When he had the beguiling look in his eyes, she found him difficult to refuse. And he *was* being a good sport about the whole thing. After being brought here under false pretenses, he had a right to be angry. Instead, he was playing along, taking the whole thing in stride. In fact, he seemed to be enjoying it. She supposed she might as well try to, as well. It was her birthday, after all. But dancing with Jake, being held in his arms—the mere thought of it made her feel shaky inside.

"One dance, Maggie?"

Face it, Maggie, she told herself as she stared up into his warm, brown eyes. *You want to dance with the man. Don't fight everything so much. Remember Millicent's advice. Give it a chance.*

With a sigh of defeat, she rose silently, and Jake gave her a smile of encouragement as he led her to the center of the floor. Then he took her into his arms, and for just a moment, Maggie thought every bone in her body was going to dissolve simultaneously.

She closed her eyes to better savor the sensations washing over her. His hand was firm but gentle in the small of her back, feeling familiar to her yet new. He entwined the fingers of his other hand with hers and pressed her trembling hand against his solid, muscled chest. The scent of him—masculine, unique, utterly appealing—surrounded her and set a swarm of butterflies loose in her stomach. She could easily stay like this forever, she decided, as a wave of pure contentment washed over her. With a small, almost inaudible sigh, she let her cheek rest against his shoulder and slowly relaxed in his arms, putting aside for just a moment all of the doubts and questions that plagued her about this man. For once, for the space of this brief dance, she would simply enjoy being held in his sure, strong arms.

Jake felt the stiffness in her body ease as she nestled against his shoulder. He dropped his chin and brushed his cheek against her hair, inhaling the subtle, sweet fragrance that clung to it. She felt so good in his arms. She always had. Soft and appealing and somehow fragile, in a way that brought out his protective instinct and made him want to keep her safe and sheltered. In fact, he would like nothing better than to spend the rest of his life doing exactly that.

For the first time all evening, he relaxed, too. Until this very moment he'd been afraid that she would bolt. It was obvious that she was uncomfortable with the contrived situation. And he was sure the twins would hear about it later. But personally, he had no complaints. In fact, he'd been trying for weeks to figure out a way to get Maggie alone so that he could try to begin rebuilding a relationship with her. So far he'd failed miserably.

He couldn't fault her caution. And at least she was pleasant to him, which was more than he would probably be in her place, he admitted. It was a start. But only a start. Before he could hope to make any progress, he had to find a way to break through the barrier she'd erected between them so that he could begin to rebuild her trust level, make her realize that he was a different man than the one who had walked out on her twelve years ago. And tonight was a good time to start, thanks to the twins.

When the music ended they drew apart reluctantly, and Jake smiled tenderly down into her dreamy eyes.

"See? That wasn't so bad, was it?" His tone was teasing, but unmistakably husky.

She shook her head, not trusting her own voice.

The twins appeared with their salads then, and slowly, as they worked their way through the meal that had been prepared with love, if not finesse, Maggie began to truly relax. Jake told her amusing stories about his travels, and she found herself admiring his wit and self-deprecating humor. He also gave her an update on his relationship with his father—still strained, though improving—and the progress he was making on his lesson plans for the coming school year.

But he also drew her out, skillfully and with sincere interest. Maggie didn't know if it was the romantic atmosphere that loosened her tongue, or just Jake's adept probing, but she opened up more than she expected. She even admitted her secret aspiration to give serious art a try, now that the girls were grown and ready to leave for college.

"I think you should, Maggie. I've seen some of your work, and I'm very impressed. I'm no expert, but didn't you say that your friend—the gallery owner—had encouraged you, too?"

She nodded. "But Philip and I...well, we go back a long way. He has a wonderful eye for art, but I'm afraid he may not be that impartial when it comes to my work."

This was the opening Jake had been waiting for ever since the day in her studio when she'd made a similar remark, and he wasn't about to let it pass. Even though he wasn't sure he wanted to hear the answer, he had to know. "You've mentioned him before," he remarked with studied casualness. "I suppose you might have a point about the impartiality issue if you and he are…well, close."

Maggie tipped her head and studied him.

"If you want to know whether Philip and I are romantically involved, why don't you just ask, Jake?" she said bluntly.

He felt his neck grow red. "I guess I didn't want you to think I was prying, and take offense."

She shrugged. "Actually, we explored a romantic relationship once. Shortly after I moved here. But there just wasn't any…*passion* might be the best word, I suppose. Philip's wife died ten years ago, and even though he's lonely, no one ever came along who compared to her, I guess. As for me, well, it was kind of the same story. Plus, I had a ready-made family in tow." Before he could ask a follow-up question about her "same story" comment, she quickly asked one of her own. "And what about you, Jake? Why didn't you ever marry?"

He looked at her steadily. "For the same reason you didn't, I suspect."

They gazed at each other for a moment in silence, and then she glanced down, suddenly uncertain. Did he mean what she thought he meant? Had he cared about her all these years, as she had cared about him, held back unconsciously by a love that had never died?

He reached for her hand then, and she was forced to meet his gaze. "However, lately I've been thinking more and more about settling down, getting married, raising a family—the whole nine yards."

His implication was clear. But even clearer was his

comment about wanting a family, Maggie thought with
a frown, that single reference suddenly casting a pall
over her evening. She vaguely recalled that he'd mentioned a family once before, but it hadn't really registered at the time. Now it hit home.

He saw the sudden furrow on her brow, and a mirror
image appeared on his own. Had he revealed too much
too soon? "Maggie? Is something wrong?"

She forced herself to smile. "No. It's probably a
good time for you to…to get married and start a family,
if that's what you want. Raising kids is an experience
everyone should have."

One time. She hadn't said that, but the implication
was clear, Jake realized. She was telling him that she'd
done the family scene, that if a family was in his future,
it wouldn't be a future that was linked with hers. He
could understand how she felt. Raising twins, especially when one had had a medical problem, would
have been difficult enough for two people, let alone
one. But it was different when the responsibility was
shared.

Before he could suggest that, however, the twins appeared at the door carrying a birthday cake topped with
glowing candles. As they launched into a spirited ren-
dition of "Happy Birthday," Jake gave her a look that
said, "We'll continue this later" before joining in the
refrain.

The twins set the cake before Maggie with a triumphant flourish.

"Make a wish, Aunt Maggie," Allison instructed.

"But don't tell," Abby added. "Or it won't come
true."

It was the same instruction she'd always given them,
and she smiled. Her gaze met Jake's over the golden

light of the candles, but she couldn't read the enigmatic expression in his eyes. Was he wondering whether her wish would have anything to do with him? she reflected. But that would remain her secret.

She took a deep breath and blew out the candles on the first try, to the applause of her small audience. Then Jake reached down next to the table and retrieved two small packages, which he held out to her.

"Happy birthday, Maggie."

"Oh, Jake, you didn't have to do this!" she protested.

"Of course I did. What's a birthday party without presents? Actually, the small one is from me and the larger one is from Dad, who sends his best wishes."

Maggie took them as the girls quickly and efficiently cut and served the cake. Then, despite her entreaties to stay and join the celebration, they whisked the cake away and returned to the kitchen to enjoy their dessert, leaving the guest of honor once more alone with her dinner companion. Maggie shook her head resignedly.

"Their single-minded determination is amazing. Especially when I think about all the years I struggled to get them to concentrate on their homework," Maggie noted wryly.

Jake chuckled. "I have to admit, I'm impressed by their thoroughness." He took a sip of coffee and nodded toward the packages on the table. "Aren't you going to open your presents?"

She chose Howard's first, exclaiming over the intricate pair of wooden candlesticks that were nestled in tissue. "Oh, Jake, these are lovely! Did Pop make them? I thought he didn't do woodworking anymore?"

"He doesn't. He's had these for years. He made them right before Mom died."

Maggie's face grew thoughtful. "I saw all his wood-working equipment in the garage the day I tried to fix your plumbing," she reflected. "You know, it would probably be really good for him to get back into this. It's not too taxing physically, and it would give him something productive to do."

"I agree. But he hasn't show any interest in picking it up again."

"There's a fair coming up at church," Maggie mused aloud. "We have it every fall. A lot of area crafters exhibit and sell their work. And the church sponsors a booth where we sell donated items. Maybe Pop would make a few things for us, since it's for charity. It might be a way to get him back into it."

"It's certainly worth a try," Jake concurred. "But I doubt he'll be receptive to the idea if it comes from me."

"Then I'll talk to him tomorrow," Maggie decided, carefully laying aside the candlesticks as she turned her attention to Jake's present. When she tore the wrapping off she was delighted to discover a leather-bound travel diary, with a note scrawled on the first page.

To Maggie,
May all your travels be exciting—and may they all lead you home.
Jake.

She looked over at him, touched by the thoughtful gift—and the thought-provoking inscription. "Thank you, Jake."

"You're welcome. I hope your upcoming trip is the first of many."

They focused on the cake, then, and just as they finished the twins made another appearance.

"Why don't you two go sit on the porch while we clean up," Abby suggested.

Jake grinned. "Sounds good to me." He stood up and reached for Maggie's hand. She glanced over at the twins who were, as she expected, positively beaming. She intended to have a long talk with those young women later, but for the moment she'd let them hold on to their misguided romantic fantasy. So, with a "Why fight it?" look, she placed her hand in Jake's and stood up, strolling with him in silence to the front door.

Once outside, she carefully withdrew her hand from his. The evening was drawing to a close, and though she'd enjoyed spending the time with Jake, she didn't want to get used to it.

"Those two," she declared in exasperation, stepping away from him to stand at the porch railing and look out over the moon-silvered bay. "What would they have done if my birthday hadn't been on a Sunday? Any other day the inn would have been full of guests."

Jake noted the physical separation she'd established. And he knew why. Her defenses had started to crumble just a bit tonight, and she was scared. But he wasn't about to let that wall come back up, not yet, anyway. He moved behind her and brought one hand up to rest lightly on her shoulder.

"Somehow I think they would have found a way."

Maggie heard the amusement in his voice, felt his breath close to her ear. So much for her plan to put some space between them. He was so close that she was afraid he would be able to tell that she was trembling. "You're probably right," she admitted, grateful that at least her voice wasn't shaking.

"Well, shall we sit? Or would you rather walk a little?"

Maggie glanced at the wicker porch swing, a perfect invitation to romance—obviously what the twins had in mind—and quickly made her choice. "Let's walk."

"I think the girls will be disappointed," Jake countered with a grin.

"Too bad. They've had their way all evening."

Maggie moved purposefully toward the porch steps, certain that walking was a far safer alternative than sitting next to Jake on the porch swing. But when he reached for her hand, laced his fingers through hers and led her into the moonlit night, she suddenly wasn't so sure.

Chapter Nine

"Are you chilly?"

Maggie glanced up at Jake. Obviously he'd felt her shiver, but she could hardly tell him it was caused more by the warm, tingly feeling his presence evoked than by the cool night air. She swallowed and shook her head.

"No. I'm fine."

Which wasn't true, either. Not when he was stroking her clasped hand with his thumb and smiling at her with that tender look in his brown eyes.

"Well, you're welcome to my jacket if you need it."

That was the *last* thing she needed at the moment, Maggie decided. Having him place his jacket around her shoulders would not do a thing to calm her rapidly accelerating pulse rate.

"Thanks."

Jake seemed content to stroll in silence after that, and Maggie gladly followed his lead. She didn't trust her voice anyway.

After a few minutes, Jake paused and nodded toward

the water. "Looks like a good spot for a view of the bay. Can your shoes handle the path?"

Maggie glanced down at her slender-heeled pumps, then at the gravel path he'd indicated. Her shoes would handle the detour with no problem, she decided. But she wasn't so sure about herself. The path led to a small dock that jutted out into the silver-flecked water—the perfect spot for a romantic tryst. Is that what Jake had in mind? she wondered nervously. Better to play this safe and take the out he'd offered her, she concluded. But when she opened her mouth to decline, different words emerged instead.

"They should be okay."

He smiled then, a smile so warm and tender, it made her toes tingle and her stomach flutter—and convinced her that she'd just made a big mistake.

But he didn't give her time for second thoughts. He took her arm and silently guided her down the narrow path to the water's edge, then onto the rough wooden planks of the dock. They walked to the railing, and as she gazed over the moonlit sea, she realized that the gentle cadence of the waves lapping against the shore was much steadier than her pulse. That was even *more* true when Jake draped an arm casually around her shoulders, making her heart jump to her throat. What had she gotten herself into? she thought in sudden panic. She was attracted to Jake, yes. But she wasn't ready for this. Not yet. And maybe never. She still had too many tangled issues and emotions to work through.

Jake felt Maggie trembling, knew she was scared, knew she was still grappling with her feelings for him and fighting their mutual attraction every step of the way. He couldn't blame her. She was afraid of being hurt again, afraid to let herself believe that maybe this time things would be different. But they had to get past that eventually if anything was ever to develop between them. Which was exactly what he had in mind.

Once upon a time, he had never even considered a future without Maggie. He felt the same way now. The challenge was to convince her of that.

A drop of water flicked against his cheek, and he glanced up at the sky with a frown, surprised to discover that a dark cloud had crept up behind them. But he wasn't ready to go back to the inn. He nodded toward the small, abandoned shed they'd passed at the end of the dock and took Maggie's arm.

"Come on. I'd hate to see that spectacular dress ruined."

She followed his lead unprotestingly, pausing only when he stopped to push open the rickety door of the structure. The hinges objected with a loud squeak, but the door reluctantly gave way, and he ushered her inside.

Maggie took a quick inventory of the shed as she stepped over the threshold. When the girls were younger she'd brought them to this dock a few times to fish, not wanting to deprive them of any of the experiences they might have had with a father. She'd peeked into the old fishing shack, but never ventured inside. It looked more dilapidated than ever, she assessed, noting that the spaces between the weathered gray clapboards had widened considerably through the years. The floorboards had long since rotted away, leaving hard-packed dirt and rock in their place. But at least it was relatively even, she thought, as she walked over to a framed opening in the wall that had once been a window. Amazingly enough, the roof still seemed reasonably watertight. It would do as a shelter from the storm, she decided.

But what about the storm inside of her? she wondered, as memories of another rainy day suddenly came flooding back with an intensity that took her breath away. In a shed much like this one, her life had changed forever, she recalled. It was her sixteenth birthday—twenty-one years ago—but right now it seemed like yesterday.

Maggie glanced up at the sky and wrinkled her nose as the first raindrops splattered again the asphalt, leaving dark splotches in their wake.

"Oh, great! Now it's going to rain on my birthday!" she complained as they pedaled side by side down the country lane.

Jake laughed. "Sorry about that, squirt. But I have no control over the weather."

She made a face at him. "Very funny. And will you please stop calling me that?"

He grinned. "Why?"

"Because I'm not. At least, not anymore."

"My, my. Aren't we getting uppity now that we're sixteen," he teased.

Maggie made another face, then pointed to a small, seemingly abandoned shed off to the side of the road. "Let's go in there till the rain stops." Without waiting for him to reply, she rode off the pavement and onto the bumpy ground.

Jake followed her lead, and as they reached the ramshackle structure the rain suddenly turned into a downpour. They dropped their bikes and dashed for cover.

"Wow! Where did *that* come from?" Maggie said breathlessly. When they'd loaded their bikes into the rack on Howard West's car earlier in the day, there hadn't been a cloud in the sky. Nor had there been any when they'd started their ride an hour ago.

"I guess the clouds crept up behind us while we were riding," Jake replied easily. He glanced up at the sky. "I think it will pass quickly. Might as well make ourselves comfortable in the meantime."

Maggie glanced around skeptically. The rain beat a noisy refrain on the rusted tin roof, but at least the floor was dry, she noted, as she started to sit down.

"Watch that mouse!" Jake exclaimed, then laughed when Maggie jumped. "Just kidding."

She glared at him. "Very funny."

He looked around. "Actually, I think we're alone here. But I promise to defend you if any cheese eaters show up." He lowered his tall frame to the floor and leaned back against the wall, drawing his knees up and clasping his hands around his legs.

Maggie looked around doubtfully, then sat down gingerly in the middle of the floor where she could keep a three-hundred-and-sixty-degree lookout for small, unwanted visitors. She dusted her hands on her khaki shorts and crossed her legs, then glanced at Jake. Her eyes widened in alarm and she gasped, pointing behind him.

"Is that a poisonous spider?"

Jake jerked away from the wall and turned to look. Maggie's sudden eruption of giggles told him he'd been had.

"Gotcha!" she declared gleefully.

Jake's eyes narrowed and he gave her a disgruntled look. "How old are you again? Sixteen—or six?"

"You did it to me," she pointed out.

"Once is okay. Getting back isn't," he declared with a tone of superiority.

Maggie gazed at him speculatively. In a way she was glad it had rained, glad they'd found this isolated shelter. Because she had something she wanted to ask him. After all, Jake was more than a year older than she was. He was popular with the girls, dated a lot. In another week he'd be going off to college. Today would be her best chance to pose the question that had been burning in her mind for weeks. But she just wasn't quite sure how to go about it.

"Jake?" Her voice was suddenly tentative, uncertain. "Can I ask you something?"

"Sure." His eyes were closed now, his head dropped back against the rough planks of the wall. He looked very comfortable, and Maggie hated to bother him with this, but he was her only hope.

"Um...well, I've been wondering...I mean, I know this is kind of a weird question, but...well...how do people learn how to kiss?"

That got his attention. His eyelids flew open and he stared at her, startled.

"What?"

Her face grew pink and she dropped her gaze. "I need to find out how people learn to kiss," she repeated, acutely embarrassed.

He grinned. "Ah, the squirt must be growing up."

She blushed furiously and scooted back against the far wall, suddenly wishing some poisonous creature *would* bite her and put her quickly—and mercifully— out of her misery. "Just forget I asked, okay?" she muttered, her shoulders hunched miserably.

Jake looked over at her bowed head, instantly contrite. He and Maggie had been friends since his parents moved onto her block when he was six, and he'd enjoyed their easy give-and-take ever since. She was a good sport and lots of fun to be with. More fun than anyone he'd ever met, in fact. But she was also easily hurt. Obviously she'd had to muster all of her courage to ask him about such a personal subject, and instead of realizing how embarrassed she was, he'd given her a hard time. Jake scooted over and sat in front of her, reaching out to touch her stiff shoulder.

"Maggie, I'm sorry." His voice was gentle, all traces of teasing gone.

She refused to look at him. "It was a dumb question anyway."

Her voice was muffled, and she seemed on the verge of tears. Which only made him feel worse.

"It's not a dumb question."

"Yes, it is."

"No, it's not. And I'm sorry I made a joke of it. I guess I just never thought about you growing up and thinking about those kinds of things."

She sniffed and risked a glance at him, her eyes frustrated. "Well, I am, Jake. And I do. Most of my friends date now. They talk about…stuff…and I feel so ignorant. I don't even know how to kiss, and they…they're way past that stage. I even turned down a date with Joe Carroll last week because I'm afraid he'll think I'm…well, that I don't know what I'm doing. And I don't!" she wailed.

Jake frowned darkly. "Joe Carroll asked you out?"

She nodded. "Why are you so surprised? Don't you think I'm the kind of girl guys would want to ask out?"

Actually, he'd never thought about it one way or the other. But the idea of Maggie going out with Joe Carroll, who acted like he was the next Casanova, made his blood run cold. Maggie was too sweet and innocent to go out with a guy like that.

"I'm not pretty enough. Is that what you think?" Maggie's miserable voice interrupted his thoughts when he didn't respond.

Jake stared at her. He'd never thought about that, either, to be honest. Maggie was…well, Maggie. She was cute. She had pretty hair. He liked her turned-up nose. He'd just never thought about her in those kinds of terms. But clearly she needed some reassurance, and the least he could do was build up her confidence— and give her some warnings.

"Of course you're pretty," he declared gallantly. "Too pretty, maybe. You need to be careful around guys like Joe. He expects a whole lot more out of a date than a kiss, from what I hear."

"Really?" She stared at him wide-eyed.

"Uh-huh."

She sighed. "Oh, well, it doesn't matter anyway. I don't even know how to do *that,* let alone anything else."

"You just need to practice," Jake told her. "That's how I learned."

"Yeah?"

"Mmm-hmm."

"But…who would I practice with?"

He looked at her for a moment as an idea suddenly took shape in his mind. "Well, I suppose you could practice with me," he offered slowly. "*I* could teach you."

She stared at him again. "You?"

"Yeah. What's wrong with me?" he asked, offended.

"Well…I don't know. It just seems kind of…weird,

you know? I mean, it's not exactly…romantic…or anything."

"So? That's probably good. This way there's no pressure."

She considered the idea for a moment, her head tipped to one side. "Yeah, you're right," she conceded. In fact, the idea made a lot of sense, the more she thought about it. She scooted closer and looked up at him expectantly. "Okay. What do I do?"

Jake shifted uncomfortably. He was in this too far now to back out, but it *was* weird, as she said. Besides, *she* might think he was an expert at this. But at the moment his limited experience seemed hardly adequate to qualify him as an instructor. However, his seventeen-year-old ego wasn't about to let him admit that. He'd just have to try and pull this off.

"You don't really have to *do* anything. The guy usually takes the lead." Like Joe Carroll, Jake thought grimly. He took more than the lead if he had half a chance, to hear him boast. Maggie needed to be prepared for guys like that, had to learn not to be swept away by their nice words and what, to her, would be sophisticated technique. The more she knew before she got into a situation like that, the better.

"So when he *does* take the lead, is that when the kissing starts?"

"Yeah. Usually."

"Okay." She looked up at him, but when he remained unmoving she frowned. "So…are you going to show me?"

Jake took a deep breath. Maggie now seemed at ease. He was the one who suddenly felt uncomfortable. He *had* made a promise, though. "Yeah, I am." He took a deep breath and leaned forward, and she followed his lead. But instead of their lips connecting, their noses collided. Maggie threw back her head and erupted into a fit of giggles.

"This isn't how it happens in the movies," she declared, her shoulders shaking with laughter.

Jake gave her a stern look. "This isn't going to work if you keep giggling," he admonished her.

Maggie stifled the giggles—with difficulty. "Sorry. Can we try that again?"

This time their lips briefly connected, but when Jake backed off and checked out her reaction, *disappointed* was the only word that came to mind. He frowned at her in irritation.

"Now what's wrong?"

"Is that it?" she asked, crestfallen.

Jake's seventeen-year-old pride took a nosedive. This lesson was getting a lot more complicated than he'd anticipated.

"Maggie, are you really sure you want me to teach you all this?"

Her face fell. "I don't have anyone else to ask, Jake," she replied quietly. Then she dropped her gaze and played with the edge of her shorts. "But if you don't want to, that's okay. I understand."

The plaintive note in her voice tugged at his heart, and he reached down and tilted her chin up with a gentle finger. "I said I'd teach you, and I will," he told her softly. Then, calling on every bit of his limited experience, he set out to do just that.

He reached over and touched her hair, surprised at its softness as it drifted through his fingers. Then he cupped her face with this hands and combed back through her flame-colored tresses, loosening her barrettes in the process until her hair tumbled freely around her shoulders. He stroked her face, the skin soft and silky beneath his fingers. But she was too far away, he decided. He reached down to her waist and pulled her toward him, until her knees touched his as they sat cross-legged facing each other, their faces only inches apart.

At this range, Jake noticed the flecks of gold in her deep green eyes. Funny, he'd never even paid any attention to their color before. But they were beautiful eyes, he realized, expressive and—at the moment—a bit dazed. So maybe his technique wasn't so bad after all, he thought, pleased. His confidence bolstered, he reached over and traced the outline of her lips with his fingertip, a whisper-soft touch that made her gasp. Her lips parted ever so slightly—and oh-so-invitingly. She'd be putty in Joe Carroll's hands, he thought, suddenly glad they'd pursued this today. At least now she'd have some idea what to expect, be a little more prepared if some guy tried to take advantage of her innocence and inexperience.

Jake let his hands drop to her shoulders, then framed her face with his hands, marvelling at the incredible softness of her skin. As she gazed up at him, so trustingly, his heart suddenly did something very strange. It stopped, just for a second, then raced on.

Jake didn't pause to analyze his reaction. Instead, he leaned forward to claim her lips, softly tasting them, before he captured her mouth in a kiss that was perhaps a bit short on technique but very long on passion.

Maggie had no idea what was happening to her. This had all started out so innocently, two old friends out for a bike ride. Her request of Jake had seemed simple enough: Tell me how people learn to kiss. But the results were far from simple. From the moment he'd begun running his fingers through her hair, her heartbeat had gone haywire. Her stomach felt funny, and she couldn't seem to breathe right. And now...now, as his lips possessed hers, she thought she was going to drown in the flood of sensations washing over her.

How could he never have noticed before that she had grown up? Jake wondered in amazement. It was obvious in her delicate curves, in her softness, in the small sounds she made as he continued to kiss her. He'd always thought of Maggie as a kid, a pal, someone to ride bikes and shoot baskets with. But he didn't think of her as a kid right now. The frantic beat of the rain on the tin roof couldn't compete with the beating of their hearts as their embrace escalated.

It was Jake who finally realized that things were moving too fast and he broke away abruptly. Somewhere along the way this "lesson" had gotten out of hand, their roles changing from instructor and student to man and woman. And as Jake gazed down into Maggie's dazed eyes, he realized something else had changed, as well. Namely his life. Somehow he knew it would never be the same again.

Maggie stared up at him, then reached out to wonderingly trace the contours of his face. She heard his sharply indrawn breath, then he captured her hand in his, stilling its sensual movement. She could see the tension in his face, feel the thudding of his heart and realized with awe that she had drawn this passionate response from him. But she felt no less moved. She drew a deep, shaky breath, and when she spoke her voice was unsteady.

"Wow!" she breathed.

He tried to smile but couldn't quite pull it off. "Yeah. Wow!"

"Jake, I…I never expected to feel like…well, anything like this. I feel so…I don't know…fluttery inside. And shaky. And scared. But good, too. All at once. Is it…is it because I've never done this before?"

Slowly he shook his head. "I don't think so, Maggie. I feel the same way, and I've kissed a fair number of girls."

She struggled to sit up, and he saw with a frown that her hands were shaking badly. He should have been gentler, moved more slowly, he chided himself. She'd never even been kissed before. Of course, better him than Joe Carroll, he consoled himself. At least he'd had the decency to back off. He doubted Joe would have been as noble.

Jake put his arm around Maggie and pulled her against him until her head rested on his shoulder, smiling as he rubbed his cheek against her hair.

"You know, I never thought of you—of us—romantically before," she said in a small, uncertain voice.

"Me, neither. But I do now." He stroked her arm. "And you know what? I like it."

"So do I," she replied softly.

"You know something else? I have a feeling this may be the start of something pretty wonderful."

She snuggled closer. "I have the same feeling."

He backed off just far enough to look down into her emerald eyes, and the warmth of his smile filled her with joy. "Happy birthday, Maggie." And then he leaned down and claimed her lips in a tender kiss filled with sweet promise.

Maggie drew a deep, shaky breath as she stared at the silvered bay through the rough opening in the wall.

She wrapped her arms around her body, holding the memories close for just a moment longer, memories of the day their friendship had ripened into romance. The images had seemed too vivid, so real—so lovely. She hated to let them go.

Had taking shelter in the old fishing shack prompted similar memories in Jake? she suddenly wondered, turning toward him. He was gazing at her silently.

"Seems like old times, doesn't it, squirt?" he said quietly, and she had her answer.

Maggie swallowed with difficulty, and turned back to the window. "Yes," she whispered.

She felt him move behind her, and her breath caught in her throat as he placed his hands on her shoulders and stroked them lightly.

"It's still there, isn't it, Maggie?" he murmured, his voice rough with emotion.

"What?" she choked out, knowing only too well what he meant.

With firm but gentle hands he turned her to face him so that she had to look directly into his eyes.

"This," he replied, and slowly reached over to trace the soft curve of her mouth with a whisper touch.

She closed her eyes and shuddered, willing herself to walk away, knowing she couldn't.

"Jake, I...things have changed. We're not the same people anymore."

"Not everything has changed."

She swallowed, and a pulse began to beat erratically in the delicate hollow of her throat. His gaze dropped to it for a moment, swept over the expanse of skin that had turned to alabaster in the moonlight, then came back to her eyes.

"We should go back," she suggested, a touch of desperation in her voice.

"I wish we could," he replied, and she knew he wasn't talking about the inn. "But the best we can do is start over. Tonight. Right now."

And then slowly, very slowly, he leaned toward her until his lips, familiar and warm and tender, closed over hers.

With a soft sigh, Maggie gave up the fight and melted into his arms. She'd intuitively known this moment would come since the day she stepped into the dining room seven weeks ago and found him there. It had been a losing struggle from the beginning, she acknowledged. Right or wrong, she wanted this moment in the arms of the man she'd always loved.

She was aware that the muscular contours of his chest were more developed, harder, than she remembered. And his arms were stronger, more sure, than she recalled, holding her with a practiced skill that had been absent twelve years ago. His mouth moved over hers with a new adeptness. The passion, though—that was the same. Just more intense.

Mostly she simply gave herself up to the moment, reveling in the exquisite joy of Jake's embrace. She returned his kiss tentatively at first, but his lips coaxed hers into a fuller response. She sighed softly as he cradled her head in one palm, his fingers tangled in her hair. Jake deepened the kiss, and she could feel the hard, uneven thudding of his heart as he pressed her closer. She offered no resistance. Couldn't have even if she'd wanted to.

Jake wasn't usually a man who lost control. He'd learned a great deal about discipline over the last dozen years, but it was a virtue that deserted him at the moment. Even as he told himself not to push, it was almost as if he was trying to make up for twelve long, parched years in one kiss. He had been so afraid she would reject his overture, that her fear would make her back off. But the fact that she had allowed him to claim her lips gave him hope for the future.

With a shuddering sigh, Jake at last raised his head and pressed hers close against his chest, holding her tightly. He had to stop now, before this got out of hand. He wasn't seventeen anymore, even if he felt like he was.

For several minutes neither spoke. Jake could feel Maggie trembling in his arms, and he didn't feel any too steady himself. Not only had their attraction endured through the years, it had intensified, he realized. The question now was, what were they going to do about it?

When her quivering finally eased, and when he finally felt able to carry on a coherent conversation, he gently pulled away from her, though he kept his arms looped around her waist. Their gazes met—his smoldering, hers dazed. With great effort, Jake summoned up the semblance of a smile.

"Wow."

"I...I think that's my line," she replied in a choked voice.

"I'm stealing it."

"Jake, I—I don't know if this is wise. I don't think I'm ready to...to..."

"Trust me again?" he finished softly, when her voice trailed off.

She stared at him, and warm color suffused her face at his blunt—and accurate—assessment of her feelings.

"It's okay, Maggie," he assured her softly. "I'm not

asking you to—not yet, not after all these years. We need to give this some time. But the magic is still there. We both know that. I'd like to see where it leads.''

Maggie swallowed. He was being direct about his intentions, and she respected that. She owed him no less. "Jake, I have a good life now. I've been…content. I thought that love had…that it wasn't the Lord's will for me. But I think I could…that we might…'' She paused and turned away in frustration, reaching up to swipe at an errant tear. "See what you do to me? I'm a wreck. And it will be worse if I let myself…if I let myself care and then…'' She paused, and Jake stepped in to finish the sentence again, much as he hated to.

"And then I disappear.''

She turned to look at him and nodded slowly.

"I'm not going to leave again, Maggie,'' he promised her, his intense gaze locked on hers. "I'm here to stay this time.''

She searched his eyes, wanting desperately to believe him. But he'd turned her world upside down once, and she had vowed never to let anyone do that again. How could she be sure this time?

Jake read the uncertainty in her eyes. "Just give me a chance, Maggie. That's all I ask. Spend some time with me. Just the two of us.''

Maggie sighed. After tonight, there was no way she could refuse. She might be foolishly walking headfirst into danger, but Millicent Trent was right. Not very many people got a second chance at love. She'd be a fool to let it slip by without even considering it.

"All right, Jake. But right now we really do need to get back. The twins will be wondering what happened to us.''

He grinned. ''I think their imaginations will fill in the blanks. They're probably celebrating the success of their strategy right now.''

Maggie took the hand he extended, and as he laced his fingers with hers, she suspected he was right. She knew that the notion of a rekindled romance between their aunt and Jake made the twins feel hopeful and excited. She ought to chastise them for their unrealistic expectations. But how could she, when her heart suddenly felt the same way?

Chapter Ten

Jake tossed his jacket onto the couch, set his briefcase on the floor and reached up to massage his neck. It had been a day full of meetings as the faculty prepared for the new school year, and he was tired. Classes started in a week and Jake was inundated with lesson plans and paperwork. The latter was no problem, of course. His years in the navy had prepared him for that, he mused, his mouth quirking up into a wry smile.

The lesson plans were another story. Teaching a course here and there during his career in the service was one thing. Planning a full load of classes for an entire semester was another. But not much could dampen his spirits after yesterday's dinner with Maggie. His heart felt lighter than it had in years.

A sudden thud from the direction of the garage drew his attention. What in the world was his father up to? he wondered, heading out to investigate.

When Jake reached the door to the garage, he paused only long enough to note that Howard was struggling to lift one of the boxes containing his woodworking tools. Then he strode rapidly across the floor and reached for it before the older man could protest.

"This is too heavy for you, Dad."

"I could have managed it," Howard declared stubbornly.

Jake didn't argue the point. They both knew he wasn't supposed to do heavy lifting or strenuous work of any kind. Making an issue out of it would only lead to an argument or cause his father to retreat into miffed silence. So instead, Jake nodded toward the once neatly stacked boxes, which were now in disarray. "What are you doing anyway?"

Howard stuck his hands in his pockets. "Maggie called. They need some craft items for a booth at the church fair, and she asked me if I'd make a few things. I couldn't say no, not after she's been so nice and all since I got here. But I need to set up my equipment."

Jake deposited the box on the floor and surveyed the garage. There was a workbench in one corner, and he nodded toward it. "Will that spot work?"

"That'll do. I just need to set up the saw and lathe."

"I'll take care of it for you after dinner."

"I can do it myself."

Jake planted his hands on his hips and turned to face his father. They were going to have to address the issue anyway, it seemed. "Dad, this equipment is too heavy for you to lift," he said evenly. "You know that. Why didn't you just wait until I got home?"

Howard shrugged. "Didn't want to be a bother."

Jake's tone—and stance—softened at the unexpected response, and he reached over and laid a hand on his father's stiff shoulder. "You're not a bother, Dad."

The older man glanced down, his shoulders hunched.

"I just feel in the way these days. Maybe I can at least do something productive for the church."

Jake frowned. Did his father really feel that useless? Maggie had intimated as much, but Jake had been so busy getting ready for school—and worrying about his relationship with her—that he hadn't really thought much about how his father was feeling. Maybe he needed to.

"Well, we'll set it up tonight. Tomorrow we can run into Bangor and buy whatever wood and supplies you need. And a couple of space heaters, so you can work out here when the weather gets cooler."

Howard looked at him warily. "I don't want to put you out."

Jake's gaze was steady and direct. "I'm glad to do it, Dad," he said firmly.

As Jake prepared for bed later that night, he thought about his conversation with his father and how they'd worked side by side earlier in the evening to set up the workshop, Jake doing the physical work, Howard providing the direction. It reminded him of younger, happier times with his father. Maybe, just maybe, they were finally taking the first tentative steps toward a true reconciliation, he thought hopefully.

He recalled Maggie's promise to pray for them, and his own conclusion that it would take a miracle to put things right between him and his father. Jake had always been skeptical of miracles. But perhaps he was about to see one come to pass after all.

"Please, Aunt Maggie?"

Maggie stared at the twins. They'd ganged up on her again, and she couldn't seem to come up with a reason to say no. Ever since her birthday the week before, they'd been grinning like the proverbial Cheshire cat, dropping hints about her and Jake, urging her to call him, to accept his invitations for dinner, to sit on the porch with him when he dropped by unexpectedly in the evening. But she needed some space to mentally regroup after their last tumultuous encounter. Those few minutes in the fishing shed had caused her too many sleepless nights.

"Won't you do it for *us*, Aunt Maggie?" Allison cajoled.

Maggie sighed, realizing she'd lost this battle. If the twins wanted her to invite Jake to accompany them to the airport in Bangor when they departed for college in two days, how could she disappoint them?

"All right. You guys win. I'll ask. But remember, he's getting ready for school, too," she warned. "So don't be surprised if he can't make it."

"He'll make it," Abby predicted with a knowing smile.

And she was right. In fact, he not only agreed to go, he offered to drive.

When the big day arrived, Jake showed up right on time, dressed in a pair of khaki slacks and a cotton fisherman's sweater that emphasized the broadness of his chest and enhanced his rugged good looks. His smile of welcome for her was warm and lingering, and the smoky look in his eyes wasn't missed by the perceptive twins. She saw them exchange a secret smile and shook her head. Hopeless romantics, the two of them.

The twins chattered excitedly all the way to Bangor, plying Jake with questions about his overseas travels, and Maggie was content to just sit back and listen to the lively banter. Between her sleepless nights and the rush to take care of all the last-minute details that going off to college entailed—not to mention running the inn—she was exhausted. Up till now the girls' enthusiasm had been contagious and had kept her adrenaline flowing. It was a happy, exciting time for them—the start of a new life—and she was pleased that their excellent academic performance had earned them both scholarships to the universities of their choice. Those scholarships, combined with their parents' insurance money—most of which had been put into a trust fund—would offer them security for many years to come. Their futures looked bright, and they had much to be happy and thankful for.

But late at night these last couple of weeks, when all the tumult ceased and she lay alone in bed, Maggie was overcome with a vague sense of melancholy. For the twins, college was a beginning. For her, it was an ending. Their departure marked the end of the life she had known for most of her adult years. Their laughter and teasing had filled her days, and the girls had provided her with an outlet for the bountiful love that filled her heart. Now they would build their own lives, apart from her, and eventually, special men would come along to claim their hearts. That was what she hoped for them anyway. She wanted their lives to be full and rich, filled with love and a satisfying career and children. It was just that she would miss them terribly. They had been her purpose, her anchor, and she felt suddenly adrift and strangely empty.

It wasn't until Abby was getting ready to board the plane that the girls themselves got teary-eyed. They'd never been apart for any great length of time, and now they were heading in two different directions, away from each other and the only home they could remember. Abby clung first to Allison, then to Maggie, as Jake stepped discreetly into the background.

"I'll miss you both so much!" she said, her voice suddenly shaky and uncertain.

"Call me every day, okay?" Allison implored.

"I promise."

"Goodbye, Aunt Maggie. And thank you...for everything."

Maggie's own eyes grew misty, but she struggled to maintain her composure as she hugged Abby again. She wanted this to be a happy moment for them, not a sad one. "Believe it or not, I loved every minute of it. Even the old days, when you and Allison used to delight in confusing me about who was who."

"I guess we were pretty bad about that," Abby admitted with a sheepish grin.

"Well, I survived. I even managed to guide two girls through adolescence at once without losing my sanity. Don't I get a medal or something?"

"Would a kiss and a hug do instead?" Abby asked with a laugh.

Maggie smiled. "I think that would be an even better reward."

Abby embraced her, and Maggie blinked back her tears.

"Now get on that plane before it leaves without you. I can't run after the plane like I used to run after the school bus!"

Abby grinned. "Yeah, I remember. Alli, you'll call, right?" Her voice was anxious as she hugged her twin.

"Count on it."

"You too, Aunt Maggie?"

"Absolutely. Now scoot. The bus is leaving," Maggie teased, trying valiantly to keep her smile in place.

"Okay." She hefted her knapsack and headed down the ramp.

Maggie and Allison waved until she was out of sight, and then, half an hour later, it was Allison's turn.

As Jake watched in the background, giving the two a moment alone, he wondered what was going through Maggie's mind. She seemed upbeat, happy. But he'd caught the glimmer of tears in her eyes more than once today. And as Allison disappeared from view, the sudden slump in Maggie's shoulders confirmed his suspicion that saying goodbye to the twins was one of the more difficult moments in her life. She suddenly looked lost—and very alone. He tossed his empty disposable coffee cup into a nearby receptacle and quickly strode toward her.

Maggie felt Jake lace his fingers through hers, and she blinked rapidly before looking up at him, struggling to smile. The understanding look in his eyes made it even more difficult to keep her tears at bay.

"You did a good job with them, you know," he said quietly, brushing his thumb reassuringly over the back of her hand. "They're lovely, intelligent, confident young women with their heads on straight and hearts that reflect an upbringing filled with kindness and love."

How was it that he'd known exactly the right thing to say? she wondered incredulously, trying to swallow past the lump in her throat. In the moments before he'd walked over, she'd been asking herself those very kinds of questions. Had she done everything she could to prepare them for what was ahead? Would the values she'd instilled in them survive their college years? Had their single-parent upbringing provided enough love and support and stability? Had she given them an adequate sense of self-worth, a solid enough grounding in their faith, to sustain them through whatever lay ahead? Jake seemed to think so. She didn't know if he was right. But hearing him say it made her feel better, and for that she was grateful.

"Thank you. I tried my best. I suppose that's all any of us can do. And I hope you're right. I hope it was good enough."

He draped his arm around her shoulders. "I don't think you have to worry about those two, Maggie. You raised them to be survivors. But then, they had a good example to follow."

Suddenly she was immensely grateful that the girls had insisted Jake come along today. His presence somehow helped ease the loneliness of their departure.

"Thank you for coming today, Jake. It was a lot tougher than I expected, saying goodbye. I—I'm going to miss those two! It will be so strange to be alone after all these years."

Jake turned to face her, letting one hand rest lightly at her waist as he tenderly stroked her cheek. "You're not alone, Maggie."

She searched his eyes, discerning nothing but honesty in their depths. His intense gaze seemed to touch her very soul, willing her to believe the sincerity of his words. And she wanted to. Dear Lord, she wanted to, with every fiber of her being! But she had to be cautious. She had to be sure. She still had too many doubts, too many questions. She would move forward, yes. But slowly. Because only time would provide the answers—and the assurance—she needed.

"By the way, the date's set."

"What date?" Maggie asked distractedly as she

snagged another forkful of chicken salad. The mid-September weather was absolutely balmy, and when Philip had called and asked her to meet him for lunch at the outdoor café overlooking the bay, she couldn't refuse. Even now, her attention was focused more on enjoying the warmth of the sun seeping into her skin than on their conversation.

"The date for your show."

She stared at him. "What show?"

"The show we've been talking about for a year—remember?"

"You mean the show I never agreed to?"

"That's the one," he verified cheerily, reaching for his iced tea.

Maggie set her fork down with a clatter. "Philip, you didn't! You know I'm not ready!"

"You're ready, Maggie. You have been for a couple of years."

"But…but I never agreed to a show!"

"True. And why is that?"

Maggie bit her lip. "This is too close to my heart, Philip. You know that. I just can't take the chance. What if…what if I fail?"

Philip leaned forward and took her hand. "Maggie, there's no growth without risk. You've lived a very predictable, quiet life here for as long as I've known you. You think things through and try as hard as you can to make everything perfect. And that's worked well for you with the inn. You have a successful business and a comfortable life. But some things can't be worked out on a spreadsheet. Sometimes you have to just trust your heart. I know it's risky. I know how much your art means to you. It comes right from your heart, exposes your soul. That's why it's so good—and also why rejection is so scary. But I'm telling you, as your friend and a professional art dealer, that the risk of a show is minimal. I've shown some of your work to my friend in Bangor, and he agrees with my assessment. It will be a great opportunity for you to launch a more serious career. I'll cancel the show if you really want me to, but I think it would be a big mistake."

She frowned. "When is this show supposed to be?"

"The opening is scheduled for the first Friday in December. It will run for a month."

Maggie took a deep breath. It was a scary commitment, but Philip was right. If she ever wanted to pursue serious art, she had to make her work available for critique and review. She needed to take this opportunity.

"All right, Philip. I'll do it," she told him with sudden decision. "I guess it's time to test the waters, take a chance."

He smiled. "You won't be sorry, you know."

"I hope you're right."

"And what about the other…risky…situation in your life at the moment?" he asked, purposefully keeping his tone casual.

"What situation?"

"Jake."

Maggie glanced down and played with her chicken salad. "I'm not so sure about that one. It's even scarier."

"Well, it would be a shame to walk away from something good just because you're afraid. And that's true for everything—from a show to a relationship. Now, suppose I get off my soapbox and change the subject to something less heavy. Tell me about the girls. How are they adjusting?"

The rest of the lunch passed in companionable conversation. But Philip's words kept replaying in her mind. Was her fear protecting her—or keeping her from something good, as he had suggested? Maggie didn't know. But as she left Philip in front of the restaurant and returned to her car, she turned to the source of guidance she always relied on in times of uncertainty.

Lord, I'm confused, she confessed in the silence of her heart. *I'm starting to fall in love with Jake again, but I don't know if that's wise. He hurt me badly once, and I don't ever want to go through that pain again. But I feel You sent him here for a reason. If it's Your will that I give our love a second chance, please help me to find the courage to trust again. Because otherwise I'm afraid I'll let it slip through my fingers. And I don't want to live the rest of my life with regrets, the way Millicent has. Please—please—show me the way!*

"Pop! Over here!"

Jake turned at the sound of the familiar voice and smiled at Maggie.

"She's over there, Dad." He laid one hand on Howard's shoulder and gestured toward the church booth with the other.

"Well, let's go say hello."

Jake was more than happy to comply. He hadn't seen enough of Maggie these last two weeks, not since the girls left. September was a popular month at the inn, and she was busier than ever, without the girls to help. But no more busy than him. He had been a bit overwhelmed by the workload at school and had been left with virtually no free time. It was not a situation he was pleased about, but until he adjusted to school and her business slowed down for the winter, there didn't seem to be much he could do about it. He had to take whatever limited time he could get with her. And accompanying his father to the church fair—especially knowing Maggie was working at the booth—was as good an excuse as any to take a break from correcting papers.

He gave her a lazy smile as they approached. "Hi, Maggie."

The smoky, intimate tone in his voice brought a flush to her cheeks. "Hello, Jake." With an effort she dragged her gaze from his and turned her attention to Howard. "Hi, Pop."

"Hi, Maggie. How's business?"

"That's what I wanted to tell you. All of the things you made sold already!"

"Really?" he asked, clearly pleased.

"Yes. And not only that, Andrew Phillips—he owns the local craft alliance—wants to talk to you. They'd like to take some of your things on consignment, and he was even interested in having you teach a class."

Howard's eyes lit up. "He liked my work that much?"

Maggie nodded emphatically. "Absolutely. He said…wait, there he is over there. Andrew!" She waved at a tall, spare young man with longish hair and gestured for him to join them. He strolled over, and she made the introductions.

"I told Howard you were interested in talking with him," Maggie explained.

"Yes, I am. Could you spare me a few minutes now? Maybe have a cup of coffee or something?"

Howard was actually beaming. "Sure, sure. That is,

if my son doesn't mind waiting." He glanced at Jake, suddenly uncertain.

Jake propped his shoulder against the corner of Maggie's booth and folded his arms across his chest. "Not at all. Take your time, Dad."

He watched the two men wander off toward the refreshment area, then turned to Maggie with a smile and shook his head. "Now that, Ms. Fitzgerald, is a miracle. Did you see the way my dad's face lit up?"

She smiled. "Yes. It makes all the difference in the world when a person believes they have something to contribute. Pop just needs to feel like he can still do something worthwhile."

"Thanks to you, he does."

Maggie blushed again and shook her head. "No. You were the one who thought to bring the woodworking tools."

"But you were the one who convinced him to use them."

She shrugged. "Well, it doesn't really make any difference where the credit belongs. The important thing is that Pop seems interested in something again. And he's looking better, too, Jake. Are…are things improving at all between you two?"

"They're better. But even though we're more comfortable with each other, there's still a…a distance, I guess is the best way to describe it. I don't feel like we ever really connect at a deeper level. And frankly, I'm not sure what else I can do. School is pretty demanding right now, and I just don't have the time to focus on Dad the way I'd like to. I'm not used to dealing with boys that age, and it's a real challenge. In fact, to be perfectly honest, I sometimes feel like I'm in over my head."

"Your father raised two boys," Maggie said thoughtfully. "Maybe he could offer you a few tips. Have you talked to him about your job, or any of the kids?"

Jake frowned and shook his head. "I don't think he's interested. He's never asked about my work."

"Maybe he's afraid that you don't want his advice."

Jake considered that. She might have a point. During the last twelve years he hadn't exactly shared a lot of his life with his father. Why should the older man expect him to start now?

"I guess it couldn't hurt to try," Jake conceded.

"Well, most people are flattered when asked for advice. And your father really does have a lot of experience with boys. You might actually..."

"Next Wednesday, then?"

Andrew's voice interrupted their conversation, and they turned as the two men approached.

"Let me check with my son." Howard looked at Jake. "Andrew would like me to come by the shop next Wednesday and look things over, maybe work out a schedule for a class. Would it put you out to run me over after school?"

"I'd be happy to, Dad."

Howard turned back to Andrew and stuck out his hand. "It's nice to meet you, young man."

"My pleasure. I'll see you Wednesday."

"Sounds like things went well," Maggie observed with a smile.

Howard nodded, looking pleased. "Yes, they did. Nice young fellow. He's a potter. It's good to talk to people who appreciate handcrafted work."

"Could be a whole new career for you, Pop," Maggie pointed out.

"Could be, at that." He turned back to Jake. "I appreciate the ride Wednesday," he said stiffly.

"No problem, Dad."

"Well, if I'm going to be making things for the shop, I need to take inventory. You ready to go?"

"Sure." Jake turned to Maggie, the warmth of his smile mirrored in his eyes. "Thanks."

Before she realized his intent, he reached over and touched her cheek, then let his hand travel to her nape. He exerted gentle pressure and drew her close for a tender kiss. When he backed off she was clearly flustered, and Jake wondered if he'd been too impulsive. But it had been three long weeks since her birthday, three weeks with nothing but the memory of their embrace in the fishing shack to sustain him. He needed to reassure himself that she hadn't had second thoughts about pursuing their relationship.

He searched her eyes, and when their gazes locked for a mesmerizing moment, he had all the reassurance he needed. "I'll be by later this week, Maggie," he said in a voice only she could hear. "We need to talk."

She nodded, unwilling to trust her voice.

He smiled, then glanced at his father. "Ready, Dad?"

The older man nodded. "Whenever you are." Howard looked at Maggie quizzically, then turned and walked away.

"I'm surprised she let you do that," he muttered as Jake fell into step beside him.

"I think she's beginning to realize that I've changed, Dad," Jake replied quietly. "At least, I hope she is."

The older man paused and regarded his son silently for a moment. Jake tensed, waiting for a derogatory comment, but instead Howard simply turned and continued toward the car. "Let's go home," he said gruffly, over his shoulder. "I've got some projects to start."

Jake followed, trying to absorb the significance of what had just occurred. Not only had his father refrained from making a disparaging remark, but even more important, he had used the word *home* for the first time. It was a small thing, Jake knew. But it was a start.

Chapter Eleven

Jake dropped his briefcase on the couch and sniffed appreciatively. Since the beginning of the school year, his father had taken over the chore of cooking dinner. The meal was never fancy, given Howard's limited culinary skills, but the gesture was greatly appreciated by Jake. He was usually tired when he got home, and definitely not in the mood to cook. His father's willingness to step in and handle KP was a godsend. Especially tonight.

As Jake strolled toward the kitchen, he mulled over the encounter he'd had with one of the freshmen this afternoon. Actually, *confrontation* might be a better description, he thought grimly. The last thing he needed in this "learning-the-ropes" phase of his new career was a smart-aleck kid mouthing off at him. He supposed he could—and perhaps should—report the insubordination to the dean. But that could be the death knell for a budding maritime career, and he was reluctant to take such a drastic measure so early in the semester. Besides, there was something about the boy that troubled him. A look in his eyes of…bleakness; that was the word that came to mind. And desperation. They were barely discernible under his veneer of insolence, but they were there, Jake was certain. He just didn't know what to do about it.

"Hi, Dad." He paused in the doorway. "What's for dinner?"

His father shrugged. "Just meat loaf. I used to make it for myself at home sometimes, after your mother died. She made it better than I do, though."

"Well, it sure smells good."

Howard turned to set the table, pausing for a moment to study Jake. "You look tired."

Jake sighed and reached around to rub the stiff muscles in his neck. "It was a long day."

"Well, I imagine teaching is quite a change from the navy. Takes a while to get used to, I expect." Howard placed the cutlery beside the plates. "Go ahead and change if you want. Dinner'll be ready in fifteen minutes."

When Jake reappeared a few minutes later wearing worn jeans and a sweatshirt, his father nodded to the table. "Have a seat. It's almost ready."

"Can I help with anything?"

"Two cooks in the kitchen is one too many. That's what your mother always used to say, and she was right."

Jake eased his long frame into the chair, watching as Howard bustled about. His father was moving with much more purpose and energy these last few days, he realized. Thanks to Maggie. Getting his father back into woodworking had been a terrific idea, and she had known just how to go about it. Considering the success of that strategy, he decided to talk to his father about school, ask his advice. Maggie had been batting a thousand so far, after all. And he *was* at a loss about how to deal with his problem student. Perhaps his father could offer a few insights. It couldn't hurt to ask anyway.

Halfway through the meal, his father gave him the perfect opening.

"I saw some of the students from the academy walking down the road today. They look like fine young men," he observed.

Jake nodded. "They are. Most of them. But I've got one freshman—I just can't figure out what's going on in his head."

Howard looked over at Jake quizzically. "What's his problem?"

Jake sighed. "I wish I knew. I checked his transcripts, and he's obviously bright. But he's only doing the bare minimum to survive in my class—and apparently in his other classes, as well. He's sullen and withdrawn and just itching for a fight. We had a confrontation after class today, as a matter of fact. I told him I expected more, and essentially he said that as long as he turned in the assignments it wasn't any of my business how well he did. That I should just grade his papers and buzz off."

"Sounds like somebody needs to give that boy a good talking to."

Jake nodded. "You're right. But he doesn't let anybody get close enough. Whenever I see him he's alone."

"Well, I'm not surprised, with that kind of attitude."

"The thing is, Dad, he has a sort of…hopeless…look in his eyes," Jake said pensively, his brow furrowed. "Like he's worried and scared and…I don't know. I just sense there's something wrong. I'd like to reach out to him, try to help, but I don't know how," he admitted with a frustrated sigh.

Howard stopped eating and peered across the table at Jake, obviously surprised by his son's admission. There was a moment of silence, and when he spoke, his voice was cautious.

"Sounds like something's on his mind, all right. Probably could use a sympathetic ear. But you're a stranger, Jake. It's pretty hard to trust a stranger, especially one who's an authority figure."

"Yeah. I suppose so."

"You know, going away to school can be a pretty scary thing. That could be part of it. But it sounds to me like maybe something's going on at home, too. Something that's tearing him up inside. Lots of times people get belligerent when they're faced with a situation that scares them, especially if it's something they can't control."

Jake wondered if his father realized that insight might apply in his own case, but as the older man thoughtfully buttered a piece of bread, his focus was clearly in the past.

"I remember one time when Rob was in sixth grade, the teacher called us up and said he was picking fights," he recalled. "Well, you know that wasn't like Rob at all. So I took him out to the woods the next weekend to help me chop some logs. Just the two of us. Your mother packed a nice lunch, hot chocolate and sandwiches, and while we were eating I started to ask about school, casual-like, and how things were going. Just kind of opened the lines of communication, I think they call it these days. Anyway, 'fore we left, I found out Rob was scared to death your mother was sick.

Overheard us talking about the Nelsons, but misunder- stood and thought it was your mom who had to have surgery. Amazing how things improved once he got that worry off his mind.''

Jake stared at his father. ''I never knew anything about that.''

Howard shrugged. ''No reason for you to. Anyhow, might not be a bad idea, if you really want to find out what's going on with this boy, to take him out for a cup of coffee or something. Let him know you're will- ing to listen, away from the classroom. More as a friend than a teacher—you know what I mean? Sounds like he could use a friend.''

Jake looked at his father speculatively. Maggie was right, it seemed. Not only did the older man have some good insights, but he'd been more than willing to share them.

''That sounds like good advice, Dad,'' he said with quiet sincerity. ''Thanks. I'll give it a try.''

The older man gave what appeared to be an indif- ferent shrug, but Jake knew his father was flattered.

''Might not work. But it couldn't hurt to try,'' How- ard replied. Then he rose and began clearing the table. ''How about some apple pie? Can't say I baked it my- self, but you'll probably be just as happy I didn't.''

Jake sent his father an astonished look. This was the first time in years he had shown Jake any humor. Could a gesture as simple as a mere request for advice make such a difference? Jake marveled. Apparently it could. Because as Howard deposited the dishes in the sink and prepared to cut the pie, something else astonishing happened. For the first time in years, Jake heard his father whistle.

* * *

Maggie glanced at her watch for the tenth time in fewer minutes and told herself to calm down. Just because Jake was coming over was no reason for her nerves to go haywire. Unfortunately, her nerves weren't listening to reason, she thought wryly, as another swarm of butterflies fluttered through her stomach.

She sat down in the porch swing, hoping its gentle, rhythmic motion would calm her jitters. She was certain that Jake wanted to pick up where they'd left off the night of her birthday, and she was afraid. Afraid that by allowing their relationship to progress, she was exposing her heart to danger. But she still cared for him. To deny it was useless. She still found him attractive, still responded to his touch. But more than that, she still felt as she had so many years ago—that God had meant Jake and no one else to be her husband. In fact, she felt it even more strongly now than before. Which seemed odd, after all they'd been through.

The crunch of tires on gravel interrupted her thoughts, and her heartbeat quickened as her gaze flew to the small parking lot. She recognized the small, sensible car Jake had purchased—a far cry from the impractical sporty number he used to crave—and watched as he unfolded his long frame and stood gazing out to sea, his strong profile thrown into sharp relief by the setting sun. He stayed there, motionless, for a long moment, seeming to savor the scene. It was a lovely view, and Maggie herself had often paused to admire it. But it was not something Jake would have appreciated—or even noticed—a dozen years ago, she reflected. It was just one of the many things about him that had changed.

And yet, at least one thing had stayed the same. He

was every bit as handsome as he'd always been—tall, confident in bearing, with an easy, heart-melting smile that could still turn her legs to rubber. He was the kind of man who would stand out in any gathering—and who could have had his pick of women through the years.

And yet...he'd never married. Had even implied that she was the reason for his single status. Maggie wanted to believe that was true, wanted to think that the love he'd once felt for her had endured—just as hers had for him.

At the same time, she wasn't a starry-eyed sixteen-year-old anymore. She was an adult who knew better than to let her emotions rule her life. She was determined to approach the situation as logically and as objectively as she could. It was true that everything she'd seen since he'd returned indicated that Jake had matured, that he was now a man who understood the concept of honor and responsibility, who could be counted on in good times *and* bad. And Maggie *wanted* to believe the evidence that was rapidly accumulating in his favor. But only time would tell if the changes were real—and lasting.

He didn't notice her in the shadows, so as he reached to press the bell she spoke softly.

"Hello, Jake."

He turned in surprise, and a slow, lazy smile played across his lips. She looked so good! he thought. Her shapely legs, covered in khaki slacks, were tucked under her, and she'd thrown a green sweater carelessly over her shoulders to ward off the evening chill. In the fading light, her flame-colored hair took on a life of its own. She wore it down tonight, as he preferred, and it softly and flatteringly framed her porcelain complexion. Right now, at this moment, she looked no older than she had that summer twenty-one years before, on the day of their eventful bike ride. And she made him feel exactly as he had on that same memorable, long-ago day—breathless, eager and deeply stirred. But he wasn't a seventeen-year-old bundle of hormones anymore, he reminded himself. Even if he did *feel* like one. *Control* was the operative word here.

"Hi." The deep, husky timbre of his voice was something he *couldn't* control, however. And it wasn't lost on Maggie, he realized, noting the soft blush that crept up her cheeks.

"Would you like some coffee?"

He shook his head. "No, thanks. Why don't we just sit out here for a while?"

"Okay." She lowered her feet to the floor and scooted over to make room for him. The swing creaked in protest as he sat down, and he turned to her with a grin.

"Are you sure this is safe?"

No, she thought in silent panic as he casually draped an arm across the back of the swing and gently brushed his fingers over her shoulder. *It isn't safe at all. Not for me!*

"Perfectly safe," she replied, struggling to keep her voice even. "We check it every season."

He smiled at her then, that tender smile she knew so well. "I've missed you," he told her softly.

"You just saw me at the fair."

"That was four days ago. And besides, there were too many people around."

The corners of her mouth tipped up. "That didn't stop you from…"

When her blush deepened and her voice trailed off,

he grinned. "Kissing you? No, as a matter of fact it didn't. It could easily become a habit," he warned, reaching out to seductively trace the contours of her lips with a gentle finger.

Maggie's breath caught in her throat at the intimate gesture, and her heart began to bang painfully against her rib cage.

"But I have to admit I prefer more privacy. Take this spot, for instance. I think the twins had the right idea on your birthday. It's very romantic here." He cupped her chin in his hand and let his gaze lovingly, lingeringly caress her face. The conflict in her eyes, the war between desire and prudence, was apparent. But equally apparent was the longing in their depths—and the invitation.

Jake tried to resist. Valiantly. He told himself that she wasn't even aware of her silent plea. That he needed to move slowly. That he needed to reach deep into his reserves of discipline and simply back off. But he was only human, after all. And desire suppressed for twelve long years was a difficult thing to control, especially when the object of that desire sat only inches away, looking so appealing and ready to be kissed.

With a sigh of capitulation to forces stronger than he seemed able to resist, Jake gave up the fight and leaned down to tenderly claim the sweet lips of the woman he loved. His intention was to keep the kiss simple and swift. Make it long enough to let her know he cared and had missed her, but short enough not to make her nervous, he cautioned himself. But somehow it didn't turn out that way.

Because from the moment their lips met, Jake was overwhelmed by a sense of urgency that took his breath away. Maggie felt so good in his arms, so right, as if

she belonged there always. He framed her delicate face
with his strong hands, his lips eager and hungry as he
kissed her with an abandon that surprised them both.
The initially gentle, tentative touching of lips escalated
rapidly to an embrace that spoke eloquently of love and
longing, reflecting twelve long years of parched emotions.

What surprised Jake more than his unexpected loss
of control was Maggie's acquiescence. He had felt her
tense initially, as if taken aback by the intensity of his
embrace, but within seconds she was returning his kiss
with a passion that equaled his own. Without breaking
contact with her lips, he shifted their positions so that
she was cradled in his arms. She sighed softly, and he
continued to kiss her, with a hunger that only Maggie's
sweet lips could satisfy.

Maggie was only vaguely aware of their change in
position. All she knew was that she wanted to stay in
Jake's embrace forever, feeling cherished and loved
and desired. With a sigh, she put her arms around his
neck and strained to draw him even closer, letting her
fingers explore the soft hair at the base of his neck.
Jake reciprocated by combing his fingers through her
thick tresses, and she felt her heartbeat quicken at his
touch.

Jake was thrown by the feelings of tenderness and
desire that nearly overwhelmed him. How had he lived
without her sweet love to sustain him all these years?
he asked himself wonderingly. Now that he'd found
her again, he couldn't imagine a future without her.

When at last Jake reluctantly released her lips, she
lay passively in his arms, staring up at him with a
slightly dazed expression that he suspected mirrored his
own. He hadn't intended their evening to begin this

way. But once in her presence, all his good intentions had evaporated, he acknowledged, as he gently brushed a few errant tendrils of hair back from her face. She tentatively reached up, as if to touch his cheek, then dropped her hand.

"Why did you stop?" He took her hand and laced his fingers through hers, then pressed it against his cheek.

She colored and removed her hand from his, then eased herself to the other side of the swing. She wasn't sure what had come over her just now, but if taking things slowly was her plan, this was not exactly the way to start. Distractedly she ran her fingers through the tangled waves of her hair, trying futilely to restore it to order.

"Jake…I think that…well, I think it's obvious that we're still…attracted to each other on the…on the physical level," she stammered. "But there are other levels that are equally important—if not more important. I—I need to focus on those, but I can't even think straight when you…when I'm…when we're close," she said haltingly, obviously flustered. "And there are issues we need to deal with—*I* need to deal with— things I still need to work through. I don't want to lose sight of those."

That wasn't exactly what Jake wanted to hear, but he saw her point. All of the other realities of his life— and their relationship—got pretty fuzzy for him, too, when her soft, pliant body melted against him and her lips were warm and willing beneath his. He drew a deep, slightly unsteady breath.

"So…no more kissing—is that what you're saying?" He tried for a teasing tone but didn't quite pull it off.

"No, of course not. It's just that…well, I think we need to keep it in perspective, that's all."

He wondered if she had any idea just what she was asking. Maintaining his perspective—let alone his equilibrium—around Maggie was almost impossible. But if that's what she wanted, he'd give it his best shot, he resolved. With a crooked grin, he draped his arm casually around her shoulders, though he felt anything but casual. His body was clamoring with unfulfilled needs—which weren't going to be fulfilled anytime soon, it appeared. So he'd better just get used to it.

"How about the old arm around the shoulder? Is that out of bounds, too?"

"No." She snuggled close and pulled her legs up beside her as Jake set the swing gently rocking.

It was sweet agony to have her soft curves cuddled so close, but he'd get through this, he resolved, gritting his teeth. He had to. *Change the subject,* he told himself desperately. *Focus on something else.* He struggled to find a topic, and was immensely grateful when Maggie took the initiative.

"Your dad seemed pleased about the fair Sunday."

"He was. He spent the rest of the afternoon making a list of supplies. I drove him over to Bangor to pick up everything yesterday. He's happy as a clam—or should I say lobster, here in Maine?—now that he's got a project. I have to practically force him to stop every night. You were right about him needing to have something to do that would make him feel worthwhile. And you were right about something else, too."

She turned to look up at him. "What?"

"Your idea to talk to dad about school. I tried it Monday night. I think he was a little shocked, but he did open up. And offered some pretty good advice along the way, I might add. Thanks to him, I think I'm finally starting to connect with one of my problem students.''

''Really?'' Her eyes were bright, her smile warm and genuine. ''I'm so glad, Jake! What did he suggest?'' She listened interestedly as he recapped his father's suggestion. ''And it's working?''

''So far. I invited Paul—that's the student's name—to meet me in the canteen for coffee yesterday. I wasn't sure he'd come, but he did. He hasn't said much yet, but I picked up enough to suspect that there was a major trauma of some sort in his life shortly before he left for school. Something to do with his parents, I think. I invited him to meet me again tomorrow between classes, and I'm hoping he'll come. I'd like to help him through this, whatever it is, if I can.''

''Did you tell your father?''

He chuckled. ''You've heard the phrase, 'Pleased as punch'?''

Maggie smiled and settled back against Jake. ''That's good. I'm glad you two are getting along better.''

''We still have a long way to go, Maggie.''

''But at least you're moving in the right direction.''

They swung quietly for a few minutes, her head nestled contentedly on his shoulder, the muffled night sounds peaceful and soothing. When Jake finally broke the silence, his husky voice was close to her ear.

''It's good to have you in my arms again, Maggie.''

She swallowed past the lump in her throat. ''I was just thinking the same thing,'' she confessed softly.

''I know you need some time. And I'm not trying to rush you. But I think you know where I hope this is heading.''

She'd have to be a fool not to. But there was so much still to be dealt with. So much that she wasn't yet *ready* to deal with. And she hadn't expected him to be quite so up-front about his intentions—not yet, anyway. "There are...issues...Jake."

"You mean beyond the obvious?" They both knew he was referring to her struggle to overcome lingering doubts about his reliability and honor.

She nodded. Maggie hadn't really planned to get into a heavy discussion tonight. But there was one issue in particular that had to be discussed sooner or later, and sooner was probably better from a self-preservation standpoint. Jake wasn't going to like what she had to say. In fact, he might dislike it enough to reconsider his feelings. But it would be better to know that now, before she got any more involved, she told herself resolutely as she drew a deep breath.

"You mentioned once that you wanted a family." Her voice was quiet, subdued. "But I've already had a family, Jake. I don't regret a minute of it, but it's a demanding job, and I've spent the last twelve years doing it. So much of my adult life has been spent doing what I *had* to do. Now...now I want to focus on the things I *want* to do for a while. Like go to Europe, pursue my art." She paused and stared down unseeingly, absently running her finger over the crease in her slacks. "I guess that sounds selfish, doesn't it?" she finished in a small voice.

Jake frowned and stroked her arm comfortingly. "No. *Selfish* is hardly a word I would use to describe you, Maggie."

She leaned away and looked up at him in the dim light, trying to read his eyes. "Do you understand how I feel, Jake?" she asked anxiously.

"Well, it's not exactly what I wanted to hear," he admitted, "but I do understand." He stroked her cheek and gave her a rueful smile that was touched with melancholy. "Our timing always seems to be off, doesn't it? First you were saddled with responsibilities that tied you down. Now you're free, and I'm saddled with responsibilities that tie me down. And as for a family—it would be different this time, you know. Two people sharing the responsibility for one child is a whole lot easier than one person trying to raise two children."

"I accept that in theory, Jake," she conceded. "But life has a way of tearing theories to shreds. And plans can fall apart in the blink of an eye."

He couldn't argue with that. Their own broken engagement was a perfect example of plans gone awry. And his presence here in Maine was another. Three years ago, if someone had told him he'd end up being a land-bound teacher, sharing a cottage with his father in rural Maine, he'd have laughed in their face.

Maggie frowned as the silence between them lengthened. She'd known since the day he talked about a family that her feelings on the subject could be a major hurdle to their relationship, had dreaded having to deal with the issue. They were at two ends of the spectrum. Jake wanted a family. She didn't—at least, not in the near future. And with her biological clock beginning to tick rather loudly, it might come down to the near future—or not at all.

Maggie felt a wave of despair sweep over her. Why did the Lord always make the choices so difficult? she wondered helplessly. Twelve years ago, her choice had been a family or Jake. Now it seemed that it might come down to Jake and a family—or no Jake. That thought chilled her, but she saw no way around it. Not unless she gave up her own dreams. And she'd done that once. She couldn't do it again—not even for Jake.

"I'm sorry, Jake," she said quietly at last. "I do understand your desire for a family. It's a beautiful thing, raising children, watching them develop and grow and become caring, responsible adults. But I—I can't make any promises. Maybe in a year or two I'll feel differently, but right now I'm just not ready to even consider it."

Jake absently brushed his fingers up and down her arm, his frown deepening. He'd been so caught up in his rediscovery of Maggie that he really hadn't thought much about the family issue, though she had alluded to her feelings on the subject a few weeks before, he admitted. It just hadn't been something he wanted to deal with at that moment. Or at all, if he was honest. There had been enough barriers already between himself and the woman he loved. Why did life often seem to consist entirely of hurdles and detours? he railed silently.

Jake sighed. The evening had taken an unexpectedly heavy turn. He still hoped that when her trust level grew, the notion of a family based on shared responsibilities would become more palatable. In the meantime, she needed the space, the freedom, that the twins' departure had given her. He didn't begrudge her that. She'd earned it. He wanted her to make that trip to Europe, to see all the places she'd always dreamed of. He only wished he could go with her.

"I'm not sure what the answer is, Maggie," he admitted, gently stroking her arm. "But maybe it's one of those things we should just place in the hands of the Lord. I can't help but believe He brought us together for some reason. Maybe, if we give this some time,

He'll eventually let us in on His plans and show us the way."

She turned and looked up at him, tipping her head. "That's funny, Jake. I can't ever remember you talking about faith or trust in the Lord before."

He chuckled softly. "Well, Dad's been dragging me to church every Sunday. Some of it must be rubbing off." Then his voice grew more serious. "Besides, the older I get, the more I realize how much help I need finding my way through this maze of a world. Going back to church, thinking about my faith again—well, it's been a great help. It seems to give me more of a sense of direction. I'm beginning to realize what I've been missing all these years by not turning to the Lord when I needed help."

Yet another new dimension to Jake, Maggie thought wonderingly. And he was right about trusting in the Lord. He would reveal His plan for them in His own time—which, as she'd learned through the years, wasn't always *her* time. She just needed to be patient.

"All right, Jake. Let's just give it some time."

"How about starting Sunday? We could go hiking over on Isle au Haut. I hear it's spectacular."

She nodded. "It is. The twins and I have spent some lovely days over there. It's wild and rugged and isolated—a wonderful spot to get away from it all."

They swung in silence for a few moments, and when he spoke, his voice was thoughtful. "Maggie?"

"Mmm-hmm?"

"You know that comment you made earlier? About keeping kissing in perspective?"

"Mmm-hmm."

"It's not going to be easy, you know. Not when it's

the first thing I think of every time I'm near you—and most of the time when I'm not.''

She blushed at his frankness. "It's—it's a problem for me, too," she admitted.

She heard a chuckle rumble deep in his chest and was relieved that at least he seemed to be taking her ground rules in good humor. "Well, as long as I don't have to suffer alone, maybe it won't be so bad."

"Besides, I didn't rule out kissing entirely, you know," she reminded him. She doubted whether she could even if she wanted to.

"Are good-night kisses acceptable, then?" he inquired hopefully, a smile tugging at the corners of his mouth.

"Absolutely."

"Well, in that case…" He glanced at his watch and feigned a yawn. "I think it's time to say good-night. Don't you?"

She chuckled and shook her head. "You're incorrigible, you know."

"Guilty," he admitted promptly. And then his eyes grew serious. "At least when it comes to you." He reached over and drew a finger gently down the line of her cheek. "Good night, Maggie," he murmured softly, and then his lips closed over hers.

This time the kiss was gentle, a thing to be slowly savored as they absorbed each exquisite nuance of sensation. Now that they had agreed to let time be their friend, the earlier urgency of their embrace was replaced by a tender exploration and leisurely rediscovery that spoke of understanding and promise and hope.

Maggie had no idea what the future held for them. But for the first time since Jake had come back into her life, she felt a sense of peace and calm. For now that she had stopped struggling so hard to resolve their issues on her own and had put her trust in the Lord, her soul felt refreshed. She didn't know the destination of their relationship, but her heart felt sure that He would guide them in right paths.

Chapter Twelve

As the blaze of fall colors began to burn brightly on the coastal landscape, so, too, did the blaze of love burn with ever-growing fervor in Maggie's heart. Sundays became "their" day, and after early-morning services together she and Jake explored the back roads and quaint byways of their adopted state. Sometimes Howard went with them, but usually he declined their invitation, insisting that three was a crowd.

And so, from popular Acadia National Park to remote Schoodic Point, their love blossomed once again on the splendor of the Maine coast. The twins regularly demanded progress reports, and though Maggie tried to play it low-key, even *she* could hear the joyful lilt in her voice every time she mentioned Jake. The girls, of course, were delighted—but no less so than Maggie. She'd been so afraid that her fragile bubble of happiness would burst, that one day she'd wake up to find herself once more alone. Yet her fears seemed groundless. Each moment she spent with Jake was more perfect than the last.

In fact, everything seemed almost *too* perfect. And life was far from perfect, as she well knew. Yet her hours with Jake disputed that reality. Each time he protectively enfolded her fingers in his strong, bronzed hand; each time his warm, brown eyes smiled down into hers; each time he held her in his arms and tenderly claimed her lips, Maggie felt a renewal, a rebirth, a reawakening. Joy and hope filled her heart as the love she'd kept locked away for so long gradually began to find release. For Maggie, who had long ago ruthlessly stifled romantic fantasies and the notion of happy endings, it was a dream come true.

That "dream-come-true" quality was brought home to her most clearly on Thanksgiving Day when she glanced around the table, her heart overflowing with love. The twins looked radiant and vivacious, chattering about college life and clearly thriving in the challenging academic environment. Howard had filled out and looked well on the road to recovery. And Jake... Maggie's eyes softened as they met his warm, intimate gaze across the table. Jake made her understand the real meaning of Thanksgiving. Loving him, and being loved in return, filled her with gratitude—and hope. For Maggie sensed they were close to a resolution of their issues.

In fact, she had a feeling this Christmas might bring a very special present her way, one she'd thought never to receive again. She glanced down at her bare left hand as she reached for the basket of rolls. Maybe...maybe in a month it wouldn't look so bare, she thought, as a delicious tingle of excitement and anticipation raced along her spine. And wouldn't the girls love a spring wedding?

Jake turned the corner and drove slowly through the pelting, icy rain, a troubled frown on his face. Though

Paul had eventually opened up and taken Jake into his confidence, in the end it hadn't made much difference. He was withdrawing at the end of the semester.

Jake let out a long, frustrated sigh. The boy had been dealing with a lot, no question about it. First, a few weeks before leaving for school, his parents had announced their intention to divorce. That was hard enough to accept. But the reason had made it even worse. His father, whom Paul had always looked up to and admired, had admitted to an affair and made it clear that he wanted to marry the other woman. Paul had not only felt betrayed and abandoned himself, but as the only child he'd been left to comfort his devastated mother. It was a difficult position to be in at any age, but especially for a seventeen-year-old still in the process of growing up himself.

Jake believed that his talks with Paul had helped a great deal, that the sympathetic ear he'd offered had provided a much-needed outlet and sounding board for the angry, hurt young man. Slowly, over the last few weeks, he had begun to calm down, settle in. His work improved and he began to socialize more.

And then he'd been hit with the news that his mother had cancer, so far advanced that there was nothing the doctors could do. She'd been given four to six months, at best. And because she had no one else to love and support her through the ordeal to come, he had decided to go home, to be with her during the difficult days ahead. Jake knew Paul had struggled with the decision, knew he didn't want to withdraw from school. In the end he'd made a courageous choice, and Jake admired him for it. But it was just so unfair, he thought in frustration, his fingers tightening on the wheel as he pulled to a stop in front of the cottage.

Jake forced himself to take a long, steadying breath before he slowly climbed out of the car and turned up his collar against the biting wind and cold rain. He slammed the door and strode up the walk, stopping abruptly when he realized that there was a ladder directly in his path. He frowned and glanced up—to find his father perched precariously on one of the top rungs, at roof level. A sudden gust of the relentless wind slapped a stinging sheet of sleet against his face, and he shivered.

"Dad!" he shouted, trying to be heard above the gale.

His father half turned and peered down at him.

"What are you doing up there?" Jake demanded angrily, his lips taut.

"The gutter's blocked. Had a waterfall right above the front door," the older man called in reply.

It wasn't the first time lately that Jake had found his father engaged in an activity that was far too strenuous for him. Now that the older man was feeling better, he was beginning to act as if he'd never had a heart attack. But today was the worst transgression so far. He shouldn't be on a ladder in *any* weather, let alone what seemed to be the beginning of a southwester.

"I'll fix it later. Come down here right now!"

Even through the gray curtain of rain and sleet, Jake could see the sudden, defiant lift of the older man's chin. "I was only trying to help. And you're not in the navy anymore, you know. So stop giving orders."

A muscle in Jake's jaw clenched and he took a deep breath, struggling for control. "Will you *please* come down and go inside where it's warm? We're both get-

ting soaked and I, for one, don't intend to get pneu-
monia.''

With that he skirted the ladder and strode into the
house, banging the door behind him.

By the time Howard followed a couple of minutes
later, Jake had stripped off his wet coat and hung it to
drip in the bathroom. His father glared at him as he
entered, then stomped into the bathroom and threw his
own drenched coat into the tub. When he returned, Jake
was waiting for him, his fists planted on his hips, his
lips compressed into a thin line.

"Okay, Dad. Let's talk about this. I can't be here to
watch you all day. You know what you're supposed to
do and what you're not supposed to do. This—" he
gestured toward the front door "—is *not* on the list of
'do's,' and you know it."

Howard gave him a resentful glare. "I'm not one of
your students, Jake. Or some enlisted man you can order around. I feel fine. I'm tired of being treated like
an invalid. I can do what I want. You're not my
keeper."

"Yes, I am. I promised Mom years ago—and Rob
more recently—that I'd take care of you. And I intend
to do just that."

"That's the only reason you let me come up here,
isn't it? Because you promised your mother and Rob.
Well, I don't need charity. I can do just fine on my
own."

"Right," Jake replied sarcastically. "Like that little
escapade I just witnessed outside. Suppose you'd
fallen? Or put too much strain on your heart? You
could be dead right now—or at the very least, in the
hospital."

"Maybe I'd be more welcome there."

"That's a fine thing to say."

"Well, it's true. You haven't wanted me around in years," the older man declared bitterly.

"I invited you to live with me, didn't I?"

Howard gave a snort of disgust. "Sure. But only because you promised your mother and Rob. Maybe if you'd bothered to come around once in a while, Clara wouldn't have died—five years ago today, not that you'd remember. You broke her heart, Jake. Just like you broke Maggie's."

Jake drew in a sharp breath. His father's harsh words cut deeply, leaving a gaping wound in his soul. He struck back without even stopping to think, wanting to hurt as badly as he'd just been hurt. "You didn't exactly act like you wanted me around. It wouldn't have killed you to try and understand how I felt. Maybe if you hadn't been so stubborn, we could have worked this out years ago. Maybe it's as much your fault as mine that Mom's gone."

Howard's face went white with shock and anger. He gripped the back of the chair and the look he gave Jake was scathing. Yet there was pain in his eyes as well, raw and unmistakable. "That's a terrible thing to say," he rasped hoarsely.

Yes, it was, Jake admitted, silently cursing his loss of control, shocked at the words he'd just uttered. And more were poised for release, despite his efforts to hold them back. Words that, once spoken, could never be retracted. They'd said too much already, possibly irreparably damaging the fragile relationship they'd built these last few weeks. It was time to stop this tirade, before it got even more emotional and hateful. With one last look at his father, Jake brushed past him and retrieved his damp coat from the bathroom, shrugging into it as he headed toward the front door.

"Where are you going?" Howard demanded, his voice quivering with anger.

"Out. I need to cool down before I say anything else I'll end up regretting."

And then he stepped outside, slamming the door shut behind him.

The sleet continued unabated, but Jake hardly noticed as he drove mindlessly to a nearby spot that overlooked the turbulent, storm-tossed coast. He sat there for a long time as the elements battered his car much as his father's words had battered his soul. So many old hurts had surfaced, so many suppressed emotions had been released. But not in a healthy way. They'd ended up accusing each other of terrible things. All this time, while Jake thought their relationship was stabilizing, his father had been harboring a deep-seated anger against him, borne of blame and resentment. And, in many ways, Jake had felt the same toward the older man, he admitted. No wonder their "progress" had been so slow. Now it had not only come to a grinding halt, but regressed dramatically.

Jake sighed and raked his fingers helplessly through his hair as a wave of despair washed over him. His father clearly didn't enjoy living with him. Was only doing so under duress. But he couldn't go back to Rob's—not yet, anyway. Though Rob had finally connected with a firm that seemed interested in hiring him, his life was still in an uproar and there was a strong possibility he and his family would have to move. So what options did that leave for Howard?

Jake didn't have the answer to that question. And he probably wasn't going to come up with one in the next few hours, he thought with a weary, dispirited sigh. He might as well go home, as unappealing as that prospect was.

All in all, he decided, it had been one lousy day.

And it didn't get any better when he stepped inside the door and his glance fell on his father's suitcase. Now what was going on? He closed his eyes and drew in a long breath, then let it out slowly.

He could hear his father rattling pans in the kitchen, and slowly, with reluctance, he made his way in that direction, pausing at the doorway just in time to see his father emptying what appeared to be a pot of beef stew into the garbage disposal. The act seemed somehow symbolic of far more than dinner going down the drain, he thought, his gut twisting painfully.

"What's with the suitcase, Dad?" he asked, striving for an even tone.

"I'm going to visit Rob for a week. I called, and he said it was okay. There's a flight out of Bangor in the morning. I'll take a cab."

Jake sighed. "I'll drive you."

"That's not necessary," the older man replied stiffly.

"I'll drive you, Dad. Let's not argue about that, too."

Howard reacted to that statement with silence. And *silence* was the operative word during the drive to Bangor the next morning. The few comments Jake tried to make were promptly rebuffed, so he finally gave up. Only when Howard was preparing to board the plane did he get more than a grunt for an answer.

"When are you coming back, Dad?"

"I'll take a cab to the house."

"I'll pick you up. Just tell me the day and time. Or I'll call the airline and find out."

Howard gave him a withering look, but provided the information—with obvious reluctance.

"Have a good trip," Jake said.

Howard didn't reply, and as Jake watched him trudge down the ramp to the plane, he jammed his hands into his pockets in frustration. How would the two of them ever work out their differences? Or maybe the real question was whether they even could, he acknowledged with a disheartened sigh. He desperately wanted to make things work between them, but he was beginning to think this was one mission that was destined for failure.

Jake was oblivious to his surroundings as he drove back to Castine, his mind desperately seeking a solution to a situation that appeared to have none. Why the retirement home caught his eye he didn't know, but he eased his foot off the accelerator slightly and looked at it with a frown as he drove past. He'd seen it before, of course, but for the first time he examined it with a critical eye. It seemed to be a nice place. Well kept, with spacious grounds in an attractive setting. Maybe... But even as the thought crossed his mind, Jake pushed it aside. How could he even consider such a possibility when he'd promised his mother that he'd never send Howard to an "old folks" home, as she called them?

And yet...he'd also promised to take care of his father. Given the recent turn of events, he was beginning to doubt whether it was possible to keep both promises. His father clearly didn't want to live with him. And Jake couldn't be there all the time to take care of the older man, who was beginning to take chances with his health. Maybe, in the short term, a retirement home was the best solution. His father would have companionship, and better care than Jake could provide. They certainly wouldn't let him climb on ladders, for one thing. And it would only be temporary, until Rob was settled again. His father liked living with Rob. Rob liked having him. Ultimately Jake was sure Howard would move back in with his first-born. Until then, he might be a lot happier—and healthier—away from his younger son.

Yet the thought of packing the older man off turned Jake's stomach. Yes, things were bad between them. But surely there was a way to smooth out their relationship. There had to be. Only, he didn't have a clue what it was, not after last night. And he was reaching the point of desperation. They couldn't live as they had those first few weeks. The tension had been almost unbearable. That in itself was bad for his father's health. The retirement home wasn't a great solution, Jake acknowledged. But maybe his father would welcome the chance to get out from under Jake's roof. At the very least, Jake decided to check the place out. He didn't think it was the answer, but it couldn't hurt to consider all the options.

Maggie's gaze sought and came to rest on Jake's tall, distinguished form across the gallery, and she smiled. He was half turned away from her, engaged in conversation with a patron, looking incredibly handsome in a crisply starched white shirt and dark gray suit that sat well on his broad shoulders. It was the first time all evening that Maggie had been alone, and she savored the respite, heady with elation at the praise her work had received during the opening reception for her show, basking in this moment of glory. And yet…as she lovingly traced the contours of Jake's strong profile, she knew that her happiness tonight was magnified because he was here to share her moment of triumph. His presence made her joy complete.

"And you were worried about having this show."

Maggie turned at Philip's gently chiding voice and smiled. "You were right. I guess I was ready after all."

Philip glanced at Jake, then back at Maggie, and smiled. "For a lot of things, it seems. I take it you two have worked things out?"

She colored faintly and turned to gaze again at Jake, a whisper of a smile softening her lips. "We're getting there. We still have issues, but…I don't know. Somehow I sense we'll work them out."

Philip put his hand on Maggie's shoulder. "I'm happy for you, you know. About this—" he gestured with one hand around the gallery "—and about that." He nodded toward Jake. "You deserve all the happiness life has to offer, Maggie."

"Thank you, Philip," she said softly. "But I'm trying not to rush things. I want to be sensible about this."

Just then Jake turned and glanced around the room, his gaze restless and searching until it came to rest on Maggie. He gave her a slow, lazy smile that warmed her all the way from her toes to her nose, and she heard Philip chuckle.

"Maggie, honey, I know your intentions are good. But trust me. Jake is past the sensible stage. And forgive me for saying it, but so are you. In fact, I'm guessing that wedding bells will be in the air in the not-too-distant future."

Maggie blushed. She didn't even try to deny Philip's words. Because the truth was she felt the same.

* * *

Maggie's eyes were glowing as she set the Sunday paper down on the kitchen table. A review of her work—brief, but highly complimentary—had made the Boston paper! A wave of elation washed over her, and she was filled with a deep sense of satisfaction and accomplishment—and a compelling need to share the news with Jake—in person. He would be thrilled, too. She'd see him in church in two hours—but she couldn't wait!

With uncharacteristic impulsiveness, she tucked the paper carefully into a tote bag, added four of the large cinnamon rolls she'd baked last night and headed out the door. Maybe her impromptu visit would cheer Jake up, even without the news she was bearing. He hadn't shared many of the details about the latest falling-out with his father, sparing her the worry during this last week as she fretted about her opening, but she knew it was serious if Howard had actually gone down to Rob's. She hoped Jake would tell her more about it now that the opening had passed.

Maggie grinned at Jake's look of surprise half an hour later when he answered her ring. She'd never shown up uninvited before, and he was clearly taken aback—but just as clearly pleased.

"Maggie!" He drew her inside, pulling her into his arms as he kicked the door shut with his foot and buried his face in her hair. For a long moment he just held her, loving the feel of her soft, slim body wrapped in his arms. Less than five minutes ago he'd been wishing—praying—for just such a visit, and it seemed the Lord had heard his plea. The last week had been hell as he'd wrestled with the problem of what to do about his father, and he was running out of time. Howard was returning late this afternoon, and Jake still hadn't figured out how to deal with the situation. All he knew with absolute certainty was that they couldn't go on as they had before.

But now, with Maggie in his arms, her sweetness enveloping him, he somehow felt better.

Maggie snuggled closer against Jake's broad, solid chest. His embrace today spoke less of passion than of the need for comfort and solace, almost as if he was drawing strength from her mere physical presence. It was a much different sensation than the usual amorous nature of their touches, but oddly enough, Maggie found it as powerfully affecting in a different way. She remained motionless as he held her, his hands stroking the curve of her slender back.

When at last he drew away, he looped his arms loosely around her waist and smiled down at her.

"Hi." His eyes were warm and tender, his voice husky and intimate.

"Hi yourself," she replied softly, playing with a button on his shirt.

"I'm glad you're here."

"I sort of got that impression. Do you want to talk about it?"

"About what?"

"About why you're so glad to see me."

"You mean beyond the obvious reason?"

"Mmm-hmm."

"Actually, I'd rather talk about you. What's the occasion?"

"What do you mean?"

"Well, you've never shown up on my doorstep uninvited before. Not that you need to wait for an invitation, you understand. It's just a first. And I hope not a last."

She smiled and blushed. "I had some good news, and I wanted to share it with you."

"I could use some good news. Let's have it."

She reached into her tote bag and withdrew the Boston paper, already turned back to the right page, and handed it to him, her eyes glowing.

He tilted his head and smiled, loving the way her eyes lit up when she was happy. She was like a warm ray of sun, a balm on his troubled soul. He reached over and gently stroked her face, letting a long, lean finger trace its way from her temple to her chin, following the delicate curve of her jaw. Her eyes ignited at his touch, and he was tempted to take her in his arms again, to taste her sweet lips until all coherent thoughts were driven from his mind and he was lost in the wonder of her love.

But first he needed to focus on the paper, he told himself. If it was important enough to bring her over without an invitation, it deserved his full attention. So, reluctantly he transferred his gaze. As he scanned the complimentary article, his lips curved into a slow smile, and when at last he turned to her, his eyes held a special warmth.

"I would certainly call that an auspicious beginning, Maggie. I'm very proud of you," he said with quiet honesty. "And in case I haven't told you lately, you are one amazing and incredible woman—not to mention talented, intelligent and drop-dead gorgeous."

Maggie flushed with pleasure at his compliments. "That might be overstating it just a bit."

"Nope. I never exaggerate."

She laughed, so filled with joy that it simply came bubbling to the surface. All of the pieces of her life were finally falling into place. She'd raised the girls well and sent them on their way in the world. She'd taken a bold step and successfully launched a serious art career. And the only man who'd ever touched her heart had come back into her life and offered her his love. The long, dry years, often filled with drudgery, seemed suddenly a distant memory. She'd made it through the hard times, and now, at last, it seemed that the Lord was rewarding her for her diligence and hard work. Her heart felt lighter than it had in years, and her face was radiant as she looked up at Jake.

"I think you're pretty special, too, you know. In fact, now that we've formed a mutual admiration society, I would say a celebration is in order." She lifted the bag. "I brought some homemade cinnamon rolls."

"Now that's the best offer I've had all day," Jake declared with a grin. He draped an arm around her shoulders and guided her toward the kitchen. Maggie's enthusiasm and euphoric mood were catching, and he found himself feeling better—and more hopeful—by the minute. "I'll pour the coffee if you want to nuke those for a minute."

"Okay."

Maggie tore the foil off the cinnamon rolls, put three of them on a plate and set the timer on the microwave. "Jake, do you have some plastic wrap? I want to leave one of these for your dad."

"Sure. In the drawer, on the right. Boy, they smell great already!"

Maggie smiled and pulled out the drawer. "They're pretty hard to resist, if I do say so myself. My guests always…"

Maggie's voice faltered and her smile froze as the words *Water's Edge Retirement Community* screamed up at her from a brochure, Jake's name prominent on the mailing label. Her stomach clenched into a cold knot, and she gripped the edge of the counter as the world tilted strangely. All of her dreams, all of her hopes, suddenly seemed to dissolve like an ethereal vapor on a frosty morning.

Maggie wanted to shut the drawer again, pretend she'd never seen that brochure, but she knew she couldn't erase it from her memory so easily. Nor could she deny its implication. The man she loved, the man she had come to believe was honorable and could be counted on to remain steadfast in bad times, was reneging on his promise to his mother. He was throwing in the towel on his relationship with his father because things had gotten rough. Or at the very least *considering* throwing in the towel. And as far as she was concerned, that was bad enough. The future that had moments before looked so full of hope and promise now seemed bleak and empty.

"Your guests always what?" Jake prompted over his shoulder as he poured their coffee. When she didn't respond, he frowned and turned toward her.

Jake knew immediately that something was wrong. Very wrong. Her body was rigid, and she was gripping the edge of the counter so fiercely that her knuckles were white. Her face was mostly turned away from him, but what little he could see was colorless. His gut clenched in sudden alarm, and he moved toward her in three long strides, placing one arm around her shoulders.

"Maggie? What's wrong?" he asked urgently.

She looked up at him, and he was jolted by her eyes, dull and glazed with shock. Panic swept over him and he gripped her shoulders, his gaze locked on hers.

"Maggie, what is it? Tell me. Let me help."

As she stared at him, Jake was able to read beyond the shock in her eyes. There was pain and confusion and disillusionment in their depths as well. His frown deepened as he mechanically reached down to close the drawer that separated them. And that's when he saw the brochure.

With a sickening jolt, he came to the obvious conclusion. Maggie had finally given him her trust, had come to believe that he was man who kept his promises and could be counted on to stand fast no matter what the circumstance, and now she had found stark evidence to the contrary.

Silently Jake cursed his carelessness. He'd meant to put that brochure in his room, had barely looked at it when it arrived, feeling in his heart that it wasn't the answer to his dilemma. But Maggie wasn't going to believe him, not now, not considering the look of betrayal in her eyes. And he couldn't blame her. He'd made a mistake in a moment of weakness, and though he recognized it as such now, he knew that for her, the fact that he'd even *considered* such an option indicated that he held his promise as less than sacred.

She began to tremble, and Jake tried desperately to think of something, anything, to undo the damage. But no words came to mind. Instead he silently guided her to the table and gently forced her to sit down, then pulled up a chair beside her. Jake reached for her hand, and she looked at him dully as he laced his fingers through hers.

"Maggie, will you listen if I try to explain?"

"Is there an explanation?" Her voice was flat and lifeless.

"Yes. Although it's not one you'll want to hear, I

suspect. But I'd like to tell you anyway. Will you listen?'' he repeated.

When she didn't respond, Jake took a deep breath and spoke anyway. "You know that Dad and I have had a rough time of it from the beginning, Maggie. I've made no secret of that. But I was really starting to think that we'd turned a corner. I won't say things between us were completely comfortable, but we were getting along. Life was pleasant enough.

"Then, last Monday, everything just fell apart. I'd had a bad day at school, and I came home to find Dad up on a ladder in the middle of that sleet storm. I was a little too heavy-handed in my reaction, I guess, and Dad took offense. The next thing I knew we were accusing each other of some pretty terrible things. Including the death of my mother.''

Maggie gasped, and Jake nodded soberly. "Yeah, it got that bad. On top of everything, it was five years to the day Mom died. Emotions were running pretty high on both sides. Suffice it to say, the situation was pretty tense by the time I walked out to cool off. When I got back, Dad's bags were packed. He left the next morning for Rob's.''

Jake paused and stared down unseeingly at the oak table. "I don't know what made me request that information on the retirement home, Maggie. Desperation, I guess. I just felt that I couldn't keep my promise to Mom *and* make sure Dad was taken care of. And I think living with me is the last thing in the world he wants. He's unhappy here, and stressed, which isn't good for his health. I just didn't know what to do. I passed that retirement home on the way back from the airport, and figured it couldn't hurt to check it out. The brochure came yesterday. To be honest, it's not something I even want to consider. But I just don't know what's best for Dad anymore. Do you understand at all how I feel?''

Maggie tried. Desperately. But she was too numb to even think. "At the moment, Jake, not very much is clear to me," she said shakily. "But I know one thing. A promise is a promise. No one ever said life was easy. But we can't just walk away from our commitments. If you give your word, you keep it. Period. It's a matter of honor. And if people don't honor their promises, how can there ever be any trust?"

Jake flinched. Maggie's words had been said without rancor, but they hit home nonetheless. And she was right. He'd made a mistake—and it was apparent that it was going to cost him dearly. Maybe even the woman he loved.

She stood up then, and Jake was instantly on his feet, as well. "Don't go yet, Maggie. Please."

"I need to be alone for a while, Jake."

"Will you call me later?"

There was a pause, and when she looked at him her eyes were guarded and distant. "I don't know."

Jake felt like someone had just delivered a well-placed blow to his abdomen. He couldn't let the woman he loved walk out of his life. But he didn't know how to stop her.

She gathered up her purse and bag, and he followed her to the door, futilely searching for something to say that would make her reconsider. When she turned on the threshold and looked at him, her eyes were filled with anguish and brimming with tears. His stomach tightened into a painful knot, and he wanted to reach out to her, gather her in his arms, tell her that he loved her and would never do anything to hurt her. But he doubted whether she would believe him. Why should she? He'd hurt her once before. And now he'd done it again. What was that old saying? Fool Me Once, Shame On You; Fool Me Twice, Shame On Me. And Maggie was no fool. Hurt and betrayed a second time, he was afraid she would simply choose to cut her losses and go on alone. She was strong enough to do it. But he wasn't strong enough to go on without her. He needed her. Desperately. For the rest of his life.

"Goodbye, Jake." Her voice was quiet, and though a tremor ran through it, he heard the finality in the words.

And as he watched helplessly while she turned and walked out into the cold rain, the rest of his life suddenly loomed emptily before him.

Chapter Thirteen

Jake turned into the church parking lot and pulled into a vacant spot by the front door.

"What are we doing here?" Howard demanded, giving his son a suspicious look.

Jake shut off the engine and angled himself toward his father, resting his arm on the back of the seat. Ever since the fiasco with Maggie this morning, he'd been praying for guidance about how to mend the rift with his father. But no one upstairs seemed to be listening. And then suddenly, on the drive to Bangor, a plan had formed in his mind. He wasn't sure it would work. In fact, he figured the odds were fifty-fifty at best. But he knew in his heart that this was the only way he and his father might have a chance at a true reconciliation. And so he had to try. He took a deep, calming breath and gazed steadily at the older man.

"I'd like to talk with you, Dad. On neutral ground. In a place where we can't shout, and where maybe some greater power will guide our conversation. I couldn't think of a better spot than here, in the house of the Lord.''

His father's eyes were guarded. "What do you want to talk about?"

"Us."

Howard shifted uncomfortably and turned away, staring straight ahead. "Seems like we've done enough talking already. Maybe too much."

"Too much of the kind you're referring to," Jake agreed. "I have something different in mind. Will you give me a few minutes?"

While Howard considered the request, Jake waited quietly, his physical stillness giving away none of his inner turmoil. Only when his father grunted his assent did he realize he'd been holding his breath, and he let it out in a long, relieved sigh.

They didn't speak again until they were seated in a back row in the quiet, dim church. It was peaceful there, and conducive to the kind of talk Jake had in mind. He just prayed that his father would be receptive.

Jake hadn't really prepared the speech he was about to give. There hadn't been time. So he silently asked the Lord to help him find the right words to express what was in his heart.

"I guess it's no secret that things have been rough between us for a long time, Dad," he began slowly, a frown creasing his brow. "Twelve years, to be exact. You didn't approve of my decision to leave Maggie and join the navy, and pretty much told me to my face that I was being selfish and irresponsible. I didn't want to hear that then. It hurt too much. The truth often does."

His father turned sharply to look at him, his face registering surprise.

Jake smiled wryly. "I guess you never expected me to admit that you were right, did you? There's stubborn blood in this family, you know. And a lot of pride. Too much, sometimes. I think that's what got us into trouble through the years. I was too stubborn and proud to admit I was wrong, even though in my heart I knew it was true. Then, to make things worse, the man I had always loved and admired, who I never wanted to disappoint, had rejected me. So...I rejected him.

"It wasn't a rational decision, Dad. It was reactive, a way to protect my heart from the pain of knowing that I had disappointed you and hurt Maggie. After that, we just seemed to grow further and further apart. It's not something I ever wanted. The truth is, I missed you all these years. I missed your humor and your kindness and your guidance. And I missed your love."

He reached over and gripped the older man's hand, the hand that more than thirty-five years before had been extended to him in encouragement as he took his first few struggling steps. Jake was breaking new ground today, too, taking new, faltering steps in their relationship, and he was as much afraid of falling now as he probably had been then.

"Dad, I'm sorry for all the pain I've caused you through the years. I'm sorry I wasn't there for Mom—and you—when you needed me most. I want to try and make things right, but I need your help. That's what I'm asking for today. I've been on my own for twelve years now, and one of the things I discovered is that I need you now as much as I ever did. Maybe more. Please give me another chance."

Jake thought he saw the glint of moisture in the older man's eyes before he averted his glance, but he couldn't be sure. *Please, Lord, if ever you listened to a prodigal son, hear my voice today,* he prayed fervently. *I want Dad back in my life—not to make things right with Maggie, but because it's the right thing to do. For Dad and me.*

Several long moments of silence passed, and Jake saw this father's Adam's apple bob. When Howard at last turned back to his son, he seemed less stiff, less aloof than he had at any time since coming to Maine.

"I know your mother would have wanted this, Jake," he said, his voice catching. "It was one of the last things she prayed for before she died. Fact is…I always wanted it, too. But it was like you said, we sort of took our positions and just dug in. Neither of us was willing to budge. Can't say it did either of us any good. And it sure did make your mother sad. She called me a stubborn fool more than once, told me you'd come back in a flash if I gave you half a chance. Guess she was right after all. Clara had a way of knowing about those things. I should have listened to her. But that West pride got in the way, I expect. Couldn't bring myself to admit that maybe I was a little too hard on you. Not that I agreed with what you did. Still don't. But it was a lot to take on at such a young age. Looking back, I can understand how it must have been pretty overwhelming. I guess Maggie can, too, seeing as how you two are getting along so well these days."

Jake didn't correct him. The situation with Maggie was too fresh, too raw, to even discuss. He would find a way to deal with it later. He had to. His future depended on it. But at the moment, he had another relationship to mend.

"Does that mean you're willing to make a fresh start?"

Howard nodded slowly, his face thoughtful. "I expect we'll still have our differences, though," he warned.

Jake smiled wryly. "I'm sure we will. The key is to agree up front that we'll work them out instead of building walls. We just need to keep the lines of communication open, just like you did with Rob all those years ago."

Howard smiled, and the bleakness that had earlier been in his eyes was replaced by a new warmth. "Even if it takes hot chocolate and sandwiches in the woods?"

Jake grinned. "*Especially* if it takes that. Maggie's converted me to hot chocolate. I even prefer it over a gin and tonic."

"That girl always was a good influence on you," Howard declared with a smile. "I'm glad she's back in your life."

A shadow crossed Jake's eyes, but he kept his smile firmly in place. "So am I, Dad. But we have run into a bit of a roadblock," he admitted. He couldn't say much more, not without revealing *why* they were having a problem, and there was no need to tell his father about the retirement home. That idea was already history, had been almost from the moment he'd sent for the brochure.

"Nothing serious, I hope," his father said in concern.

"We'll work it out," Jake replied with more confidence than he felt. But he had to think positively. Because he couldn't face the alternative. "Are you ready to go home?" he inquired, changing the subject before his father probed more deeply.

Howard nodded. "I don't want to overstay our welcome here in the Lord's house. I expect He has more important problems to deal with than ours."

"I expect He does," Jake agreed as he stood up. "But I'm grateful He helped us through this one."

Now if only He would do the same for him and Maggie.

Maggie paced back and forth in the living room, agitated and unsettled. This time, when Jake called, he hadn't let her put him off as he had on the numerous other occasions he'd phoned. Tonight he'd simply asked if she would be home and announced he was coming over.

She paused in front of the fireplace and gazed down into the flickering flames, a troubled frown creasing her brow. Since the day she'd walked out of Jake's house almost three weeks ago, her emotions had been on a roller coaster. They'd run the gamut from devastation to bleakness to loneliness to grief to anger. She'd berated herself over and over again for allowing her trust to be betrayed a second time—and by the *same* man! How big of a fool could she be?

She'd asked herself repeatedly if she had overreacted. And always the answer came back the same. No. Jake had made a sacred promise to his mother, literally as she was dying, and until recently he had gone to admirable lengths to keep it. Everything he'd done and said in the months he'd been here had seemed to indicate he was a changed man, a man who understood the meaning of duty and honor and responsibility.

Maggie understood Jake's frustration and sense of helplessness over his relationship with his father. She'd had similar moments during the girls' growing-up years, when they'd clashed and said things they'd later regretted. It happened. But you didn't deal with it by turning your back on the problem, by simply shoving it out of sight. You talked about it. You worked things through. You made amends and went on. You didn't walk out.

Yet that's exactly what Jake had contemplated doing when things got rough. The very fact that he'd even *considered* breaking his promise scared Maggie to death. Because if he'd done that with Howard when things got dicey, how did she know he wouldn't do it with her?

And that was one fear she couldn't handle. Life was filled with uncertainties. She knew that. But if she ever married, she wanted to do so secure in the knowledge that the sacred vows of "for better, for worse" would be honored by the man to whom she'd given her heart. And she was no longer sure Jake was that man.

The doorbell interrupted her thoughts, and she jerked convulsively, one hand involuntarily going to her throat. She didn't feel ready to face Jake. Then again, she doubted she ever would. So they might as well get this over with, she thought resignedly.

When she reached the front door, she took a slow, deep breath, then pulled it open.

For a long, silent moment, Jake simply looked at her, his breath making frosty clouds in the still, cold air. He was wearing a suede, sheepskin-lined jacket over dark brown corduroy slacks, and his hands were shoved deep into the pockets. The shadowy light on the porch highlighted the haggard planes of his face, and Maggie suspected he'd suffered as many sleepless nights as she had.

"Hello, Maggie."

She moved aside to let him enter. "Hello, Jake."

He stepped in and shrugged out of his jacket, watching as she silently hung it on a hook on the wall. Except for Sunday services, he'd seen nothing of her since the day she walked out of his house. The faint bluish shadows under her eyes, the subtle lines of tension around her mouth, were mute evidence of the strain she'd been under, and his gut clenched painfully. It seemed all he ever brought this woman he loved was pain and uncertainty, when what he really wanted to give her was joy and peace.

Of all the failures in his life, his relationship with Maggie was the one that affected him most deeply. He wanted to take her in his arms right now, to hold her until she knew beyond the shadow of a doubt that he loved her with every fiber of his being. But that was not the way to convince her. He had another plan in mind. Not one he particularly liked, but at least he felt it had a chance to succeed.

She turned back to him then, her eyes guarded and distant. "Let's go into the living room. I have a fire going."

She chose a chair set slightly apart from the others, and Jake sat down on the couch. He leaned forward intensely, his forearms resting on his thighs, his hands clasped.

"Thank you for seeing me, Maggie."

"I suppose we had to talk sooner or later."

"Well, it was tonight or not for several months. Dad and I are going to Rob's tomorrow for Christmas. We won't be back until after you leave for Europe."

That jolted her, and Maggie's eyes widened in surprise. "When did you decide to do that?"

"Last week. Rob invited us, and Dad wanted to go. It will be a good chance for all of us to have some family time together. It's not the way I anticipated spending Christmas, but given the circumstances, I thought it might be for the best.''

Maggie's throat constricted, and the ache in her heart intensified as she turned to gaze unseeingly into the fire. She blinked to hold back the tears that suddenly welled in her eyes, berating herself for her lack of control, and took a deep breath before she spoke.

''You're probably right.'' How she managed such a calm, controlled tone when her insides were in turmoil she never knew.

Jake nodded wearily. ''But I couldn't leave with things so unresolved between us.'' He frowned and raked his fingers through his hair, then restlessly stood and moved beside the fire, gripping the mantle with one hand as he stared down into the flickering flames. When at last he turned to her, his eyes were troubled. ''The fact is, Maggie, the whole retirement home idea was a bust, from start to finish. I'm not even sure why I sent for that brochure, except that I was desperate. I wanted to keep my promise to my mother, but I also knew Dad was unhappy, which wasn't good for his health. I was between the proverbial rock and a hard place.

''I guess what it comes down to is this—I'm human. I make mistakes. And that was a big one. But I never pursued it beyond sending for that brochure. Because I realized, even before you walked out, that I had to try harder to make things work with Dad. The two of us had been living under the same roof for months, but we'd never really connected, never really opened up and been honest with each other, never dealt directly with the issues that divided us. And so I decided to tackle them head-on when he got back.''

He paused and dropped down on the ottoman in

front of her, his eyes so close that she could see the gold flecks in their depths. As well as the sincerity.

"It worked, Maggie. The last three weeks have been the best we've had in twelve years. We admitted to each other where we'd fallen short and agreed to try our best to make things work. And we are. I know we'll still have some rough times. I think that's the nature of any human relationship. But we'll get through them. Because we both want it to work."

He reached for her hand then, and Maggie's breath caught in her throat. It took only this simple touch to reawaken all the longing she'd so ruthlessly crushed since she'd walked out of his house.

"The fact is, Maggie, I feel the same about us. I have almost since the day I took shelter here from the mist. I never realized how lonely the last twelve years had been until then. I know you're disappointed and disillusioned right now. I know you think I betrayed your trust. But I do honor my commitments. I'm a different man in a lot of ways than the twenty-five-year-old who walked out on you twelve years ago. What I did then was wrong, and I make no excuses. All I can do is give you my word that it will never happen again. The retirement home fiasco notwithstanding, I've learned a lot about duty and honor and responsibility in these last dozen years. I can't promise that I won't make mistakes. But I can promise you that in the end I'll always do the right thing. Because I love you with all my heart. And I always will."

The tears in Maggie's eyes were close to spilling over. With every fiber of her being she wanted to believe him. But hurt had made her cautious. And so had the need for self-preservation.

Jake watched the play of emotions across Maggie's

face. He saw the yearning and the love in her eyes, but also the uncertainty and fear. It was what he expected. What he had come prepared to address. Slowly he reached into the pocket of his slacks and withdrew a small, square box, then flipped it open to reveal a sparkling solitaire.

Maggie's eyes grew wide as she gazed at the dazzling ring. "Isn't that…that's the ring…" Her voice trailed off.

"It's the same ring, Maggie. I kept it all these years. I never knew why—until I came to Maine and found you again."

Maggie's voice was thick with unshed tears, and a sob caught in her throat when she spoke. "Jake, I…I don't know what to…"

He reached over and placed a gentle fingertip against her lips. "I'm asking you to marry me, Maggie. But I'm not asking you for an answer right now. In fact, I don't want one tonight. Because whatever you decide, I want you to be absolutely sure. No second thoughts, no regrets. All I'm asking is that you take the ring with you to Europe, as a reminder of my love. Think about my proposal. Give yourself time. And then, when you get back, we'll talk about it again."

Maggie's mind was whirling. This was the Christmas present she'd anticipated with such joy at Thanksgiving. Now…now it left her confused and uncertain—yet filled with a sudden, buoyant hope. But there was still a major unresolved issue between them that had nothing to do with their recent falling-out.

"Jake…there's still something we haven't dealt with," she reminded him in a choked voice. "The family issue. I haven't changed my mind on that."

He looked at her steadily. "But I have. I've given it

a lot of thought, Maggie. And bottom line, while I'd like to have children, if it comes down to a choice between you and a family, there's no contest. I love you, and that's enough for me. Anything else would be a bonus. Whatever you decide is fine with me.''

Maggie felt her throat tighten at the love and tenderness—and absolute certainty—reflected in Jake's eyes.

''You seem awfully sure.''

''That's because I am. It's not so hard to make compromises when you love someone as much as I love you. Besides, I don't come without strings, either.''

She frowned. ''What do you mean?''

''Think about it, Maggie. I'll bring an aging parent to this union. A lot of women wouldn't want to take that on. You faced marriage once before saddled with a pretty overwhelming responsibility. In a way, you will again.''

Maggie smiled and shook her head. ''Jake, I love Pop. I don't consider him a burden in any way. In fact, before…well, before we had this problem, I was thinking down the road that maybe if things…well… progressed between us, we might want to live here. And we could turn the little guest cottage into a place for your dad. That way he'd be close by, but still have a sense of independence.''

Jake's heart overflowed with love for this incredible woman who was so giving, who always thought of others. Dear Lord, how was he going to survive the next three months without her? And he couldn't even bring himself to consider beyond that if, in the end, she rejected his proposal.

''You are one special woman, Maggie Fitzgerald,'' he declared huskily. He was tempted to demonstrate the depth of his feelings in a nonverbal way, but he restrained himself—with great effort. Calling on every ounce of his willpower, he stood up, then reached down and pulled her to her feet. For a long moment they simply gazed into each other's eyes, both wanting more, both trying desperately to remain in control.

"Will you take the ring, Maggie?" Jake finally asked, his voice rough with emotion. "Not as a commitment—but as a reminder of my love?"

She nodded. "Yes." Her voice was a mere whisper, and she clutched the small velvet box tightly to her breast. "You know, I...I almost wish I wasn't going now," she admitted tremulously.

Jake shook his head firmly. "Don't feel that way. Savor every minute of this experience. You owe that to yourself after all these years. And I'll be here when you get back."

"I'll...I'll miss you, Jake."

He reached for her then, groaning softly as he pulled her fiercely against him and buried his face in her hair. How could he leave without at least one brief kiss to sustain him during the long months to come? That wasn't too much to ask, was it?

He backed up slightly and gazed down into Maggie's eyes. They were filled with yearning, and his own deepened with passion. No, it wasn't too much. They both wanted this. Needed it. Silently he let one hand travel around her neck, beneath her hair, to cup the back of her head. And then he bent down and gently, tenderly claimed her sweet lips.

Maggie responded willingly, knowing that this moment would be a memory to take with her, to hold in her heart, during the long, solitary months ahead. His lips, warm and lingering, moved over hers, seeking, tasting, reigniting the flames of desire that had smoldered in her heart these last few weeks. But all too soon, with evident reluctance, he drew back. The smile he gave her seemed forced, and his voice sounded strained.

"I'd better go."

Several more moments passed before he released her, however, and when he did it was with obvious effort. She followed him to the hall, watched silently as he shrugged into his coat, walked beside him to the door. He turned there, reaching out once more to touch her face, his gaze locked on hers.

"Bon voyage, Maggie. Think of me."

And then he was gone.

Maggie knew that Jake was doing the right thing, the noble thing, giving her time to sort through her feelings and be sure of her decision. But for just a moment, she was tempted to throw caution to the wind, fling open the door and run impulsively into his arms. It was what her heart told her to do. But her heart had led her astray before, she reminded herself. And so, with a decisive click she locked the door and turned back to the living room. She would take the time he'd offered her to think things through. It was the wise thing to do.

But it wouldn't be easy.

Chapter Fourteen

Jake smiled as he read Maggie's account of her adventures at the Trevi Fountain in Rome. He wasn't surprised that several locals had tried to pick her up. She might be nearing forty, but she was still one gorgeous woman.

"Good news from Maggie?" his father inquired, setting a mug in front of Jake. They had gotten into the habit of sharing hot chocolate—and some conversation—each evening before going to bed.

Jake chuckled. "Seems the Italians are a good judge of beauty after all."

Howard raised his eyebrows. "Oh? Are they asking her for dates?"

Jake smiled. He doubted that "dates" were what they were after, but he let it pass. "Mmm-hmm. But she's holding her own. Sounds like she's having a wonderful time. The art classes are going well, and she says she's made some great strides with her painting."

"Glad to hear it. But I'll sure be glad when she

comes back. Seems kind of quiet around here without her."

Jake's smile faded. "Yeah."

"You never said much the night you went to say goodbye to her, Jake," Howard said carefully. "I don't want to pry, but...did you two work things out?"

Jake glanced down into his half-empty mug and sighed. "I don't know, Dad. But...well, I guess there's no reason to keep it a secret. I asked her to marry me."

Howard's eyes widened in surprise. "You did? What did she say?"

"I didn't ask for an answer. All I asked her to do was think about it while she was gone, and let me know when she got back."

Howard drained his cup and rose thoughtfully. He paused by Jake's chair and placed a hand on the younger man's shoulders. "Maggie will come around, son. You'll see. You're a good man, and she'll realize that in time."

Jake stared after his father, his throat tightening with emotion. The future of his relationship with Maggie might still be uncertain, but at least he and his father had reconnected. His father had just touched him with affection for the first time in years. And he'd called him "a good man." That small gesture, those few words, meant more to Jake than all of his other accomplishments combined.

Now if only Maggie would come to the same conclusion.

Maggie tipped her face back to the sun and sighed contentedly as Parisian street life bustled around her. Her fabulous European adventure was drawing to a close, but it had been everything she'd hoped. She felt

steeped in great art, had soaked it up until her soul was
satiated. And she'd learned so much! The classes had
been tremendous, and she'd produced some of her best
work on this trip, shipping it home to Philip as she
completed it. His enthusiastic response had reaffirmed
her opinion that she'd made great strides.

With only two weeks left in her sojourn, her
thoughts were now beginning to turn to home, and she
reached up to finger the ring that hung on a slender
gold chain around her neck. Soon she would have to
make her decision. Maggie knew, with absolute certainty, that she loved Jake. She also knew, with equal
certainty, that she was afraid. So the question came
down to this: Was she willing to take the risk that love
entailed? To trust her heart completely to this man who
had walked out on her once before? A man who she
had come to believe was now capable of true commitment—but whose unexpected lapse had shaken her
trust?

Maggie knew what the twins thought. They'd
summed it up in three pithy words. *Go for it.* Philip
had said much the same thing. And Maggie felt in her
heart they were right. She knew that nothing good
came without risk. Yet she was still afraid. She'd
prayed daily for guidance, asked for a sign, for direction, but so far the Lord hadn't responded to her plea.

Maggie sighed and reached for the mail she'd just
picked up. There was a letter from Jake, she noted, her
lips curving up into a smile. He wrote practically every
other day. And one from Pop, she saw with surprise.
Those would be letters to savor. So she put them aside
and opened the large brown envelope from Philip, who
sorted through her mail at home and passed on things
that looked important. She peered inside and withdrew

a small package with an unfamiliar New York return address. Curiously she tore off the brown wrapping to find a little box cocooned inside a letter. Quickly she scanned the single sheet of paper.

Dear Ms. Fitzgerald,
Millicent Trent gave this to me and asked that I send it to you. I am sorry to inform you that she passed away last week after a brief illness. But she did so at peace with the Lord, and with joy. She said she wanted you to have this because you would understand, and that she hoped your story turns out happier than hers. She also asked me to remind you that very few people get a second chance, and to consider carefully before you let yours slip away. I confess I don't understand the message, but Millicent said you would. May the Lord keep you in His care.

The letter was signed by a Reverend Thomas Wilson.

Maggie's eyes filled with tears as she removed the lid from the small box and gazed down at the two-part heart pendant nestled inside. She was deeply touched by Millicent's gift, for she knew that of all the woman's possessions, this was the one that meant the most to her. Perhaps in death she would at last find the reconciliation that had eluded her in life, Maggie thought wistfully, as she silently asked the Lord to watch over her friend.

Wiping a hand across her eyes, Maggie reached next for Pop's letter. It was brief, and written very much in character.

Hi, Maggie.
I got your address from Jake. I hope you're having

fun. We're not. Don't get me wrong. Things are
good between Jake and me. Real good. Jake
turned out fine after all, and I'm proud to have
him for a son. But he's been moping around the
house like a lovesick puppy, and it's driving me
crazy. So please come home soon and put him out
of his misery. He misses you a lot. So do I.

Maggie smiled through her tears. Obviously Pop and
Jake were getting along fine. Jake had told her he'd
make it work, and he had. There was an undertone of
affection in Pop's letter that conveyed even more
clearly than the words that the two of them were back
on track.

And then she settled back in her chair and opened
Jake's letter. His notes were typically chatty and warm
as he filled her in on his daily life, making her feel that
she was sitting next to him on the couch while he
shared his day's adventures. But it was always the
opening and closing that she reread several times. He
never failed to remind her how much he missed her or
that he was counting the days until her return. Though
he never pressed for an answer to his proposal, she
could sense hope—and anxiety—in every line. The
closing of today's letter especially tugged at her heart.

The days are long, Maggie, and without the sound
of your voice and your sparkling eyes, they seem
empty. The nights are even worse. I find sleep
more and more elusive as I anticipate your return.
I hope that you're faring better than I am on that
score. And then again, maybe I don't. In my heart,
I hope you miss me as desperately as I

miss you. I don't know what hell holds for those who sin, but I feel that in the agony of uncertainty I've endured during these last few weeks I have somehow made reparation for at least some of my transgressions. I love you, Maggie. More with each day that passes. I look forward to the moment I can tell you that again face-to-face. Until then, know that thoughts of you fill my days—and nights.

Maggie's eyes grew misty again, and she drew in a long, unsteady breath. This was the most direct Jake had been about his feelings. Until now his letters had been mostly lighthearted, written to make her smile, not cry. But now he was baring his soul, letting her know just how much her answer meant to him. It was a courageous thing to do, giving someone the power to hurt you that way. But it was honest. And from the heart. And it touched her deeply.

Maggie pressed his letter to her breast as she extracted Millicent's pendant from the tiny box and cradled it in her hand. She thought about the gift of love Jake was offering her. And she thought about Millicent's sad story of love thrown away. She thought also about all that Jake had done in the last few months to prove his steadfastness and his ability to honor a promise. How he had diligently cared for his father and painstakingly rebuilt that relationship. How he came to her aid when she was ill. How he stayed by her side at the hospital, and was there for her to lean on during the twins' emotional send-off to college. Since coming back into her life, he had never once failed to be there when she needed him.

And suddenly the image of the painting she was just

now completing came to mind. With a startling flash of insight, she realized that while she had been asking the Lord for a sign to help her make her decision, it had literally been in front of her for weeks. For she now knew that she had made her decision long ago, in the hills above Florence. She'd just been too afraid to admit it. But today's letters had brought everything sharply into focus and banished her fear.

With a sudden, joyful lightening of her heart, Maggie gathered up her letters and headed back to her room.

Jake shoved his hands into his pockets and drew a long, unsteady breath. It had been three months since he'd said goodbye to Maggie. Three eternal, lonely months. She'd written regularly, but letters didn't ease the ache in his heart, nor did they fill his days with joy and laughter and his nights with tenderness and love.

He sighed and reached up to loosen his tie as he gazed out into the night. Nothing seemed right without Maggie. He needed her. The thought that she might ultimately reject his proposal had plagued him incessantly, etched faint lines of worry at the corners of his eyes. And yet he knew he had done the right thing. He'd given her the time she needed to be sure. Because he didn't want her to commit to him unless she felt the same absolute certainty, trust and deep, abiding love for him that he felt for her.

Jake heard a door open and he turned slowly, his gaze softening into a smile as Maggie entered. She always looked beautiful to him, but never more so than right now, as she walked toward him resplendent in her wedding finery. He held her at arm's length for a moment when she joined him, letting his gaze move over her slowly and lingeringly, memorizing every nuance of her appearance as she stood before him, more dazzling in her radiance than the illuminated Eiffel Tower visible behind her through the French doors on the balcony.

Her hair was drawn back on one side with a cluster of sweetheart roses and baby's breath, a miniature reflection of the bouquet she'd carried as they were married just hours before. Her tea-length white silk gown, subtly patterned to shimmer in the light, was simply but elegantly cut, with slightly puffed sleeves and a sweetheart neckline. Around her neck she wore Millicent's heart pendant, the two halves seamlessly joined by the hands of a master jeweler. Jake would never forget the expression of joy and certainty on her face as they'd exchanged their vows in the tiny chapel she'd reserved. Illuminated only by the mosaic of late-afternoon light as it filtered through the intricate stained-glass windows, with the fragrance of roses sweetly perfuming the air, it had been the perfect, intimate spot for them to exchange the vows that had been so long delayed.

"You look breathtaking," Jake said huskily, the warmth in his eyes making her tremble with joy—and anticipation.

She smiled, and a becoming blush rose in her cheeks. "Actually, I feel pretty breath*less*," she admitted.

He chuckled. "It has been a bit of a whirlwind, hasn't it?" Since her phone call a week ago, life had moved into high gear. Thank heaven her call had coincided with Spring Break! But even if it hadn't, nothing could have kept him from her side.

"Everything happened so fast that I can hardly believe it's real."

"You're not sorry, are you?" he asked worriedly. "Would you rather we had waited, been married at home?"

She smiled and shook her head. "No. We waited long enough. And once I decided, I was determined to have that Paris honeymoon after all."

His eyes deepened with passion, and he reached for her. But when she held back, he looked down at her questioningly.

"Jake, before we…we…well, I have something I'd like to give you first," she stammered.

He smiled indulgently. "Since I've already waited years for this moment, I suppose I can hold out a few more minutes."

"I'll be right back," she promised, extricating herself gently from his arms. She disappeared into the bedroom of their suite, and returned a moment later with a large package wrapped in silver paper. As she held it out to him, she noticed that he'd placed two small packages with white bows on the coffee table.

"Looks like we both had the same idea," he commented with a smile.

"I didn't expect a present, Jake. Not on such short notice," she protested.

"I've had these for a long time, Maggie," he told her quietly. "They were just waiting for this moment."

He sat on the couch and drew Maggie down beside him, then tore off the shiny paper of his package to reveal an impressionistic painting of a man, woman and small child on a hillside picnic, visible only from the back, surrounded by a golden light. The man and woman were seated, and he had his arm around the child. He was pointing into the distance, and the woman's hand rested on the man's shoulder as she leaned close to him. A feeling of intrinsic love and serenity and unity pervaded the painting, making the viewer yearn to be part of the idyllic family scene.

Jake examined the exquisite painting silently, then drew a deep breath as he turned to his wife and shook his head in awe. "This is wonderful, Maggie!" he said in a hushed voice. "All of your work is excellent, but…well, this stands apart. You always paint from the heart, but this…it captures something, some essence, I've never seen before in your work."

"It comes even more from the heart than you realize, Jake," she told him softly.

He looked at her curiously. "What do you mean?"

"I thought a lot about us while I've been here. I knew from the beginning that I loved you. That was never a question. But I was so afraid of being hurt again. I just couldn't decide what to do. I asked the Lord for guidance, but I never seemed to get an answer.

"And then last week I was sitting at a sidewalk café, and I thought about this painting, which I started in Florence. Suddenly I realized I'd made my decision— about a couple of things—a long time ago."

She drew a deep breath and looked at him, her gaze steady and certain. "That's us, Jake. You and me…and our child. I never even realized it until a few days ago. My heart's known for weeks what I wanted to do. It just took a little longer for the message to reach my mind."

Carefully Jake set the painting down, then he reached for her and pulled her close.

"Oh, Maggie." His voice broke, and he buried his face in her hair, holding her tightly. "Are you sure? You're not doing this just because you know I want it?"

"Partly," she admitted, her voice muffled against his chest. "But I'm doing it for me, too. I want to raise our child—together—if the Lord chooses to bless us with one. I want part of us, what we have together, to live on. And I want to share our love with a child."

He drew a deep, shuddering breath, and when he pulled back, the tenderness, love and gratitude reflected on his face brought a lump to her throat.

"I love you, Maggie."

"I love you, too. With all my heart." Her own voice broke on the last word, and he reached over to frame her face with this strong hands, his thumbs gentle as they stroked her damp cheeks.

"Now it's your turn." He retrieved the two small packages, handing her the smaller one first.

Maggie tore off the wrapping and lifted the lid of the small box to reveal an antique, gold-filigreed locket. She flipped it open to find two tiny photos— one of she and Jake taken when they were about nine and ten, and one of them taken by the twins on her last birthday. Those two photos seemed to reaffirm what her heart had long known—that their lives had always been destined to join.

"That was Mom's locket," Jake told her. "I found it when I was cleaning out the house for Dad. Her mother gave it to her when she turned twenty, and it was always one of her most treasured possessions. I know she'd want you to have it. And so do I."

"Oh, Jake! It's lovely! Thank you."

He handed her the other package and waited silently as she tore off the wrapping, raised the lid and carefully folded back the tissue paper. With unsteady hands she withdrew a small, framed document, and her breath caught in her throat as she was immediately transported back to another time and place. At the top, in careful lettering, were the words *Official Document*. Below that it read, "I, Jake West, and I, Maggie Fitzgerald, promise to always be friends forever and ever, no matter what happens." It was dated twenty-eight years before, and they'd each signed it in their childish scrawls. Their mothers had signed also, as witnesses.

"I'd forgotten all about this," she whispered.

"I found it in my mother's fireproof 'treasure box' the same day I found the locket," Jake said quietly. "I meant those words then, Maggie. And I mean them now."

Maggie could no longer hold back her tears. They streamed down her cheeks unchecked as she stared down at the yellowed document in her hands. She thought about the gifts they had just exchanged—the locket that had once belonged to Jake's mother, this sentimental document, her painting. None of them had much, if any, monetary value. But they were worth far more than gold to her, for they came from the heart and were born of love. A cherished line from Matthew came suddenly to mind—"For where thy treasure is, there also will thy heart be."

Maggie looked up at Jake, and he reached over to gently brush her tears away.

"No more tears, Maggie. There've been enough of those in this relationship." He reached down and drew her to her feet, guiding her to the French doors that looked out onto the lights of Paris, the illuminated Eiffel Tower rising majestically into the night sky.

"Remember how we used to talk about Paris? How we thought it was so romantic, and how we dreamed of spending our honeymoon here?" he asked softly.

She nodded, a smile of gentle remembrance touching her lips. "Mmm-hmm."

He turned to face her, his hands resting gently at her waist. She looked up at him, and the intensity—and fire—in his eyes made her breathless. "Well, our honeymoon might have been a little delayed. But I promise you this, my love. I'll spend the rest of my life making up for lost time. Starting right now."

Then he took her hand and drew her back inside, closing the door on the lights of Paris before he pulled her into his waiting arms. And as his lips claimed hers, in a kiss filled with promise and passion, Maggie said a silent prayer of thanks. After all these years, she had at last come home to the man she loved. And it was where she belonged. For always.

Epilogue

Two and a half years later

"Allison, will you run down to the cottage and tell Pop dinner's almost ready?"

"Sure." Allison pulled off a piece of the turkey that stood waiting to be carried to the table and popped it into her mouth. "Mmm. Fantastic! Sure beats the food in the dorms," she declared with a grin.

"Well, you'll only have to put up with the food for one more semester," Maggie reminded her with a smile. "I still can't believe you two are graduating in less than six months!"

"We can't, either," Abby chimed in. "Watch out, world, here we come!"

Maggie laughed. "Amen to that!"

Jake ambled into the kitchen, sniffed appreciatively and headed straight for the turkey. "That smells great!" he pronounced.

But just as he reached for a piece, Maggie stepped

in his way. "If everyone eats their turkey in the kitchen, I'll end up having mine alone in the dining room," she complained good-naturedly. "And that's no way to spend Thanksgiving."

"Well, I have to nibble on something," Jake declared. Without giving her a chance to elude his grasp, he reached for her and pulled her into a dip. "I guess your ear will have to do."

Abby giggled. "You two act like you're still on your honeymoon."

Jake's eyes, only inches from Maggie's, softened and he smiled tenderly. "That's because we still feel like we are," he replied as he held her close.

Abby sighed dramatically. "That's s-o-o-o romantic. I sure hope I meet somebody like you when I'm ready to get married," she told Jake.

"I hope you do too, honey," Maggie agreed before Jake muffled her lips in a lingering kiss.

"Mmm," he murmured. "I like this idea. Start with dessert."

Maggie laughed softly. "That's all you're going to get if you don't let me up before everything burns."

"That's all I need," he countered, raising one eyebrow wickedly.

She blushed. "Well, I don't think the others would agree to defer dinner until after you have...dessert."

With an exaggerated sigh, he slowly released her. "Oh, all right. I suppose I have to be a good sport about this."

"Pop's on his way," Allison informed them as she breezed back into the kitchen.

"Okay, let's get this show on the road, then. Everybody grab a dish and let's eat!"

It took a few minutes for everyone to settle in, and

then they joined hands and bowed their heads as Jake spoke.

"Lord, we thank You today for all the blessings You've given us this past year. For the joy You've sent our way, for good health, for the family ties that bind us to one another with deep, abiding love. Thank You also for watching over us and guiding us through each day, for letting us feel Your loving presence so strongly in our lives. Help us always to be grateful for all that we have, not only today, but every day of the year. Amen."

As Maggie raised her eyes, she was filled with a sense of absolute peace and deep contentment. All of the people she cared about most were with her today, and that alone made her heart overflow with gratitude. Her gaze moved around the table. Pop, who loved living in his own little cottage and now had a thriving woodworking business. Allison and Abby, still incurable romantics, ready to launch their own careers. And Jake. She gazed at him lovingly as he carved the turkey. Every moment with him had been a joy. Each day their relationship grew and deepened and took on new dimensions.

At that moment, one of those dimensions began to loudly demand attention, and Maggie's gaze moved to the high chair next to Jake. Her lips curved up softly and her eyes took on a new tenderness as she gazed at the newest member of their family. For the last nine months, Michael had joyfully disrupted their household, and they'd loved every minute of it. True to his word, Jake had gone out of his way to make sure that this time raising a child was a shared experience. He'd attended every childbirth class, coached her through labor, took most of the night feedings and changed more than his share of diapers. And Maggie loved him more every day.

As Michael demonstrated his hunger in a particularly vocal way, Jake turned to him with a smile. "Hold on there, big fella," he said, reaching over to tenderly ruffle the toddler's auburn locks.

Then he glanced at Maggie, and they smiled across the table at each other. It was a smile filled with tenderness, understanding, joy and love. Especially love. Because both of them realized how very blessed they were to have been given a second chance to find their destiny. And how close they'd come to losing it.

Though no words were spoken, Maggie knew what Jake was thinking. She could read it in his eyes. And it mirrored her thoughts exactly.

It didn't get any better than this.

*   *   *   *   *

Dear Reader,

When my husband and I were married nine years ago, the priest who officiated at the ceremony spoke about the extraordinary gift of ordinary love—how remarkable it was that love could flourish amid the stresses and tribulations of day-to-day life. He went on to point out that it was the everyday kindnesses and caring gestures—more than the fleeting euphoric moments—that formed the solid foundation of lasting love. And he said that this "ordinary" love was to be celebrated and held up as an example to others.

Although I was too caught up in the "euphoric moment" of the wedding to fully appreciate his message that day, ultimately I recognized its truth—and broadened my definition of "romance." Yes, it's still that enchanted evening when you see a stranger across a crowded room. And it's still that heart-stopping moment when two hearts touch for the first time. But it's so much more! It encompasses all of the levels on which two lives intertwine—intellectual, emotional and spiritual, as well as physical.

I try to capture this multidimensional nature of love in all of my books. But it is perhaps especially present in *It Had to Be You,* which focuses on growth and change in a long-term relationship. I hope you enjoy reading about Jake and Maggie's reawakening love as much as I enjoyed writing about it.

Sincerely,

Irene Hannon